Another Family Reunion Novel
In the Wisdom of the Ancestors Series
— Book 17 —

ALL IN THE FAMILY

ANN JEFFRIES

Published and Distributed By
New View Literature
820 67th Avenue N, #7603
Myrtle Beach, South Carolina 29572
www.newviewliterature.com

Editing: Jessica Tilles

Cover and Interior design: TWA Solutions

All In the Family
ISBN: 978-1-941603-45-1 (Print)
ISBN: 978-1-941603-46-8 (eBook)
Library of Congress Registration Number: ______________________

First printing August 2019

For inquiries, contact the publisher.

ALL IN THE FAMILY

ANN JEFFRIES

Acknowledgments

I bow in humble appreciation to:

The Creator

My Ancestors

Military families everywhere

Carolina Forest Authors' Club

Faithful family, friends, and Fans

The journey continues and the struggle for literary
perfection shall never end

I remain faithfully yours,

Ann Jeffries

Titles in the Ann Jeffries'
Family Reunion–Wisdom of the Ancestors Series

In paperback and e-book formats:

Southern Exposures
Another Point of View
Northern Exposures
Uncommon Choices
An Unguarded Moment
Moments To Remember
The Better Part of Valor
Walking on Uneven Ground
Ask Me No Questions...I'll Tell You No Lies
Touch Me In The Morning
All Goodbyes Aren't Gone
A Different Frame of Mind
Judicial Indiscretion
Crystal Clear Persuasion
Sweet Justice
Bittersweet Memories
All in the Family

In the Audiobook Format:

Southern Exposures Produced by Ginger Walton
Another Point of View Produced by Glen Pavlovich
Northern Exposures Produced by CJ McAlister
An Unguarded Moment Produced by Richard Dennis Johnson
Moments To Remember Produced by Richard Dennis Johnson
The Better Part of Valor Produced by Richard Dennis Johnson
Walking on Uneven Ground Produced by Richard Dennis Johnson
Ask Me No Questions...I'll Tell You No Lies Produced by Pam Dougherty
Touch Me In The Morning Produced by Ginger Walton
All Goodbyes Aren't Gone Produced by Julian Thomas
A Different Frame of Mind Produced by CJ McAlister
Judicial Indiscretion Produced by Kelley Hazen
Crystal Clear Persuasion Produced by CJ McAlister
Sweet Justice Produced by CJ McAlister

In Production:

Uncommon Choices
Bittersweet Memories

Contents

AH when will this long vveary day haue end,

and lende me leaue to come vnto my loue?

Hovv slovvly do the houres theyr numbers spend?

How slowly does sad Time his feathers moue?

Hast thee O fayrest Planet to thy home

Within the Westerne some:

Thy tyred steedes long since haue need of rest.

Long though it be, at last I see it gloome,

And the bright euening star with golden creast

Appeare out of the East.

Fayre childe of beauty, glorious lampe of loue

That all the host of heauen in rankes doost lead,

And guydest louers through the nights dread,

How chearefully thou lookest from aboue,

And seemst to laugh atweene thy twinkling light

As ioying in the sight

Of these glad many which for ioy doe sing,

That all the woods them answer and their echo ring.

— "Poem 6" by Edmund Spenser

(Written in the mid-1500s in Old English and appears how it was written.)

When You Know

Chapter 1

Tucker Cavanaugh laughed at something one of the women said, as the group of young male and female military officers exited through the Armory's big, heavy, double, front doors. His smile, his default expression, transformed his face from merely drop-dead gorgeous into movie-idol splendor. He could take a joke and often suffered in silence when people made what he considered to be "too much" over his good looks and fine physique. Tucker was just that kind of guy, though. He was beautiful on the outside as well as on the inside. The kind of young man people took notice of and even stopped whatever they were doing to stare.

Still, he never knew how to handle the adulation, accolades or the teasing; particularly when in high school, his baseball teammates tagged him "Pretty Boy." After all, he felt he had nothing to do with his appearance. Blue eyes, blond hair, and a sturdy body ran on both sides of his family. They were steeped in his DNA.

His mother was still a knockout in her forties and he looked the spitting image of his father. He came from a long line of tall, rugged Nordic stock. Some relative way back in his genealogy was a member of the peerage, a warrior; a conquering Norman come English nobleman. Folklore recounted that he married well and had one of the realm's most sought-after beauties as his mistress. So the oral history goes, although he had both a beautiful wife and a splendid mistress, his long-ago relative had quite a reputation with the ladies of the royal court because of his extraordinary good looks; an English rake of the first order. So, what people saw stamped on Tucker's face and physique, he felt, was not within his control. Nevertheless, even at twenty-one years old, he was still unaccustomed to women, like Mallorie Colbert, a female officer, in her late-twenties or early-thirties, hitting on him as she was doing now.

The sun was bright on this crisp, cold day; enough to have him put on his Ray-Bans against the still blindingly white snow, button his long, military top coat, and put on his hat, completing his spit and polish uniform. Coming out of the Armory was as far as he got when his eyes landed on the graceful, gazelle-like movements crossing his path and holding him in a state of suspended animation.

"Hey, man, let's go," Captain Ian Murray, his Commanding Officer, chided when Tucker stalled in front of him.

If Tucker heard him or any of the other officers' complaints, he, a big, six-foot, five-inch, two-hundred-pound man, was blocking their escape, he gave no indication of it. Nothing penetrated his concentration on the female runner who would have made FloJo envious of her moves. Now he knew what the statement *poetry in motion* truly meant.

"What's wrong with you, Tuck?" Mallorie asked when she noted his attention shifted away from her flirtations. She tried to follow his line-of-sight, but all she noticed were students and professors hurrying across the campus to get out of the cold wind and a few people jogging. She sensed something or someone captured his complete attention and it wasn't her.

"Nothing," he absently said. "Go ahead. I'll see you..." he said, his voice trailing off. He moved swiftly dodging people who it seemed were sauntering much slower than he. There was still a lot of snow and some ice on the ground, so he had to be careful where he stepped. With his eyes on a black hoodie and a pair of incredible legs in black cut off sweatpants, he continued to follow slowly gaining ground on the object of his attention.

He had seen her before many times, but each time he was too far away to catch up to her. This time he was determined. He ran track, too, and jogged daily, but carrying his heavy backpack, wearing hard-bottom, dress shoes on icy patches of ground, his formal, military-dress uniform, long, heavy coat, and the crowded campus, didn't allow him the luxury of a full out sprint. Plus, she had quite a head start on him. He took to the grassy area, but the snow and ice still hindered his progress there too.

A large contingent of international students, excitedly chattering, passed between him and the object of his interest. He kept bobbing and weaving, trying to break through the crowd and simultaneously keep the woman in sight, but when he cleared the group, the hooded female runner was nowhere to be seen. Nevertheless, Tucker jogged to the last spot where he saw her and turned a three-hundred-sixty-degree circle trying to catch a glimpse of where the woman went. He saw, perhaps, hundreds of students and professors heading in or out of various campus buildings, but none of them wore a black hoodie, cutoff sweats, and reflective running shoes. If he had the time, he would have searched each building, but he was running late as it was. Disappointed that he hadn't found the woman, again, he headed for his dormitory to change his clothes.

Whitney Ivy Alexander didn't really have the time to spend at the auditorium with her former college roommate and current housemate, but KiLi Hakamora was beyond nervous about performing in front of others in competition. She was standing in the aisle between the stationary theatre seats with her back to the stage energetically shifting from foot to foot. The tryouts were for the holiday pageant the University's Entertainment Department was preparing to staff with talented people. KiLi convinced Whitney her moral support was crucial to her success, so here Whitney sat uncomfortably and waiting through several contestants for KiLi's turn on the stage at the microphone.

"You ought to try out, too, Whit," KiLi encouraged around the gum popping and constant motion. "You have a really good singing voice."

Whitney rolled her expressive, light, crystal-brown eyes up to the ceiling, sank further down in the theater seat, and leaned her head back, so she was looking at the beautiful fresco ceiling five stories up. KiLi insisted on calling her *Whit* despite the fact she asked her not to shorten her name. Whitney was proud of the name her parents gave her almost nineteen years ago. Her father's favorite female vocalist back in the day was Whitney Houston; the choice of names prophetic. Although, to her own ear, she didn't sound like the incredible songstress, she did have a striking resemblance to Alisha Keys, the music icon, but so did her mother. Still, others often compared the range and inflection of her vocal ability to the great Ms. Houston. Whitney's grandparents were devout fans of Whitney Houston's cousins, the famous songstress Dionne Warwick and opera great Leontyne Price.

She considered her middle name, Ivy, a gift from the woman who made it possible for her parents to meet and fall in love. Her Nana Sylvia's aunt, Hannah Ivy Benson, Whitney's great-grandaunt, was the one who many years earlier sold the house in the Georgetown section of Washington, DC, to her dad, Air Force five-star General Benjamin Staton Alexander. Although her parents were now deployed in Tokyo, Japan, she lived in that house they still owned while she attended Georgetown University's Law School.

Family folklore held that Whitney Ivy's great-grandaunt, Hannah Ivy, raised Whitney's grandmother Sylvia and her siblings while their parents and grandparents were touring the European continent as performers with the great Josephine Baker. In fact, Whitney hadn't even been a gleam in her dad's eyes back then when the house became his.

As the family history went, Washington was where her dad first met her mom, Stacy Greene, when she was just a Second Lieutenant. On their first encounter, her mom had just graduated from the Naval Academy in Annapolis, Maryland. Her dad was a Captain stationed at March Air Force base near San Diego, California. His team of pilots flew in fresh-off-the-assembly-line aircraft to replenish the supply of fighter jets for Andrews Air Force Base. Those jets were slated to fly support and security escort for the President's Air Force One.

Her dad was at the Pentagon late one evening waiting to go out on the town with a friend when in the cafeteria, he spotted the young Navy Lieutenant who would in later years become his wife. Whitney Ivy and her six siblings loved to hear her parents' courtship story told over and over again.

There were also many wonderful family stories about her uncles and aunts and their dating histories and subsequent marriages. Also about her grandparents and great-grandparents on both sides of her family. It was fascinating stuff to hear how dating mores changed from generation to generation.

Though her family was tightly knit and kept up with each other almost daily, each year Whitney looked forward to her family's Juneteenth Reunion in Summer County, South Carolina, and the Young Cousins' Academic Labor Day Beach Party along the South Carolina Grand Strand in Atlantic Beach. The annual family reunion was when hundreds of family members converged on the Town of Goodwill for ten days of unadulterated fun, education, and camaraderie. At the end of the summer, the cousins who were still in school, assembled in Atlantic Beach, at Grandaunt Hannah Ivy's Victorian mansion and camped in tents in her yard on the beach.

Not that Whitney lacked for fun or family during the rest of the year. Her Aunt Vivian Alexander Montgomery, one of her father's two younger sisters, lived less than thirty minutes away on a ranch in a rural area outside of Washington, DC, with her second husband, former basketball icon Charles "Chucky P" Montgomery, MD. Her uncle was now the head of Emergency Medical Services at Physicians' Hospital, a facility he built and owned with several other doctors. Her Aunt Vivian, a US Supreme Court Justice, was the youngest female to be robed in the High Court's history. Chuck and Vivian had thirty children her aunt adopted with either her first husband, Derrick Jackson, her second husband, Charles Montgomery, or were naturally born to them. Her aunt and uncle adopted children who were abandoned, orphaned, or had health challenges, and made them a part of the family. So, Whitney Ivy didn't lack for close family companionship while her parents and siblings were in Japan and she was in Washington, DC.

"Whit? What are you thinking about?" KiLi asked. "You haven't heard a word I've said in the last five minutes."

"For the umpteenth time, KiLi, my name is Whitney," she stressed.

"I'm glad to finally meet you, Whitney," the young man said, his hand extended. "I'm Tucker Cavanaugh."

She was slouched down in the seat with her feet crossed at the ankles and braced up on the back of the stationary seat in front of her. Wearing a pair of cutoff sweat pants after having just completed a five-mile run, she smelled a little gamey at best. Not the most auspicious way to make a new acquaintance, she ruminated, as she extended her hand to accept his. Magic. That's all she could think when their hands connected and she looked up into his mesmerizing blue eyes.

"'To finally meet me?'" she parroted around a large lump in her throat.

"I've seen you jogging on campus, like a little while ago, but I wasn't close enough to say hello. Now I am...close enough. Hello." Her hand was warm and grabbed him around his heart and squeezed.

"Hi, I'm KiLi Hakamora."

"Hi," Tucker acknowledged, not taking his eyes off of Whitney's face or letting her hand go. "Would you like to go for coffee? Please?"

"Of course, we would," KiLi answered before Whitney could reject the offer. She knew her friend shied away from even the most casual dates.

"I think the offer was for me, KiLi," Whitney said, not taking her eyes from Tucker's, "but we'll have to make it another time. I'm just here to give KiLi a little moral support. Then I have to go shower and study."

"How about we study together?"

Whitney chuckled. "Not very persistent, are you?"

"No, I'm the shy, retiring type," Tucker said.

"I'll say. You're really very introverted," Whitney said and smiled.

"The bane of my existence. So, about that study date? How about 6:00 P.M.? I'll bring pizza?"

Whitney laughed. No one had been so entertaining in trying to land a date with her before. She shrugged. What could it hurt? "If you think it will help you get over your bashfulness, it's a date. Here is my address," she said, producing a card.

He looked at the card and whistled. "Uh, nice neighborhood. Maybe I should have our first date catered."

"Maybe the second date," she suggested.

"I like the way you think. Let me give you my phone number, just in case you have some prince or potentate make a better offer to you and I get kicked to the curb."

She took the cell phone he offered and inserted her name and phone number and sent his to her phone. "I don't renege on promises I make. However, the date is only good until 6:00 P.M. At 6:01, all bets are off."

"Hey, Tuck, we're up. Let's go, man!" someone hailed him.

"Yeah, I'm coming," he said, but never took his eyes off of Whitney's face as he walked backward toward the stage. "I'll see you by five-fifty-nine, Whitney. Count on it."

"*Wow!* Talk about seriously *cute!* He is *awesome!*" KiLi exclaimed.

Yeah, no, not bad at all, Whitney thought as she watched him mount the stage two steps at a time. For a big, tall guy, he seemed surprisingly light on his feet. He reminded her of her father in height and general physique. She considered her dad drop-dead gorgeous, too. She continued to watch Tucker as he headed for the drum set in the center of the stage, sat down, and began adjusting the height of his snares, base, high hats, tom-tom, and cymbals. With his sticks in hand, he began a syncopated rhythm as he turned his head from side to side and listened to the sound each instrument made. A few more adjustments and then he led the countdown for the band beating his sticks together.

There was something unidentifiable about him beyond his incredibly good looks and great physique snagging her attention. Now he seemed to be deeply ensconced in his music to the exclusion of all else. She put her feet on the floor, leaned forward with her arms stacked and resting on the top of the stationary seat in front of her, and braced her chin on her stacked hands. She was mesmerized just watching him play. Then he smiled with his bottom lip caught between his pearl-white teeth, did this quick, sexy little neck gyration to the right and left, and let it rip with his hands and sticks a blur. Yet, the sounds which poured out were magic and streaked through her senses. Whitney sat straight up in the darkened auditorium and lost her heart in that instance.

He had an undeniable sex appeal—the deep sea-blue eyes, the rakish blond hair that curled madly around below his ears, the smile that suggested he could easily talk any female with a heartbeat into being naughty. He looked good in his dark blue US Marine Corps sweatshirt pushed up to his elbows, a pair of light- colored, knee-length shorts, and boat shoes with no socks on a cold day. His legs were long and well-muscled as were his arms and shoulders. Altogether a very attractive package.

Then he brought the old school funk and reggae with his band and had her standing up leaning forward on the back of the seat before her and taking intense notice.

After speaking with the gorgeous Whitney, Tucker was in a zone. He couldn't believe his luck. When he walked into the auditorium and saw the black hoodie and those incredibly long shapely legs in black cutoff sweats resting on the back of the seat in front of her, his blood pressure skyrocketed. He was flying now!

His hands, wrists, and feet were working in concert to beats that were almost orgasmic. He closed his eyes, sucked his bottom lip into his mouth, and let the music capture and flow through him the way his dad and granddad taught him. With her image in his head, he didn't hold back. Her smile was clean and crisp on a light, warm-brown complexion with features arranged by The Creator on a very good day. Her eyes a light, crystal brown, a perky tipped up nose, and lips that knew what to do with a smile. Her hair was a long, dark sandy brown crinkle skein. Even in a topknot ponytail, it hung down her back in a profusion of curls.

Although she wasn't dressed to impress, she did so nonetheless. She was obviously young, but she had an air of sophistication and confidence about her Tucker never experienced in other young women of his acquaintance. He sensed immediately she was intelligent and if her little half grin was any indication, she was fun to be around. He liked the combination of intelligence and fun. She didn't take herself too seriously. He had a good feeling about Whitney and he was eagerly looking forward to their study date tonight.

At the end of the set, his band members all turned to look at him, amazement showing in their smiles. A smattering of enthusiastic applause came from the few people in the auditorium, including Whitney. He smiled at her and wanted to spend more time talking with her, but he had laundry to do so he'd have something to wear tonight.

Chapter 2

After parking his Harley at the curb, Tucker bounded up the two flights of concrete steps to the wide, front, covered porch of the impressive corner multilevel brownstone. He carried his book bag over his left shoulder and two large pizzas balanced on his right hand. He was about to knock on the wide, intricately carved, wood front door when it flew open.

"Dude!" the young, light-skinned, Black man said as he and another young man came barreling out of the door. "Sorry. Didn't see you."

"That's okay. Uh, is this where Whitney lives?"

"Yeah. Hey, are those loaded pizzas?" he asked, reaching for the boxes.

Tucker pulled them back before the guy could grab it. "Yeah. It's for Whitney."

"Oh, snap! Maybe we don't have to go to dinner with the parental units after all," the other young man said.

"Mom's not gonna go for that and you know it, Ryan."

Suddenly, the door opened behind them, spilling more light onto the front porch. A very tall, porcelain-skinned man stood with one eyebrow raised, massive arms folded across his broad chest covered in a tuxedo and black tie. A diamond stud winked in his left earlobe. "Gentlemen," he pointedly acknowledged.

"Uh, hey, Dad. We, uh, we're just going next door to visit a hot second with Anna and The Fenster…"

"You thought I'd overlook you two in the head count? I'm old, but I'm not senile."

Both young men dramatically sighed when they got the icy look from the easily seven-foot tall man who was clearly only somewhere in his forties. That was when Tucker realized the two guys are teenagers and twins. They were wearing tailored tuxedos, too.

"Come on, Dad," Ryan whined. "Do Roger and I really have to go to this dinner?"

"Ask your mother," he said with a devilish glint in his keen, brown eyes. "*Now.*"

Both young men huffed and dejectedly turned to go back into the house.

"Who's your friend with the great smelling pizzas?"

"Some dude looking for Whitney."

"Oh?"

"Uh, yes, I'm Tucker Cavanaugh. Whitney and I have a study date and if I'm not standing before her in less than one minute, I'm in trouble."

"Then you'd better come in. I'm Whitney's uncle—."

"Dr. Charles Montgomery," Tucker finished before the man could answer. He switched the pizzas into his left hand and stuck out his right for a shake. "Aka, Chucky P. You're a legend in the annals of professional basketball, an all-time leading center for the Boston Celtics, in Georgetown Medical's Emergency Room, and you're the owner of Physician's Hospital in Prince George's County, Maryland."

Chuck chuckled and accepted his handshake. "Thanks for telling me who I am. Contrary to my sons' belief, I still have all of my faculties in highly-tuned, working order. You know who I am because…?"

"My dad and granddad are big fans of yours from when you played for Boston College and then went into the pros. They followed your career and took me to see you when you played your final professional game in Madison Square Garden. You had the best game of your career that night and won MVP for that series. I'm a baseball man, myself, but I was just a kid back then and was totally awed by your performance."

"What, may I ask, do you do to keep body and soul together now?"

"I'm in med school, military. I'm in my second year and I've been looking at hospitals to determine where to do my residency program. Budget cuts make it hard to find opportunities at military teaching hospitals with excellent programs. I like it here in the city, so I looked at area hospitals, yours included."

"Well, then, you're welcome here," he said, swinging the door open to the utter chaos inside.

There were people everywhere, Tucker noticed, mostly young people in every height and description dressed in a tux and black tie and females in after-five attire for a rather formal evening, but obviously not happy about it. The bedlam was reaching astronomical levels when a voice silenced the entrance hall.

"Now, my darling offspring, the answer to your question is absolutely, unequivocally, positively...wait for it... no. You may not opt out of this dinner tonight. The National Medical Association is giving your male parental unit a well-deserved award. You, my many sweet and loving unguided missiles, will all be happily in attendance to cheer like banshees in a standing ovation when he receives his award and makes his acceptance speech."

"Mom," one brave soul said, sounding aggrieved, "you or Dad receive some type of award almost every month from somebody. Can't I—."

The raised eyebrow from *The Mom* silenced the questioner.

Tucker understood why everyone quieted when U.S. Supreme Court Justice, aka *The Mom*, aka Vivian Alexander Jackson Montgomery, was in a room. The woman was awesome on television and beyond belief in person. She was tall, slim, and resembled a youthful Jada Pinkett-Smith with short hair plastered attractively to her scalp in ringlet curls.

When her magnetic eyes landed on Tucker, he held his breath a beat. "Absolutely," he said and grinned.

She stepped forward, hand extended. "You don't resemble any of my progeny, so you must be Tucker Cavanaugh, Whitney's study date. You're the reason my usually biddable niece is unwilling to dump you and to accept my last-minute invitation to join this august group for the awards dinner."

"Guilty, Madam Justice, but I'll never let it happen again."

"Well said," she commented, then turned to her brood and spread her arms open. "See, this is the kind of young person you all should aspire to be...obedient. Now, time's wasting, but let's not be rude. Say a cheerful hello and goodbye to Mr. Cavanaugh. Then, as your male parental unit is so fond of saying, 'let's head 'em up, and let's move 'em out.'" Then turning back to Tucker, with a little head nod, she said, "You'll find Whitney Ivy in the kitchen."

"Thanks," he said, gave a little military salute that had her grinning at him, and then stood a moment, watching the crowd clear out of the spacious vestibule. He turned in a circle, looking at what he could see of the beautiful, well-appointed house. It was just shy of a mansion and was even more impressive on the inside as it had been on the outside, especially the wide, Gone-With-The-Wind staircase. Then he followed the direction and voices back through a long, wide hallway past other rooms to a large, modern, eat-in kitchen.

"Go away, Uncle Bill. For the last time, I'm not going to come to work for you next summer," she said without heat.

"You don't know what you're missing, kiddo. I've got major clients in the entertainment and sports industries. You could spend time on the continent or interesting island resorts—."

"Getting absolutely nothing accomplished except a darker tan," she joked.

"Well, there is that. You'd be my special assistant; my right-hand. I could also get you in front of a camera for my summer issue of *Risqué* as one of the top-ten, young, amazing women in the world. Your new tan would look great in a swimsuit."

"If you hadn't noticed, I already have a permanent tan furnished by my parents."

"Uh, excuse me, but these pizzas are getting cold."

Whitney turned in her seat at a long kitchen trestle table that could easily seat twenty. She checked her watch. "You're late."

Her beauty held him speechless and suspended for a few heartbeats. Something special spasmed through him and arrowed straight to his heart every time he saw her. At that moment, he sincerely believed he was looking at his future. "Not true. I got waylaid on the front porch by a set of escaping teenaged male twins, Ryan and Roger; Dr. Montgomery's scrutiny and interrogation before he would let me fully into the house; Justice Montgomery's lecture on obedience; and the agony of defeat by a bunch of reluctant dinner companions."

Whitney laughed. "All right, you successfully ran the obstacle course, so you're forgiven this time. Uncle Bill, this is the not-exactly-late Tucker Cavanaugh, my study date and dinner companion for the evening. Tucker, this is William Chandler, Esquire."

"Cavanaugh," Bill acknowledged, shaking his hand. "Never argue with an intelligent woman."

"Sage advice from a man who needs no introduction, but I'm desperate to become her friend," he acknowledged. "Pizza?"

Bill chuckled. "Thanks, but no. I'm on my way out."

"Safe trip, Uncle Bill," Whitney said, giving him a long, strong hug and short kiss on the cheek.

"We'll talk when I return."

"If we must, but my decision is final. If Dad, Mom, and the offspring won't be in the country for the summer, then I'm heading for Japan."

"Nevertheless, we'll talk," he said and, after nodding to Tucker, was gone.

"You have quite a family. You're military, right?"

"I am, yes. How did you know?" Whitney asked.

"You said 'in country' which is a military term not many outsiders don't know or use," Tucker commented and placed the pizzas on the table beside stacks of legal tomes. "I'm sure I don't have to tell you William Anthony Chandler, your Uncle Bill, is one of the most respected legal minds of his generation. He's also multi-talented. He's won Academy Awards for roles he's portrayed in the movies, too, and his modeling career seems to be nothing less than stellar. I've read both of his magazines, *Stallion*, though I'm not gay, and *Risqué* for his cutting-edge slant of men's fashion. I like his line of men's clothing and scents. As I said, quite a gifted and accomplished family."

"Ha! Don't I know it," she commented as she lifted the lid on the pizza boxes and snagged a slice of each variety. "What about you? Sibs or other extended family?"

"Just my parents, two grandparents, my mom's dad and my dad's mom, and me," he answered, going to the industrial-sized sink to wash his hands and dry them with paper towels.

"Where are they? I hear bedrock Yankee in your voice."

"Poland Springs, Maine. You've got a good ear."

"Ah, no wonder you were wearing shorts and no socks."

"Socks?"

"It was very cold out today."

"Cold? Today would have been considered a heat wave in Maine, but it was a forced laundry day. I was desperate for clean clothes. That's why I couldn't stay and talk with you after my band's audition. I wanted to get cleaned up for our study date."

Whitney grinned at him. "I don't think I've ever been to Maine. What's it like there?"

"It's mostly rural. Plenty of open space. A lot of hills and forests. Only a little over one million people live there as compared to someplace like New York City, where more than eight million live in the city alone." Tucker shrugged. "That's why I like Maine. It's not overpopulated. The coast is rocky; not much beachfront, but awesome ocean views. Snow and more snow in the fall and winter. Sometimes in the spring, too. It's beautiful year-round, but I like it the most this time of year, in the fall, when the leaves turn brilliant colors. I like it a lot."

"What does your family do in Poland Springs for a living?"

"My dad's an attorney and Mom doesn't work outside our home anymore. She used to be a full-time literary agent in Boston until I came along and Dad was in law school. Now she likes to cook and tend to her garden. She still represents some of her longtime clients periodically and she edits manuscripts sometimes. My parents have known each other since they were toddlers. My grandparents, too. My granddad, my mother's father, is a carpenter. He makes furniture. My grandmother, my dad's mother, was an investigative reporter, but she mostly blogs now on state and local political issues."

"I like the way you phrased it, your mom 'doesn't work outside of your home anymore.' It tells me you value what she does as a homemaker."

"She's the best. She worked very hard every day to make sure my dad and I could go out into the world and make her proud of us," he said, laughing.

"Besides making your mom proud of you and playing your drums, what else do you like to do?" She took another slice of the loaded pizza.

"I like learning new things, playing my guitar or a piano."

"You're really good on the drums."

"Thanks, but today you were my inspiration. How did your friend do?"

She smiled at his compliment. "KiLi did well. She was selected to be in the pageant. How about you and your band?"

"We're in, too."

"That's great. What are you studying?"

"At the moment, vascular traumas. Also, organic and general chemistry, calculus, biology and physics."

"You're in med school?" Whitney asked, surprised.

"Yes, I'm in my second year and a First Lieutenant in the Marine Corps. What about you?"

"Law school, second year, but you seem so young. Too young to already be in med school."

"Twenty-one and I tested out of high school after one year. Columbia University undergrad, and tested out in three years. High scores on my MCATS. Same goes for you, it seems. You look too young to be in law school."

"Younger than you, but I also tested out. The American University in Tokyo undergrad, and tested out in two full years. High LSAT score. Legacy at Georgetown Law because of my Aunt Vivian."

"Interesting. Parents? Sibs?"

"Parents are in the military as you've already guessed. My dad is in the Air Force and my mother is in the Navy. They're both stationed in Tokyo, Japan, with my sibs, three and three, triplets."

"*Wow!* That's cool. Must run in the family."

"Yeah, both sides. How did you guess?"

"Your uncle and aunt had a bunch of twins in their brood. Also the fact your aunt and uncle were profiled on the Sweet Justice television show during Senate hearings when the President nominated your Aunt Vivian for the Supreme Court. It was an exclusive, thorough, in-depth interview and the only one permitted on their ranch in Maryland. It included their children, siblings, parents, and extended family.

"Were you there when the interview was shot?"

Whitney shook her head and quickly swallowed a bit of pizza. "Nope. I was in Japan with my family. We couldn't get away in time to come for the interview. We were there when Aunt Vivian took her oath and was robed." She didn't mention that their absence was intentional to protect their identities as much as possible from becoming a target of terrorists.

"That must have been awesome."

"It was. What type of law does your dad practice?"

"Civil, mostly contract law. He doesn't take criminal cases, but in a town the size of Poland Springs, with less than six thousand residents, everybody is related or knows everybody else, so there's not much to argue about. There aren't that many lawyers in town, so he's kept pretty busy preparing wills and trusts or property settlements." He was intently staring at her and, as if the light had dawned, his eyes widened, he snapped his fingers, and pointed at her. "Ivy!"

Surprised, she shrugged and tilted her head to one side. "What gave it away?"

"Your voice and your aunt said your middle name is Ivy. I mean, what she actually said was 'Whitney Ivy is the kitchen' otherwise, it might have taken me longer to make the connection. I remembered overhearing your roommate say you have a good singing voice. I have a good ear for sounds. The jacket on your latest CD said three of the singers are triplets. None of your CDs have your pictures on them. When I saw your performance on that HBO African Relief concert, you were in costumes that partially covered your faces and concealed your identity."

"Can you keep the secret? Not even KiLi knows and her parents and mine are friends and work together in Japan."

"I can, yes, but you're famous. How long do you think you can keep your identity and celebrity a secret?"

"I don't know, but keeping our faces out of the press and news media was the only way our parents would allow us to travel and perform live. They want us to have lives that are as normal as possible without all of the hoopla. None of us want the glitz and glitter that notoriety brings. We just enjoy singing together. Performing every once in a while to raise money at benefits for worthy causes is fun, but we don't want to make a career out of it. Especially since my sisters are five years younger than I am, it's a hobby for us right now. Our record label and distribution company agreed to the terms."

"I've played your latest CD until my friends were sick of hearing it."

Whitney smiled, pleased that he enjoyed her music, and chagrined before asking, "Can you keep another secret?"

"Sure, if you want," Tucker agreed.

"Have you heard of the French Mariah?"

He snorted. "Yeah, who hasn't? She's awesome."

"She's my grandaunt. My paternal grandmother's older sister."

He sat back in his seat and just stared at her. "Wow," he said, breathing the word. "How do you manage to keep from bursting with pride? You and your sisters have a very unique sound, your grandaunt is a world-renowned actress and songstress, and you're a part of a family of overachievers."

"You must have had accolades, too, to be so accomplished at an early age. How have you handled it?"

"Carefully," he said and laughed. "I see what you mean. Is that why you didn't audition for the pageant?"

"Yep. I know, even without my sisters' voices, as soon as I open my mouth to sing, someone would recognize my voice."

"You're right. Your latest CD is number three this week and trending up."

"Yes, I know. Uncle Bill is our agent. He told me it might be nominated for a music or video award. If we are nominated, my parents and Uncle Bill are going to tighten the security around us."

"You can't blame them."

"No, I don't have any animosity about the security measures. I know they're doing the best thing for me and my sibs, but the past two years are the first time my parents let me live on my own. Or relatively so. I don't want to jeopardize my freedom or security. My dad owns this house and I rent rooms to a few other law students in the Georgetown Law Advanced Scholars Program and to KiLi, because our parents are friends. She's in her sophomore year at Georgetown University. My parents insisted on running background checks on the law school students who live here. Uncle Bill lives here in the house, too, and keeps a close eye on me when he's in town. Anna Jones is a longtime family friend and is the majordomo for this house. She keeps an eye on everyone who comes here to visit. She lives next door with her husband, Fenster Jones."

"The concert violinist?"

"Yes. You've heard of him?"

"Of course. My grandparents enjoy classical music and I heard it a lot growing up."

"My Uncle Chuck and Aunt Vivian play music in their home all the time. They stop by often as they did today or have me out to their ranch when I can make time. Their children, my cousins, all go to school at Georgetown Academy here in town and usually come here after class or other activities until their parents pick them up to go home during the week. They've been known to camp out here if they have extracurricular activities in town or during inclement weather. We have sleepovers and binge on pizza and pop."

"I can imagine a family, as large as your uncle and aunt's, is like an invasion."

She laughed at that. "My Aunt JeNelle Towson Alexander is the junior US Senator from California and she lives here, too, when Congress is in session, which is another reason for the heightened security. Her husband, my Uncle Kenneth Alexander..."

"Who is the former governor of California..." Tucker supplied.

"Yes, and he is the owner of CompuCorrect Global. He has the security system of this house monitored twenty-four-seven by Richardson Investigations and Security. Sometimes my Aunt JeNelle brings my cousins with her when they have a break from school. It gets even more chaotic when they're in town. Also, my Uncle Gregory..."

"The fantastic basketball player known as Alexander the Great and his super-model fiancée..."

She chuckled. "Yes, Angelique comes down from New York City relatively often because Anna is Angelique's mother and Angelique owns and operates a restaurant and a bar in the city. Then there's Aunt Aretha, the youngest of my father's four sibs, who might drop in without notice, along with any number of other family members like my mother's brother, Uncle Russell Greene."

"The artist, Russell Greene?"

"Yes, you are very well informed."

"I read a lot," he said, but he actually had a photographic memory and an extremely high IQ that he never publicly mentioned. "Yet, you don't feel smothered?"

She smiled at his astute understanding. "I don't, no. I love my family, all of them very much. Although I was born in San Diego, California, and lived there until I was five years old, I grew up in Japan. My sisters and brothers were born in Japan. My parents let us come stateside as much as they could so we feel connected to our family here. That was always something to look forward to, but now that I live here, I crave seeing and being with them even more as much as possible. Every chance I get, I go to Summer County, South Carolina, where both my maternal and paternal grandparents live with a substantial number of other extended family members."

"I overheard you tell your Uncle Bill you plan to spend the summer in Japan."

"I talk with my parents and sibs every day, but I also miss not being with them. My sisters and I are writing music for our next music release. If we get fifteen new singles ready by the time I go to Japan, we'll cut a new CD. If my sibs decide to take the summer off and come here, we'll cut the new CD here. It will take us all summer to record. Also, Trey Kennard is scoring a new movie. He wants to use us to sing the title song and maybe a few others. He wants to meet with us next summer in Japan. So, if my family doesn't come here, my trip will be both pleasure and business."

"I know what you mean about missing your family. Because of med school and my military duties, I don't have a lot of time to go home for visits; not even during the holidays, but I Skype my parents frequently. They and my grandparents come to DC as often as possible. Usually three or four times a year." Tucker spotted a couple of guitar cases leaning against the kitchen wall. "May I?" He reached for one of the cases.

"Sure. Go ahead." One was an electric guitar she used to work through a melody that kept running through her head ever since she listened to Tucker and his band. Writing down the tune, she talked with Bill Chandler about it hours before Tucker's arrival. She had it pretty much locked, but it would mean a uniquely different direction in her music, her sound. Nevertheless, it was exciting enough, she wanted to share it with her sisters. After Bill listened to it several times, he thought it was well worth the risk to change the direction of her sound.

"If it's okay with you, I'd love to meet your parents the next time they're in town. I'd particularly like to talk with your father about his law practice. I haven't decided what track to follow when I start practicing law once I graduate."

He strummed the guitar pick over the strings for a couple of chords and found the instrument perfectly tuned. "It certainly can be arranged, but I imagine you're surrounded in your family by lawyers. Your Aunt Vivian's law firm is one of the youngest and most prestigious in the country."

"I am, yes, of course. However, my aunt doesn't run the Alexander, Carter, Chandler, Charles, Lightfoot, and Towson law firm anymore since she's been a judge on the Appellate and now the Supreme Court. However, it doesn't hurt that Uncle Bill lives here and he is still a founding partner in the firm. My surrogate Uncle Alan and Aunt Melissa Charles Lightfoot live across the street. They are both lawyers and founding partners in the firm. Uncle Alan is also the Attorney General for the Native American Nations. My other surrogates, Uncle David and Aunt Gloria Towson Carter, are both founding law partners and Uncle David is the firm's current managing partner and a former US Bar Association president. They were all in the Georgetown Law Scholars Program together with Aunt Vivian and lived in this house until they graduated and passed the bar. Then they started the law firm together. So I can always call on any of them to help me study, but I like to do things on my own and meet new people."

"I do, too. I'd really like to see you again," Tucker said as he continued to strum the guitar.

Whitney picked up the electric guitar and plugged it in. "Me, too. Like to see you again, too, I mean." She picked up on the rhythm he was playing and played along, improvising effortlessly around his primary tune.

"I know you're really busy and I am, too, but my band will be playing Saturday afternoon from one to three-thirty for this wedding and reception at the Washington Club. Do you think you could find time to come?"

"Don't you have to ask the bride and groom about having a guest?"

He laughed. "No, the groom, Mike Giaconni, is a member of our band. He's another guitarist and the woman he's marrying, Trisha Rossi, is his childhood sweetheart. She sometimes sings with us. You may have seen and heard them today during the audition."

She shrugged, but she frankly only paid attention to him on his drums. She had a ton of things to do this weekend, but she liked Tucker Cavanaugh...a lot...and wanted to see him again. "Sure, if you believe it's okay, I'll come."

It looked like she hung the sun the way his face lit up. She couldn't do anything but smile in return as they continued to talk while they played the guitars, smoothly moving from one tune to the next. Eventually, she shared the music she wrote that day and they played a duet together.

"Well, you two must have had a good study session if you're grinning at each other like you aced your finals," KiLi said as she entered the kitchen and headed to the beverage cooler for a soda.

Then she spotted the last slices of pizza, sat down at the table, and helped herself. "So, Tuck, you got any more like you at home?"

He laughed, looked at Whitney and shook his head. "My name is Tucker; not Tuck, KiLi."

Chapter 3

It was getting late and neither Whitney nor Tucker had studied anything except each other and the music they refined together. They continued to talk after KiLi left the kitchen to go to her bedroom. Other housemates came and went and were introduced to Tucker, but didn't stay to chat him up.

It was half-past ten when Tucker's cell phone rang. He sat up straight when he viewed the small screen. "Mom?" Tucker asked and left the call with speakers on.

"Hi, honey. I'm sorry for calling you so late, but your grandmother took a tumble today down the steps at the Court House. This is the first opportunity I've had to call you."

"Don't apologize, Mom. How is she doing?" he asked, his brows drawing together in concern and concentration.

"She's been hospitalized. It's serious. Your father and I are beside ourselves with worry. The hospital doesn't have a neurosurgeon on staff. So they're trying to find someone from Portland, but I thought maybe you might know of someone or could recommend someone we can get to come in. Time is critical."

Tucker shook his head, closed his eyes, and palmed his face with one hand dragging down his features. He wanted to be there with his family to lend moral support, but his mind wasn't functioning to conjure up someone near his home in Poland Springs, Maine, with the specialty his grandmother needed.

Whitney was listening to the conversation between Tucker and his mother. She could see the anguish on his face and hear the tension in his and his mother's voices. She took her cell phone from her pocket and called her Uncle Chuck. When she ended that conversation, she made another call before she approached Tucker, who was ending his call with his mother with the promise to get back to her as soon as possible.

"Come on, let's go," Whitney said as she stuffed her books into her backpack and handed his book bag to him. She grabbed their heavy-duty, winter coats.

"Go? Go where?" he asked, confused.

"To Maine," she said and headed to the front door.

"Wait, Whitney, I wish I could, but it would take too long to drive."

"We're not driving, so come on."

She went out the door and unlocked her vintage Pathfinder SUV in the driveway with the tags that read "EXPLORE." Tucker reluctantly got into the front seat and put his books in the back. "I don't understand."

"You will, but for now, fasten your seat belt and hope that we don't catch any red lights."

It didn't take her long to drive from the wealthy and fashionable Georgetown area of Washington, DC, via the parkway to Reagan National Airport at nearly eleven at night. She pulled into the gated, secured area where private planes were kept, and showed the guard her ID. Shortly thereafter, they pulled up to a huge hanger where a plane was being prepped for departure. "Wait here," she said to Tucker as she got out of the car and went into the office. "Hello, I'm Whitney Alexander," she said, extending her hand.

"Parrish Stone, Ms. Alexander. It's nice to meet you. I've already spoken with the doctors in Poland Springs and alerted them to our arrival."

"I should have you there in about two hours or maybe less with a good jet stream and no headwinds."

When she returned moments later, her tuxedo-clad Uncle Chuck was with her as was another man in a tuxedo. Tucker recognized the other man as one of the most renowned neurosurgeons in the country, and the top neurosurgeon at Georgetown Medical.

Tucker stood with his mouth agape when he saw Whitney approach while she talked with her uncle and Dr. Stone. Then she brought him over and introduced him.

"Tucker Cavanaugh. I've heard good things associated with your name around the hospital," Dr. Stone said as they shook hands.

"Thank you, sir. I volunteer at the hospital when I'm not in class. I've followed your career. I'm at a loss for words at the moment. I want to express my appreciation to you and Dr. Montgomery for dropping everything to do this for my family."

"That's all right. We understand," Dr. Stone said.

"Let's get aboard. Whitney's ready to go," Chuck interrupted and ushered them up the short rise of steps and into the aircraft. Chuck closed and locked the door behind them.

"Uh, where is Whitney?" Tucker asked, looking around before stowing his books in an overhead compartment of the well-appointed luxury jet aircraft and taking off his heavy winter coat.

"In the cockpit. Settle down and strap in," Chuck said to Tucker's stunned expression.

"'In the cockpit?'"

"Not to worry. Whitney is an excellent pilot. If you'd like, I don't think she'd mind if you rode shotgun. Me? I'm going to catch forty winks."

"Me, too," Parrish Stone added.

Whitney was completing her preflight checklist when Tucker came through the door to the cockpit. She didn't break her contact with the ground crew or her concentration on her tasks, but smiled when Tucker strapped in the chair to her right.

"Copy that, Washington Tower. I'm reading you five-by-five," Whitney spoke into her face mic as she continued to check the readings on what Tucker thought was an awesome array of dials and gauges. "This is Flight Alpha 4445 Zulu requesting permission to taxi, Washington Tower."

Tucker listened to Whitney while the sleek craft was pulled out of the hanger and she started the engines. Within a few minutes, they were lifting off the tarmac into the star-studded, midnight sky. Whitney continued a running commentary with the Washington Tower as the plane began to level off and banked east toward the Atlantic Ocean.

"We're off," she said to Tucker, then hung her headset around her neck. She looked at him briefly and then again checked her dials and gauges.

"You're absolutely amazing," he said seriously.

"Thanks, but I could see on your face not being there was difficult for you. I know how I would feel if something happened to one of my grandparents."

"Who does this jet belong to?"

"My Aunt Vivian owns Adventurer Executive Airlines. Another little secret you're going to have to keep. It's really not a secret that she owns the airline, but she doesn't manage the day-to-day operations. She generally keeps this jet for family trips in the US."

"How long have you been flying?"

"Officially, since I was eleven. Actually, I soloed at eight years old in an old crop duster that my Uncle Kenneth designed and he and my dad built when they were in their teens. My dad taught me to fly. He's a jet fighter pilot, but he doesn't log much flight time these days."

Tucker sat staring. "Benjamin Alexander, the Astronaut?"

She shrugged in agreement and continued checking her dashboard gauges.

"He obviously did a great job with you. You seem very comfortable flying this plane."

"I fly as often as I can. Usually, I fly something smaller when I'm heading to South Carolina for a weekend, but tonight we needed speed. This one is faster."

"I can't tell you how much this means to my family and me."

"Let's just get your grandmother back on her feet."

"My Nana," he said and smiled. "I call her Nana."

Whitney laughed. "So do I. I mean I call my grandmothers Nana, too. Nana Sylvia and Nana Helen. They're too young in mind, body, and spirit to be considered old folks. I'm fortunate to still have my maternal great-grandmother, Lula Belle Mae King, alive and well."

"Exactly. My Nana still plays tennis, goes golfing, and sails a twenty-footer single-handedly, too. She was an investigative newspaper reporter in Boston for the *Boston Globe* and she still writes a weekly blog. She's only in her sixties."

They chatted as Whitney piloted the aircraft through the clear, cold night sky. Thanks to a helpful jet stream, they landed, as Whitney predicted, less than two hours later at the small Poland Springs Municipal Airport. They climbed into a waiting seven-passenger van that took them directly to the hospital.

It wasn't a particularly large facility, Whitney noted. It was no larger than the hospital in Summer County, South Carolina, where her Nana Sylvia was the head of nursing and the nursing school administrator. She was also the representative to and an officer of the state nurses' association. Whitney did volunteer work at Summer County General several summers when she and her siblings came to visit their family. Those summer jobs helped her realize she didn't want a career in medicine. She enjoyed the entertainment industry, but considered it more of a hobby than a career option. Yet, she got to be around the rather large number of attorneys in her family and fell in love with the law.

Each summer, during the family's Juneteenth reunion, family members would conduct classes at the high school, Summer County Academy, in different career paths which always proved beneficial in considering career choices. Whitney Ivy was fascinated with the law and her Aunt Vivian and Cousin Donald Dixon were excellent role models. Vivian graduated from Georgetown Law and Donald from Harvard. So she was following in her aunt's and cousin's ennoble footsteps for her first career objective to practice law.

She wasn't sure she wanted to spend her entire life as a lawyer or climb the ranks to become a Supreme Court Justice like her Aunt Vivian. However, going to law school gave her a place to start and a discipline which could be the basis for whatever else she decided to do with her life. Like her cousin, Donald Dixon, he didn't practice law in a traditional manner. Rather, he worked for some type of international organization. He also traveled quite a bit many years ago. Now that he and Oceanographer Cecile Jordan were married with a growing family, he telecommuted and spent more time at home in Goodwill, Summer County, South Carolina. He also handled the legal affairs for the Dixon and the Alexander family members and specifically for Vivian and her husband Chuck when the need arose.

Whitney settled in a waiting room while Tucker, her Uncle Chuck, and Dr. Stone went to the surgical theater to prepare for Tucker's grandmother's surgery.

Hours later, Tucker stood in the doorway, still wearing his green surgical scrubs, leaning against the frame, arms folded across his chest while watching Whitney Ivy Alexander. She was sitting on a hard, plastic chair, her long, jean-clad legs and booted feet up on the coffee table, crossed at the ankles. She was wearing earbuds while reading from several thick books and making audio notes in her iPhone recording app. She seemed completely at ease in her surroundings and not the least bit disturbed by having to fly him to his family's side during this crisis in the middle of the night.

In his view, she was truly a phenomenal young woman. She stood heads above anyone he ever met. Moving toward her, he took her legs from the coffee table and sat down on it, facing her. She looked up at him, searching his eyes, expressionless. He leaned forward, took her head in his hands, and kissed her on her Kewpie-doll mouth. They looked into each other's eyes as they kissed and then slowly pulled away. Weighty moments passed while they continued to study each other, their heads only inches apart.

"She'll be okay?" Whitney asked, quietly removing the earbuds and studying the shine in Tucker's beautiful, deep blue eyes.

He nodded while gathering his composure. "I was permitted in the OR while Dr. Stone..."

Whitney listened while Tucker described the delicate brain surgery Dr. Stone performed and the work her Uncle Chuck had done on his grandmother's other injuries. She heard every word, but she knew, without a shadow of a doubt, just listening to him speak so tenderly about his Nana Felicia, Tucker Cavanaugh was shaping up to be the love of her life.

"My parents want to meet you," Tucker was saying as she clicked back from her realization. "They sent me to find you."

She smiled, but her stomach did a somersault while she busied herself, gathering her books and other paraphernalia.

Tucker carried her book bag over his left shoulder and held her left hand with his right as he guided her through the quiet hallways to an elevator that took them to the critical care unit on the third floor. A group of doctors in scrubs surrounded her uncle and Dr. Stone, asking questions and listening intently to their responses. A number of doctors, when they heard that Drs. Stone and Montgomery were flying in from Georgetown Medical, came to the hospital and were in the balcony of the operating theater, observing the medical procedure performed by these renowned doctors.

Tucker and Whitney passed the group and went into a waiting area where a very handsome man and an extremely beautiful woman sat holding hands; their foreheads pressed together, talking quietly. Another older man stood as they came into the waiting room. Without words, he reached for Whitney and fiercely hugged her.

"I'm Tucker's grandfather, Todd Adamson," he said, holding her at arm's length. "You're the young woman who saved Felicia's life. I've known her for all of her life and mine. I couldn't lose her..." he said as tears leaked out of his still deep blue eyes.

Tucker took his grandfather into his arms and kissed his temple.

Next Whitney found herself sandwiched between Tucker's father and mother in another fierce hug.

"I will always be in your debt, young lady, for what you've done for our family," Tucker's father, Leland Cavanaugh, said before he and his wife released her.

"I'm glad I could help."

"You did more than just help," Tucker's mother, Aurora, said with her pretty blue eyes shiny with tears. "You saved my mother-in-law's life. Tucker probably told you that he was allowed to be in the operating room during the surgery. He told us how difficult it all was, but Felicia should make a full recovery."

They continued to talk while Tucker's father and grandfather took him aside.

"She's a beautiful young woman it seems, inside and out," his father commented.

"I know," Tucker said, still looking at Whitney as she sat talking with his mother and reassuringly holding her hands. "Although I've seen her jogging on campus, I met her for the first time less than twenty-four hours ago. I'm in love with her. If she'll have me, I'm going to marry her." He looked at his grandfather and then his father before he looked back at Whitney Ivy Alexander. "You're looking at my future bride and the mother of our children."

Chapter 4

The sun was peeking over the horizon as Whitney landed the jet at Washington's Reagan National Airport and taxied to one of the Adventurer Executive Airline Transportation hangers. She pulled to a complete stop just outside the wide-open doors as the ground crew secured the blocks against the wheels. Whitney cut the engines and the noise they made slowly died. She stood from her seat, stretched her hands up over her head, and went to unlock the aircraft door that became short steps to the ground.

"See you later, kid," Chuck said, shaking Tucker's hand.

"Thank you, sir," he said, shaking Chuck's then Dr. Stone's hand as they deplaned. They still looked dapper in their very fashionable tuxedos.

He waited while Whitney went through her post-flight checklist and routine, then they deplaned together.

"Where do you live?" she asked as they stowed their books and climbed into her SUV.

"In a dormitory up on campus."

She drove to her home on the edge of Rock Creek Park and invited Tucker in. "Sleep here in my room for a while," she offered. "The roads are a little too icy yet this early in the morning to ride your bike. You look like you're dead on your feet and so am I."

Tucker stopped in his tracks. Whitney stopped, too, turned halfway up the wide staircase and smiled down at him.

"Come on, Tucker. I'm not propositioning you. I promise. In addition to my own bed, I have a king-sized sofa bed in my room." She extended her hand and he took it. "Besides, I'm a confirmed virgin until I marry."

That bit of information caused Tucker to audibly swallow. For all intents and purposes, so was he a virgin.

They slept for a solid six hours in the same room, but in different beds. As promised, he slept on Whitney's sofa bed while she slept in her king-sized bed. Whitney woke first when her cell phone rang.

"Hi, Dad," she said once she dragged her phone under the mountain of pillows covering her head.

"Hi, baby. I hear you did a mercy flight to Poland Springs, Maine, late last night."

"You must have talked with Uncle Chuck."

"Actually, I spoke with my sister when I couldn't reach Chuck. There's a child here in Tokyo, an orphan with a cleft lip, cheiloschisis, and cleft palate, palatoschisis, who needs medical attention. The Japanese are unwilling to expend the resources for the child's care because he is the son of an American enlisted man who was once stationed here, but transferred out and recently died in Afghanistan. The man's American family wants nothing to do with the child and the child's mother abandoned him immediately after the birth and moved away. The poor kid doesn't even have a name, so I've named him Alexander. I wondered whether my sister and Chuck would be interested in taking the child on. He's less than a month old."

"What did Aunt Vivian say?"

"She said, yes, she wants the baby, but Chuck left a reception in his honor last night to fly to Maine with you and a Marine,

Tucker Cavanaugh. She said she and Chuck would come immediately to start the paperwork for custody and adoption and to evaluate the baby's medical needs as soon as Chuck returned from Maine with you. They're already in the air on their way here.

"So how did it go with Cavanaugh's grandmother?" Benny asked his daughter.

"Her prognosis is very good, Dad. Uncle Chuck was able to tag one of the most imminent neurosurgeons in the area who happened to be at the awards dinner, too, to come with us to help Mrs. Cavanaugh. We had a few moments to spend with her, Tucker's parents, and his maternal grandfather after the surgery before we went wheels up again to come back to DC."

"Your mother and I are very proud of what you did, sweetheart."

"Thanks, Daddy, but I just did what came next just like you taught me. By the way, Dad, I think I've met my future husband."

For long, ponderous moments, silence reigned.

"Oh, hell, baby, did he have to be a Marine?"

Whitney laughed at her father's aggrieved tone. "He plays drums, piano, and the guitar. He also has a nice singing voice."

"Well, that's something," he said on a windy sigh. "Does he know he's going to marry you yet?"

"No, not yet, but he kissed me on the mouth. That was my very first real grown-up kiss and I liked it. I want to get to know him first and, of course, he's got to pass *The Mom Test* before I can propose to him in a year or two. You see, he's still in medical school. He hasn't started his residency program yet and he's only twenty-one. Of course, I have another year in law school, so assuming he passes *The Mom Test*, I can't ask him to marry me until I graduate and pass the bar exam. Even then, I think I should get established in a career and be capable of standing on my own two feet before I get married."

"Well, it gives me a few more years to be the best man in your life."

"You will always be the best man in my life, Dad. He'll just be the love of my life."

Another long moment passed before they continued to talk. They never tired of talking with each other. Though Whitney loved her mother fiercely, she considered her dad her best bud. Her father raised her alone in California for the first five years of her life while her mother was away on what she said were naval training missions.

Though her mother was never specific about what it was she was doing for those five years when no one could reach her, Whitney suspected, whatever it actually was, it wasn't training, but was covert and extremely dangerous.

Though her mother was warm and loving, she still had an edge about her, a Southside Chicago city girl quickness that said, given the right set of circumstances or provocation, she could be dangerous, lethal in fact. Although her mother was the American Naval Attaché to the Japanese government—essentially a military diplomat assigned to the US Ambassador's office—she might go away for long periods with little or no notice or explanation about what she did during her absence. Whitney and her siblings learned to ask their mother no questions, but celebrate her return each and every time.

Her mother taught her and her siblings the martial arts and how to use weapons for defense. Those factors led her and her siblings to believe their mother to be a warrior. Whitney soaked it all up like a sponge and still attended off-campus, self-defense classes and taught the martial arts to little kids when time permitted. It was also great exercise.

When the call with her father ended, she crawled out of bed and headed for her en-suite bathroom shower. When she emerged, she was dressed for the wedding.

Tucker was still quietly sleeping. Whitney went to the Keurig in the sitting alcove of her bedroom suite and brewed a large cup of strong, black coffee and made a cup of hot chocolate for herself. When it was ready, she sat on the edge of the sofa bed and looked her fill at the handsome countenance of Tucker Duncan Cavanaugh. His blond hair was a little long and charmingly messy. The five o'clock shadow on his square jaw gave him a sexy, rakish appearance, though it did not overshadow his youthfulness. He was sleeping on his back with his hard, muscular arms up above his head in a totally relaxed and vulnerable position. As she continued to watch him, his eyes opened and the blue magic studied her as she studied him.

He slowly jackknifed into a sitting position and kissed her on her mouth while they continued to study at each other. "Is that for me?" he asked, referring to the steaming cup of coffee she held.

"It is, yes. You seem like a black coffee kind of guy."

"It's the life-giving fluid. The elixir of life," he said as he brought her hand up while she continued to hold the cup to his mouth, his startling blue eyes still studying her over the rim. "I heard your cell phone earlier. Is everything all right?"

"It is, yes. My dad called to tell me he and my mom are proud of me. He learned about our flight to Maine. He also said Aunt Vivian and Uncle Chuck are on their way to Japan to adopt another baby."

"*What? Wow!* They already have so many."

"They have plenty of room for more. They adopt orphans who have health challenges or are in need of long-term, high-quality medical care the orphanages can't afford to provide. They haven't been able to save every baby they adopted, but they don't stop trying."

"That's such a selfless thing to do. It's admirable."

"I think so, too. They also take children who are abandoned and are not likely to be adopted for various reasons, usually medical. When I marry and can afford it, I would like to do the same thing."

"You're not seeing anyone special, are you?" he asked tentatively, concern narrowing his brows.

She smiled at him. "I am, yes," she said, relinquishing the coffee cup to him, took his head in her hands, and then kissed him before pulling a breath away slowly, "seeing someone very special. In fact, I told my dad this man is my future husband."

Tucker's smile was glorious. "I told my dad and granddad this morning I've met my future bride. They agreed with me. What did your dad say?"

"He asked why I picked a Marine. My mom is a Navy Admiral and my dad is an Air Force General, but according to him, a Marine is one-half step up from an Army grunt," she said, laughing at Tucker's comical, pouting expression.

"Ooh Rah!" he said, emphatically, again smiling at and then kissing the young woman who made his life brighter.

Chapter 5

The Washington Club was located on the lower level of a tall, typically nondescript, glass-and-stone, modern, office building in the heart of downtown Washington, DC. The building was usually closed on weekends except for employees who were badged in to access their offices on the upper floors. The Washington Club was a private, members-only association and opened on weekends only for special events like this wedding. Trisha Rossi and Mike Giaconni, the bride and groom, scored the lushly-appointed club only because the bride's aunt, Maria Rossi, was a member and vouched for the young couple.

Maria, a high-powered attorney, was the only family member the bride or groom would have in attendance. Their Italian families were at odds with each other and had been for decades; the epitome of the Hatfields and the McCoys in Italian families.

Mike and Trisha were both grad school students, but when they discovered Trisha's pregnancy, they decided to immediately marry rather than wait until after they graduated. Their families didn't even know they were dating or lovers. Mike and Trisha let their respective families believe they had successfully separated them in high school in the Little Italy neighborhood of New York City where they both grew up. Nothing could have been further from the truth. Mike and Trisha conspired to be together outside of their families' watchful eyes and outside of the city through undergrad and grad school, regardless of their families' feelings. Their families, though modern in some respects, were still steeped in the Old Italian tradition of arranged marriages and family vendettas. Each family was impatiently waiting for Trisha and Mike to finish grad school so they could marry them off to people of the families' choosing. Trisha's Aunt Maria was her father's older sister and the black sheep of the family. She was aware of both families' schemes, but wasn't having any part of an arranged marriage for her niece. At a much younger age, Maria, too, was subjected to her family's attempt to arrange a marriage for her to an older man she didn't even know. Her refusal to bend to her family's will was the cause of her banishment. Maria was the only family member Mike and Trisha communicated with about their dilemma and in turn, Maria was helping them marry, unbeknownst to the rest of their respective families.

Tucker met Trisha and Mike at a little hole-in-the-wall club in Harlem, New York, when he was a student at Columbia University. He was just hanging out one Friday night and went inside to listen to the reggae music the club specialized in. Mike was playing the hell out of some calypso drums, which was an oddity in and of itself. Though he wore his long, black glossy hair Rastafarian style, no one would mistake Michael Andino Giaconni for anyone other than of Italian ancestry. However, if people heard him play, but couldn't see him, they would believe he was a part of Bob Marley's original band. True also for Trisha Rossi, whose dark hair and flashing dark eyes couldn't look more Italian if she were Gina Lollobrigida's twin, but she could belt out a reggae song like a Rasta native.

Tucker and Whitney pulled into the underground parking garage in time to see Tucker's other five band members taking their musical instruments out of a van they used for transportation to and from the various gigs they played in and around the city. They had been together as a band for the last five years; Tucker was the last addition after the fateful night they met in Harlem. They were all students and made good pocket money from their gigs. Tucker, the only one in med school and the military, was the youngest member of the group. His duties sometimes made it impossible for him to join them for a gig, but fortunately, he wasn't the only drummer. He was good, but none of them felt they were irreplaceable. What they were was interchangeable. Each one of them could play more than one instrument and could sing. Although Mike recruited each one of the band members, neither claimed a leadership role in the band. That's why they called their band Changelings. They had a wide repertoire of music they could play and sing for any occasion, but they all loved what they considered a synthesis of funk and reggae. Only two of the six-member band were American of African descent, one a native of Australia, and one of Chinese descent, but their racial make-up never mattered. Their groove was tight.

Whitney found a seat away from the activity going on to set up the club for the wedding and reception. Earlier, she followed Tucker on his Harley to his dormitory and waited in her SUV, reading while he went in to shower and dress for the wedding. He returned fully dressed in less than thirty minutes with his hair still damp and smelling so good he was almost edible. Now, she watched Tucker and the other band members set up their equipment and then disappear behind closed doors.

Whitney was working on her iPhone research app when she sensed someone standing near her. She looked up quickly at the man and cataloged his face and features, then continued researching a case she would have to be prepared to brief in her Torts' class on Monday. Generally, she liked to get ahead of her class assignments so that she could do other things. However, now she was truly behind and needed to catch up.

Initially, she only expected to spend a few hours with Tucker for their study date and then put in some serious time studying for the rest of her weekend. That plan changed with one of Tucker's enigmatic smiles. They had been together since six P.M. the day before. If she weren't careful, she would throw her study plans out the window and spend the rest of the weekend studying Tucker Duncan Cavanaugh.

A tall glass of Long Island iced tea was placed on the table beside her. She looked at it and then at the man who was smiling at her.

"You've ignored me long enough. Have a drink with me and let's get to know each other better," he said, sitting down with his own drink in hand.

"Thank you, but I don't drink," she said, moving the drink away from her. Something about him made Whitney decidedly uncomfortable. Her mother taught her to trust her instincts. She watched him for a moment, cataloging his square face, dark hair and features. Not Middle Eastern she concluded, but perhaps Greek with more Nordic features like Irish or Welsh. He wasn't particularly tall, but muscularly built.

"Make an exception in this case. We've got all afternoon and evening. If you're lucky, you can also have me all night."

"If I wanted a drink, I would have gotten water for myself. The only thing I intend to do tonight is study."

"You're a student? You look like a high-fashion model."

Whitney ignored his attempts to engage her in conversation and returned to her research. That was becoming increasingly more difficult with the room filling up with wedding guests. Whitney could block out the noise, but her guard was up and she didn't feel comfortable with the man still sitting at the table next to her.

He lied and claimed all of the seats were taken and directed anyone who attempted to sit at the table to find someplace else to sit. Whitney resolved to take the first opportunity to move to another location.

Bells chimed and the crowd brought the sound down to an excited murmur. Whitney stood with everyone else and moved slightly away from the table to get a better view of the groom and his groomsmen, including Tucker, as they entered the front of the club from a side door. *He looks handsome,* Whitney thought, in his dark suit, white shirt and maroon tie. He and the other groomsmen had their hair slicked back in a decidedly Gatsby-era style. Their clothes seemed to match the period, too. All of the men wore essentially the same thing with a dark red rose as their boutonnières.

When Tucker turned his head to watch the bride enter the room, Whitney's eyes met his. He released his polar-ice-cap-melting smile until the bride and groom stood side by side. The ceremony was simple and memorable, lasting only about fifteen minutes. Once it was over, everyone applauded while the couple sealed their marriage with a long, salacious kiss.

Whitney thought this would be an opportune moment before the meal was served to change seats. She returned to the table to retrieve her small Hermès purse and coat. Her coat was still where she left it, but her purse was gone. When she stood up at the beginning of the ceremony, she distinctly remembered placing her iPhone in her purse and then hanging the purse on the back of the chair under her coat. The chair backed to a wall where no one could have passed behind her.

Another thing her mother taught her; whenever possible, sit with her back to a wall. That way, any potential attacker would be forced to come within her peripheral view; particularly if she kept scanning her environment with her head on a swivel. She looked around the chair and under the table, but her purse was nowhere in sight. Neither was the man who was sitting at the table. No one else was sitting there and no one was nearby. The expletive slipping from her lips was succinct, but not necessarily vile.

While Tucker dealt with his duties as a groomsman, Whitney continued to search for her missing purse. Her mother gave the purse to her as a birthday gift two years earlier. Stopping momentarily, she took a mental inventory of what was in her purse. She only had her iPhone, car and house keys, identification, a credit card, and less than one hundred dollars in cash in the purse. She was concerned someone could find her home and access it with her keys. It would create a security problem for everyone who lived there. Those other things could be replaced, but the sentimental value of the gift from her mother could not.

Tucker couldn't wait to get away from the endless number of photographs being taken to memorialize the wedding. He only glimpsed Whitney once while he stood waiting for the wedding ceremony to begin. To his way of thinking, she was the most gorgeous woman in the room. She wore a wine-colored, long-sleeved sheath with a deep peek-a-boo décolletage. The dress stopped just above her knees and a matching sleeveless coat with a shawl collar was floor length. The outfit complimented her pretty, light-brown complexion and her tall, slim, slightly-muscled frame. However, it didn't obscure the subtle, lush curves which shown as she walked with grace and sophistication in her stiletto platform pumps. With her seemingly yard-long skein of blended blond-to-brown hair color in a tight chignon at the nape of her neck, the long graceful column of her neck stood out in perfect profile of an ancient cameo. Her only pieces of jewelry were diamond stud earbobs and a gold chain around her neck that read FAMILY.

When he spotted Whitney sitting at a table against the wall and smiled at her, Mallorie Colbert was in his direct line of sight to Whitney and mistook his smile as being meant for her. He had a feeling Mallorie's attention to him might be problematic. More so, however, was Ian Murray, who was at the same table with Whitney. Ian was his Commanding Officer, a captain. Tucker didn't care for the man. He seemed to Tucker a bit too egotistical about his military rank. Even more troublesome was the fact he was a cock hound who claimed he could have any woman he wanted. Tucker didn't want Ian to think Whitney was available for his picking.

As soon as the photos were done, Tucker headed for Whitney.

"Hey, handsome, what's your hurry?" Mallorie Colbert asked, stepping in front of Tucker and blocking his path.

"Hello, Mallorie. I didn't know you were going to be here. I didn't think you knew Trisha or Mike well."

"I was at a party Changelings played a few weeks ago on campus. Mike said you had to work that night, but he mentioned you would be here today as one of his groomsmen and said I was welcome to come." Well, that wasn't exactly what Mike said. Rather, he only said that if Tucker didn't already have a date, she might ask him to bring her to the wedding. She moved in closer to take Tucker's hand. "Why don't we find a table where we can be alone together? They're about to serve the food."

"Uh, sorry, Mallorie, but I already have a place to sit...with a friend who came as my date."

"A date?" she asked, stepping back, clearly annoyed. "Your friends said you haven't been dating anyone and you didn't have a date for the wedding."

"My friends?"

"Yes, the band members."

"Oh. They haven't met her yet."

"Where is she?" Mallorie belligerently asked.

Annoyed with her tone, Tucker, nevertheless, looked up toward the table where he had last seen Whitney. She was standing, looking around as if she were searching for something. "She's over there near the back of the room. So, if you'll excuse me."

"You aren't going to introduce me to this date of yours?"

"Well, sure, if you'd like."

Whitney was frustrated because her purse was missing. She was cautioned by her mother to not let important things out of her sight when in public. She needed to get to a phone to call and cancel her credit card and alert her Uncle Kenneth about the potential security breach.

"Whitney? What's wrong?" Tucker asked.

She looked up, surprised. She hadn't noticed him approaching or the woman who was possessively hanging onto his arm. She was truly slipping. Her mother would not be pleased. "Oh, hi," she said and smiled distractedly. "I've misplaced my purse. May I use your phone?"

"Sure, here," he said, retrieving his phone from his pocket and passing it to her. He began to search for her purse while she was on the phone. At least that was one way to extricate himself from Mallorie's clutches. He noted Mallorie was looking daggers into Whitney's back. He knew Mallorie was interested in him on a personal level. She made it abundantly clear, but the feeling was not mutual. He thought she should recognize by now he was not interested in anything more than a professional, military relationship and, perhaps, friendship. She was a Marine Communications Specialist who was approximately thirty years old, worked at the Pentagon, but was taking Foreign Service classes on the Georgetown University campus. They were both First Lieutenants under Ian Murray's command.

"Sorry, it took longer than I thought," Whitney said, handing the phone to Tucker. "Your dad called. Your Nana is doing well.

He asked you to call him later. Oh, and your mom wanted Uncle Chuck's and Dr. Stone's contact information. I gave it to her," she said, and then extended her hand to the woman standing next to Tucker. "Hi, I'm Whitney. I apologize for my rudeness. I misplaced my purse and had to cancel my credit card." She didn't mention the questions her Uncle Kenneth raised about her safety. Her parents would be notified and so was her Uncle Bill. He was cutting his trip to New York City short and would be back in DC in a matter of hours.

Reluctantly, it seemed to Whitney, the woman took her hand. "Mallorie. You know Tucker's parents?"

"Uh, not well, but we've met," she said cautiously.

"You must have met Tucker some time ago. I didn't think his parents were in town lately."

"Not so long ago," she hedged. Becoming more and more uncomfortable with this woman's scrutiny, she looked to Tucker for cues on what this was about.

Reading Whitney's silent query, Tucker said, "Uh, Mallorie, I'm going to sit here and eat," and pulled Whitney's chair out to seat her.

"Hey, scram, kid," Ian said, coming back to the table. "You and Colbert go find someplace else to sit. This table is reserved for the lady and me."

"Captain, the lady is *my* date. Whitney Alexander, this is Captain Ian Murray."

"Hello," Whitney said. "You were sitting here before. Did you notice my purse?"

"'Your purse?' Uh, no, but you didn't say you were with anyone. You even let me buy you a drink," he accused, annoyed.

"'A drink?'" Tucker said, his brows narrowing. "Whitney doesn't drink alcohol, Captain."

"I didn't ask you for a drink," she said in her own defense.

"Table of four?" the maître d' interrupted. "We are ready to serve this section."

"Uh, Whitney?" Tucker asked. "Is this all right with you?"

"Uh, sure, why not?" she said reluctantly. She would have much rather have moved away from the prevaricator, Captain Murray and Mallorie, of-the-daggers-in-her-eyes, but the room was quieting, waiting for the grace to be said and then the food served.

They all sat. Tucker reached for her hand and smiled at her before they bowed their heads.

The meal proved to be more of an inquisition than an enjoyable conversation for Whitney. Both Ian and Mallorie asked her probing questions she and Tucker fielded and tried to turn the conversation to more neutral territory.

It became clear to Whitney, based on the questions Mallorie asked her and the insertion of innuendo about her relationship with Tucker, she was a cougar-in-training. On the other hand, Ian was an arrogant control freak who tried to impress her with his military standing and worldliness. Whitney never mentioned her mother was an Admiral and her father was a five-star General and Astronaut. Both of her parents were a part of the President's Joint Chiefs of Staff, head advisors to and for the Pacific Rim, and were the primary diplomatic contacts for intergovernmental exchanges among the Asian and African countries and Polynesian Islands including Hawaii bordering the Pacific Ocean. One couldn't be more well-connected in the military than that. They were seen by many as among the most respected in service to the United States. So, Whitney wasn't impressed with Ian's captaincy or posturing, though clearly, he thought she should be. She had experienced both traits in her parents' commands in Japan. Soldiers tried to curry favor or impress her parents through her. It annoyed her that Ian kept saying derogatory things to and about Tucker in a joking manner. She would have offered a rebuke were it not for Tucker taking her hand under the table for a short squeeze. He was reading her impatience with Ian's diatribe well. Ten minutes into any conversation, Whitney was only half listening to Ian.

As the meal wore down, people stood to salute the bride and groom, some with jokes or others with heartfelt sentiments. The groomsmen each took a short turn dancing with Trisha while Mike danced briefly with each bridesmaid. Then Tucker came back to the table and brought Whitney to the dance floor amid a lot of teasing and whistling from his band members.

Tucker held Whitney in his arms as they talked face to face. "As promised, our second date is catered."

Whitney laughed, her smile bright. "It's still technically our first date."

"Oh, no, our first date ended when you took me to my dorm to shower and change. Remember, I asked you to come to the wedding as my date. When you waited for me and brought me to the wedding, it was the beginning of our second date."

She had a pithy response and laughed at his rationale, but he never tired of making her smile or talking with her to the exclusion of everyone around them. That was evident when the dance floor was cleared without their notice. Though no music was playing, they were still talking and dancing until Mike walked up and tapped Tucker on his shoulder. That's when he and Whitney realized they were the only ones still on the dance floor.

Tucker escorted Whitney back to the table where Ian and Mallorie still sat while he went to the bandstand and picked up his guitar. The band performed several ballads as tributes to the bride and groom, but as he sang and played his guitar, Tucker's eyes often strayed to Whitney. He sang to Trisha and Mike, but his words were for Whitney Ivy Alexander.

Trisha stepped to the microphone and then turned to whisper something to her husband, who in turn whispered something to the band. Moments later, Trisha let loose with an old Chaka Khan & Rufus song, "Tell Me Something Good." Whitney believed, if she closed her eyes, she could imagine it was the songstress herself belting out the raunchy sounds.

Tucker was playing the hell out of the guitar and moving his pelvis in a way that made her humble. His startling blue eyes latched on to her as he and the other band members made the lusty, heavy breathing sounds into the microphones on the transition. Their hips moved in such a way that had the women squealing.

Tucker was glad his guitar covered his visible erection. He was looking at Whitney and imagined making love with her. The grin rimming her lips said she was possibly imaging the very same thing. He got up close to the microphone as if he would devour it and stared into her eyes as he sang the chorus with the other band members.

Trisha and Mike did a duet of another Chaka Khan & Rufus release, "Sweet Thing." Again, as Tucker sang for the audience, his eyes were on Whitney's she knew. A thrill, the likes of which she never knew before, streaked up her spine and her blood warmed. His grin grew wider and she smiled at him in return.

She noticed people looking between him and her, but paid them no attention. She laughed out loud when Tucker pointed to her while singing "Ain't Nobody Loved You Better." Her cheeks were flushed, she knew, but TNT couldn't blast the smile from her face. She mouthed the words with him, though she didn't give voice to the song for fear someone would recognize her sound.

⌒

"So, what are you doing tomorrow?" Tucker asked as they sat in Whitney's car outside of his dormitory.

"Studying," she said. "What about you?"

"Studying. Want to study together?"

Whitney laughed. "You're too much of a distraction to try to study with you around."

"Okay, so for our third date, we'll go for a run early in the morning, have bagels and coffee at this little place, Greenfield Brothers, I like to go to in Georgetown, and then we'll decide what to do for the rest of the day." He kissed her quickly and then bounded out of the car before she could answer.

"Tucker," she called after him on a windy sigh.

He just smiled, walking backward and waving until he went inside his dormitory out of sight.

Whitney drove home, and changed into a pair of jeans and a Georgetown Law sweatshirt. She scrubbed her face clean of makeup and let down her hair to get comfortable. She pulled out her textbooks and had been studying for hours in the library when Anna Menendez-Gaza Jones, a middle-aged, but still attractive woman of Peruvian descent and the house majordomo came to the library door.

"*Niña*, you have a guest."

"Who, Ms. Anna?"

"A man, a military man who brings flowers to you."

Whitney smiled to herself. Tucker! She had a hard time trying not to think about him while she worked. Although they had only parted a few hours earlier, she was glad he came to see her. "Show him in, please, Ms. Anna."

She continued to make notes while her thoughts were clear. She knew once she and Tucker were in the same room, they wouldn't get a thing done.

She smelled the flowers before Anna announced his presence. When she looked up, it wasn't Tucker Cavanaugh standing in the library. It was Ian Murray clad in his military regalia.

"Hello, again," he said to her stunned expression.

"Captain," she acknowledged, standing. "How did you know where I live?"

"Oh, I, uh, found your purse and wanted to return it to you." He placed the purse on the table next to her. "Your address was on your student ID card," he said, looking around the large, well-appointed library. "Here," he said, passing the flowers to Anna. "Put these in water." He took off his coat and passed that and his hat and gloves to Anna before he began to tour the room, looking at the books, paintings, and statuary. "Nice place," he said before coming to stand near her at the highly polished library table. "Why don't you have your maid bring us some coffee? We didn't get a chance to talk alone during the wedding. Now we have time to get better acquainted."

"Where did you find it?"

"Uh, well, someone must have turned it in at the club desk."

"Thank you for bringing my purse to me, but as you can see, I'm in the middle of studying."

"You can take the time, considering what I've gone through to return your property to you. Besides, it's extremely cold outside today."

She suspected it was he who had taken her purse in the first place, but had no proof. She would, however, follow up and question the Club's personnel about how the purse came to be in their possession.

Bill was back in town and extensively questioned her. She'd give a heads up to Bill about Ian Murray when he got back from a meeting with his law partners. She and Bill would leave no detail unexplored; especially none involving her safety and that of the residents who depended on the security of their home.

Moreover, ISIS operatives were known to target military families. Although Ian didn't look like a terrorist, his overly attentive behavior was troubling. She'd had to fend off her share of pushy men, but somehow, he seemed exceedingly aggressive. She didn't touch the purse when he placed it on the library table. Bill would raise fingerprints from her purse and run them through AFIS, the Automated Fingerprint Identification System, and then do thorough background checks on everyone's fingerprints he found.

For now, if one cup of coffee would speed Ian Murray's departure, then she would take the few minutes he requested. She sat down and stared at him. He wasn't an unattractive man for someone who may have been in his mid-thirties, but he was at least twice her age and for her, he held no interest. She sat back in her seat, her legs crossed tailor-style in the chair, and waited. He gave her a cocky grin.

"This is a very nice house. Do you live here with your parents?"

"No."

"No? Then who lives here?"

"I do, but not my parents."

"I see. So, you're in law school?"

"Yes."

Anna returned carrying the flowers in a vase and placed them on a credenza by a side window.

"Thank you, Ms. Anna. Do we have any coffee already made?"

"Yes, *Niña*, would you like some?"

"Not for me, no, but Captain Murray would like a cup."

"For you?"

"Just water for me, please, Ms. Anna. Thank you."

When Anna left the room, Whitney continued to sit quietly.

"Why are you staring? You seemed to have a lot to talk to Cavanaugh about even though his girlfriend was sitting there."

His girlfriend? Whitney wondered and struggled not to react; another trait taught to her by her mother. She sensed Ian's comment was used to elicit a response and a ruse to discourage her growing relationship with Tucker. Clearly, Ian wanted to find a way to engage her in a conversation, but she wasn't about to have a revealing chat with him. If Tucker and Mallorie were engaged in an intimate relationship, she would find out directly from Tucker. However, from what she knew of Tucker Cavanaugh, he wasn't the type of man to bring her to an event if, in fact, he had a girlfriend who would also be in attendance. That would be out of character for the young man she was beginning to trust and respect.

Anna returned and handed a bottle of cold water to her and then placed a tray on the table containing a small pot of hot coffee and a cup with a spoon and condiments in front of Ian. He never even acknowledged Anna, Whitney noted, and thought him rude.

The front door opened and a voice called out. "Anyone home?"

"In here, Aunt JeNelle. In the library," Whitney acknowledged.

Shortly, JeNelle Towson Alexander appeared at the library's double doors.

"Well, hello, babe," she said, smiling at Whitney and then giving her a warm hug and kiss on the cheek. Then she moved to hug Anna before turning toward the man in the room.

"Captain Ian Murray, US Marine Corps, my aunt, JeNelle Alexander," Whitney said as JeNelle extended her hand.

Whitney noted the captain didn't bother to stand to greet her aunt, further evidencing, in her mind, he had no respect for women.

"A pleasure to meet you, Ms. Alexander. I see beauty runs in your family."

"Uh, thank you, Captain," JeNelle said, her brows slightly drawn together. "Is everything all right, Whitney? Your parents?" she asked while taking off her coat, hat, scarf, and gloves.

"There is no problem. Captain Murray returned my missing purse. He wanted a cup of coffee as his reward."

Anna took JeNelle's coat and other things and asked, "Would you like something? I just brewed a fresh pot of coffee."

"Yes, thank you, Anna. It's brutally cold out there today. When I left California, it was seventy-five degrees and no humidity. I would love some coffee. Am I too late for dinner?"

"I'll bring your coffee. Dinner will be served whenever you are ready."

"Bless you, Anna," she said with a grateful smile. Something about the captain made her feel she should not leave her niece in the room alone with him. So, she took a seat at the library table. "Where are you stationed, Captain?"

"Here in Washington. I have command of the Reserve Officers Training Corps units at the colleges and universities in the area. The ROTC gives students financial help in exchange for military service later."

"Yes, I'm familiar with the program. So, how did you meet my niece?"

"At a wedding."

"Who got married, Whitney?"

"Friends of Tucker Cavanaugh, Mike, and Trisha Rossi Giaconni. The wedding was at the Washington Club."

"Rossi? Ah, any relation to Maria Rossi?"

"Yes, I understand that she's Trisha's aunt. Do you know her?"

"We've met. She's a lobbyist and The Washington Club is one of their private haunts. As I recall, Marie's law office is located in the building above the club."

"What do you do?" Ian rather insolently asked.

"Not enough to my way of thinking. I'm the junior US Senator from California."

"Oh," he said, a bit chagrined. "Not just a pretty face and great body then."

Both Whitney and JeNelle just stared at him without comment. He began to squirm under their intense scrutiny.

Anna returned with JeNelle's coffee and small fresh fruit, cheese and cracker tray she placed in front of JeNelle.

"Well, since you have finished your coffee, Captain, Anna will show you out," Whitney invited.

"I thought I might take you out or we could stay here since your maid is about to serve dinner."

"No, Captain. I'm not ready to eat. I have hours of studying to do. I need to get back to it."

Ian sat scrutinizing her before finally rising from his seat. "Another time then," he said. Anna was there handing him his coat, hat, and gloves. "Senator," he said, nodding at JeNelle before giving Whitney another long appraising look. "I'll see you again soon, Whitney." *Indeed, I will,* thought Ian. *I have very specific plans for Ms. Alexander.*

When he was gone, Whitney and JeNelle each sighed in relief.

"Who is he?" JeNelle asked before she bit into a wedge of cheese.

"Someone who apparently can't catch a clue."

"A little long in the tooth and pompous, too."

Whitney laughed. "Yes, somewhere between Elvis Presley and R. Kelly. My new friend, Tucker Cavanaugh, is under his command."

"Ah, the man everyone is talking about."

"He is so special, Aunt JeNelle," she said with a broad, dreamy smile.

"So I've been informed."

Whitney braced her face on her open palm. "Did you know the first time you saw Uncle Kenneth he was the one?"

A sweet smile crossed JeNelle's exceptionally beautiful face. "I think so, but your dad was trying his level best to be the man in my life. Kenneth says he also felt strongly about me, too, but he wouldn't do anything to interfere with your dad's pursuit. Of course, then you came along and everything for Benny centered on you and your mother."

"I love to hear about their story. According to them, it took a while for them to figure out they were in love with each other. Nana Sylvia said she knew it before they did."

JeNelle laughed. "Your grandmother is right. Your parents were in love long before they realized it. Your parents were focused on their careers to the exclusion of all else until you were on the way."

"Nana was also right about you and Uncle Kenneth, wasn't she?"

"Yes, she was. Is love what you're feeling for Tucker Cavanaugh?"

"Oh, yes, it is. When we met for the first time, there was this instant flash of knowledge and heat, but we're going to take our time to get to know each other."

"That's good. I'd like to meet him. Do you think he could come to dinner one night?"

"I'll ask him. We're going for a run in the morning. If he's free, maybe he'll come to dinner tomorrow?"

"That would be perfect. I don't know what my schedule will look like once the Senate resumes deliberations this coming week." She picked up her coffee cup and pushed the tray toward Whitney. "Finish this for me please, babe. I'm going to have dinner in the kitchen so you can get back to studying. Then I'm going up to my room to read, say good night to my babies, and torture your uncle with phone sex before I turn in for the night."

"Okay, Aunt JeNelle," Whitney said, laughing as they kissed cheeks. Whitney went back to her studies, dismissing Ian Murray from her thoughts.

Tucker looked at his watch. He had been studying for hours in his dorm room. He talked with his parents and both of his grandparents. They were at the hospital having a meal in his Nana Felicia's hospital room now that she was out of intensive care. She wasn't out of the woods yet, but her prognosis, according to his dad, was good. Everyone was still so grateful to Whitney for facilitating his grandmother's medical needs.

Whitney. He couldn't get her out of his head for two seconds. Rather, he wasn't trying, because he was listening to her music on his iPod while he studied. It wasn't just that she was so beautiful and had a great body. Just as he thought, she was highly intelligent and beautiful on the inside, too. He never met anyone who was as talented and knowledgeable as she. He thoroughly enjoyed just being in her company, talking with her. Morning couldn't come soon enough to see her again.

When someone knocked on his closed door, Tucker called out an acknowledgment.

Payton Bradshere, another band member, came in and stretched out on Tucker's bed. "So who was the stone, cold fox you brought to the wedding?"

"Her name is Whitney Alexander. I introduced you to her, didn't I?"

"Yeah, but you didn't give me no time to get my mack on. You can't have all the ladies, man. Pick a lane and stay in it."

"The only lady I'm interested in is Whitney."

"Not according to that Mallorie chick. She's been tracking your heels like a heat-seeking missile."

"So I've been told, but I'm not interested in her in that way."

"So does this Whitney have any friends I should know about?"

Tucker shrugged. "She's friends with KiLi Hakamora. I haven't met any of her other friends."

"Yeah, I remember her, KiLi," Payton said. "She's a singer, right? Kinda short, petite, Asian woman. She really has a set of pipes on her, though."

"I thought you were seeing Macy," Tucker commented while he continued to study.

"I am, but a man has to have a little variety in his life. I've never dated an Oriental woman. I didn't know you were into Black chicks, but I'll tell you, man, if you slip, I'll be there to pick up where you leave off. That Whitney? She's a real pearl."

Tucker just shook his head and continued studying. Payton didn't know the half of it. He knew great music, though, and if Payton knew Whitney was the lead singer for the group, Ivy, he'd freak.

When Tucker looked up again a while later, Payton was asleep. It was nearing midnight. After a moment's mental debate, he picked up his cell phone and speed dialed Whitney's number.

"Why aren't you already asleep?" she asked, with a smile in her voice.

"Because I wanted to be the last person to say good night to you."

She chuckled. "Good night, Tucker. Sleep well."

"Good night, Whitney. Until tomorrow."

They hung up.

"Wasn't that precious?"

"Out, Payton. Go sleep in your own bed."

Chapter 6

The sun was just beginning to rise as Tucker and Whitney stretched and limbered in preparation for their run. Their breaths puffed out in small white clouds that quickly dissipated in the cold, morning air. The grass, though still mostly green, where it peeked through the snow, looked like it held a light dusting of sugar crystals when the sun struck it.

Without a signal or a word passing between them, they began to run in synchronized movements behind Whitney's home on the inside edge of Rock Creek Park. They ran in tandem into the depths of the heavily forested park on a meandering, rubberized blacktop path that was cleared of snow. Other runners passed, going or coming. Occasionally, a biker would streak pass or people on in-line skates seemed hell-bent on a kamikaze mission. As Tucker and Whitney got closer to the stables, the smell of horses and hay permeated the air. To Whitney, there seemed to be an inordinate number of mounted police officers out at this time of morning. She regularly ran this path with some of her housemates early in the morning, but hadn't noticed this enhanced amount of security.

The seventeen-hundred-acre park in northwest Washington, DC, held wondrous sights and sounds; nature's beautiful plants, shrubbery and trees and a cacophony of bird song. The creek, for which the park was known, bubbled and gurgled over and around the rocks and boulders in its path, creating waterfalls and pools and ponds where deer and other woodland creatures drank and bathed. Beavers built dams and hawks built nests, making the park their home. Occasionally, human homes dotted the landscape tucked back unobtrusively in the woodland area. Her aunt's close friends, Tate and Capri McAllister Kennedy, once lived in a house near where they ran, but they moved out into the Maryland countryside once their twins were born. Tate, a college professor, was also an astronaut with her dad. Capri, like her Aunt Vivian, was an attorney, a lobbyist on Capitol Hill, had the cliffside home built by their friends, Roderick and JaiHonnah Hawkins Baylor, several years ago. Many of those homes in the park were there for hundreds of years. Like her parents' home, they skirted just inside the perimeter in zones where roads or trails were plotted and maintained.

Whitney was in a mental zone, but as always, hyper-aware of her environment; another thing her mother taught her and her siblings. She and Tucker were on the Dumbarton Oaks Trail approaching the stone bridge over a wide section of the creek when she sensed, before spotting, a detail of men and women coming toward them. The sound of crushed leaves to their right and left in the thick foliage caused her to place a restraining hand on Tucker's left, thick, muscular bicep to slow his progress.

Tucker looked down at Whitney's hand before he looked at her face. Her eyes were scanning their surroundings, concern bunching her brow. They were well into mile three and making their way through the woods toward the commercial downtown area of Georgetown when Whitney slowed to a walk.

Since she didn't seem winded, he was about to ask her what was wrong when he heard and felt a group approaching from the other side of the Dumbarton Oaks Bridge.

Suddenly, they were surrounded by figures clad in vegetation-colored regalia, making them almost indistinguishable from their woodland surroundings. Tucker grabbed Whitney's hand and pulled her into the protective shelter of his arms as they looked around at the weapons trained on them.

As the group approached and began to cross the bridge, Whitney released a breath and patted Tucker's arm. "It's okay," she said quietly. When they were in the midst of the running party, one man stepped toward Whitney.

"Good morning, Mr. President," Whitney said and grinned.

"Good morning, Whitney. Why haven't we seen you at the White House lately?"

"I'm still in law school, Sir."

"Your point would be what?"

She grinned. "That I have a full schedule?"

He shook his head full of attractive, wavy, white hair. "When your mother was under my command, she managed to make herself available for state dinners. She was quicker on her feet than you seem to be."

"Until she met my dad and moved to California."

"Are you claiming someone is taking up your free time? Is that it?"

"May I present First Lieutenant Tucker Duncan Cavanaugh, US Marine Corps? Tucker, this is President Clarence Gordon, formerly my mother's immediate CO when he was still Admiral Gordon, head of the Pacific Fleet. He chose my mother years ago right out of the Naval Academy when she graduated at the top of her class to be the XO of his staff at the Pentagon."

"At ease, Lieutenant," the President said, extending his hand to Tucker, who had been standing at attention. "Next to marrying my wife, your mother is one of the best decisions I ever made. However, I should never have let her get hooked up with that Alexander jet jockey," he said, shaking Tucker's hand. "Where are you stationed, Cavanaugh?"

"Sir! ROTC at Georgetown Medical School, Sir!"

"Ah, a doctor?"

"Sir! Yes, Sir. That's my intention."

"What are your intentions regarding my goddaughter, Marine?"

"Sir! I intend to marry her as soon as she says the word. Sir!"

"Well, for a Marine, you've got good sense," he said and laughed. "Whitney, I'm putting your young man on the White House guest list, so you have no more excuses for not attending state dinners. You know you already have code clearance. You're already on the guest list for every event. However, The General still has hopes to marry you off to one of our sons. Bring your Marine to the next state dinner so the General can get a good look at him. Come to think of it, when I tell her you've got a guy, a Marine of all things, she'll probably have you bring him to dinner in the residence."

"General Gordon may have better luck marrying one of your sons off to one of my sisters in about ten or fifteen years, Sir."

"Not if that father of yours has anything to say about it. He's still angry with me for deploying your mother for five years."

"I think Dad has pretty much gotten over that... maybe, a little. At least he doesn't stick needles in your effigy anymore," she said grinning.

"We'll see," he said, laughing and then hugged Whitney. He then extended his hand to Tucker again. "You should have been a Navy man, son."

"*Sir! Ooh Rah!* Sir!" he said, and saluted.

The President smiled and returned the salute before he and his entourage jogged away.

"Okay, that was surreal," Tucker said in a long breath.

Whitney giggled. "The tough part is yet to come. Be prepared to face the General, otherwise known as the First Lady. She's career US Army Ranger and not as amenable as the President. Let's go, Tucker," she said and resumed their run. "You're going to have to learn how to be faster on your feet now."

"So, while your father was raising you alone for five years, your mother was deployed at some undisclosed location?"

"That's right. They weren't married and I wasn't planned. However, although Mom wanted to terminate her pregnancy, Dad wasn't having it. He convinced her to go through with the pregnancy and stuck by her every step of the way for the nine months. Two days after my birth, she left San Diego unannounced. Mom never contacted my dad after I was born. As a result, he was afraid he would never see her again; never have a chance to tell her that he was in love with her. He used every contact he had to try to find her, but never did.

"My Nana Sylvia sent pictures of me to the then Admiral Gordon. In return, Mom sent one short letter to my Nana Sylvia and Granddad Bernard through the Admiral, thanking them for the pictures. After my grandparents told him about the letter, my dad took me to Admiral Gordon's office at the Pentagon with the hope that the Admiral would tell him where my mother was deployed. My dad was prepared to try to be redeployed somewhere near where my mom was stationed. The Admiral bounced me on his knee, but wouldn't tell my dad where my mother was."

"Obviously she came back. Did she ever say where she had been deployed?"

"Not a word and her return to our lives was accidental. She thought my dad married Aunt JeNelle, so she hadn't planned to see my dad again. My dad and mom were close friends and lovers who, according to them, had 'an unguarded moment' and later discovered Mom was pregnant with me. Dad proposed marriage, but Mom refused him. Nevertheless, he brought her home to

Goodwill, South Carolina, to meet his family. Mom became fast friends with my dad's family, but Mom still wouldn't marry him.

"Dad was quite a ladies' man in his day and Mom was very young and unwilling to settle down. She wanted to actively pursue her career. For Dad, this was a first," she said, laughing. "For Mom, Dad wasn't a priority. He said that blew his mind. She was a challenge that led to something more real for them than a surface relationship. They both said they weren't in love with each other; just the best of friends with benefits. Mom thought Dad was in love with Aunt JeNelle and he and I would have a better chance for a more stable life if Dad did marry Aunt JeNelle.

"So when Mom finished her tour after five years, she went to visit her father and brother in Asheville, North Carolina. That's when she learned my dad was there many times, trying to find her. Mom didn't understand why he was looking for her. After all, it had been five years since she last saw or talked with him. Since she was in Asheville, North Carolina, and wasn't far from my grandparents' home in Summer County, South Carolina, she decided to stop in to say hello on her way to Washington to be redeployed and find out why Dad was looking for her. She didn't expect to find my dad and me there visiting for Juneteenth. She also didn't expect to find out Aunt JeNelle married my Uncle Kenneth, my father's older brother, and they had two sets of twin boys by then. My dad finally talked my mom into marrying him a year later, after the first set of triplets was born."

"Your mom must still be close to the President."

"She and my dad both are. They're first line advisors to the Joint Chiefs of Staff and diplomats; military advisors to the countries that comprise the Pacific Rim. They head the US Pacific Command that coordinates the RIMPAC Naval and Air Force joint exercises with other countries in the Pacific."

"No wonder it's hard for them to get away. That's an awesome amount of responsibility."

"Yet they always make time to be together and to be with us."

"They sound like a dedicated couple."

"They are and very much in love with each other, just as your parents are."

He smiled at that and reached across the small round table to play with Whitney's fingers. They were lingering over hot cocoa and bagels with locks, onion and cream cheese at Greenfield Brothers, a small, out-of-the-way, but very popular bakery and tea and coffee shop in the heart of the Georgetown section of the city.

"I, uh, had a visitor yesterday. Your captain stopped by to return my purse," she said. She felt him take her hand more securely in his as if concerned for her safety.

"Is that all he did?" he asked.

"Well, he seemed to want more than to return my purse, which I believe he took in the first place. I can't prove it, though. Nothing was missing. The contents were all still there, including eighty-seven dollars in cash. It's a Hermès bag my mom gave to me for my birthday a few years ago. If theft were the object, I think my money and credit card would have been taken as well as my phone. The purse is in good shape because I only use it on special occasions and it's valuable. It could have been sold, but he claimed someone turned the purse in at the club's desk." She watched his expression. "You're angry."

"No, not so much angry as annoyed and concerned. Did he try anything?"

"No, not physically. I wasn't alone in the house, but I've learned how to take care of myself. He did say Mallorie is your girlfriend."

"She's not," he emphatically said, looking into her eyes, clearly frustrated. "Fidelity is very important to me, Whitney. So, if you ever have a question about my commitment to our relationship, I want you to feel free to ask me about anything you want to know. I promise I will never lie to you. It's true Mallorie frequently calls me or drops by my dorm room uninvited or tracks me down when I'm working. She's tried to ingratiate herself with my band friends. In ROTC meetings or projects, she's always sitting or standing near me, insinuating herself into whatever my assignments are."

"She's stalking you."

"She's just always around, but I haven't given her any reason to think I'm interested in her." He looked into her eyes. "I'm not concerned about Mallorie so much as I am about Ian."

"Don't be," she staunchly said, squeezing his hand. "As I've said, I know how to take care of myself. He's not the first guy who wouldn't take no for an answer. Fidelity is a critical component of a relationship for me, too. I will never lie to you either. If you ever feel insecure about whether our relationship is on track, you need only talk with me."

"You'll let me know if Ian tries to contact you again?"

"Are you going to let me know if Mallorie tries to hit on you again?"

He grinned at her. "No, of course not."

"Then enough said." She grinned at him.

Simultaneously, they leaned across the table for a brief, but powerful kiss. They were smiling at each other, like idiots, when they parted.

"Before I forget, are you busy for dinner tonight?"

"No, why?"

"My Aunt JeNelle is back in town and would like to meet you. Would you come to dinner?"

"Yes. I'd like that. It will be our fourth date."

Whitney laughed. "I'll have to write it down in my *Book of Counted Joys*."

"You keep a journal?" he asked as they disposed of their debris from their breakfast and headed for the fragrant bakery shop's door.

"No, but I'm a fan of Janice Sims' novels. She always references some sage advice from the *Book of Counted Joys*."

"You read romance novels?"

"Suspense, mostly military." She shrugged, thinking of her mother. She would never admit to anyone she suspected her mother trained as a Navy SEAL; that when she deployed without notice, it was because she was on a covert mission. "I'm not opposed to romance in a novel. What do you read for entertainment?"

He grinned and took her hand as they strolled the commercial district of Georgetown window shopping. "Suzanne Brockmann's Troubleshooters series."

Whitney smiled up at him. "I love that series!"

Neither noticed the person pacing them on the opposite side of the street.

"So, I just couldn't hold it in another moment," JeNelle Alexander said, telling a story about her experience on the US Senate. "I stood up to the lectern and said to the honorably challenged and questionable gentleman Senator, 'I'm over eighteen years of age and the fact I'm a female is a no-brainer. I'm married with eight children, but I haven't been called *a girl* since I strapped on a bra and a thong.'"

Tucker and Whitney burst out laughing at her aunt's story. Bill Chandler joined in, as did Anna and her husband, Fenster Jones. They were gathered around the kitchen table, finishing a delicious meal. When Anna rose to begin clearing the table, Tucker stayed her hands and took them in his.

"Ms. Anna," he said and kissed her knuckles, "that was absolutely the best home-cooked meal I've had since the last time I ate my mother's cooking. Thank you," he said sincerely.

She blushed prettily, her lovely dark eyes sparkling at the adulation and then hugged him.

"Now you sit, Ms. Anna, while Whitney and I clean up," he said, rising.

The six dinner companions continued to chat as they worked. Whitney started a fresh pot of coffee to go with the freshly baked Apple Brown Betty she made for dessert. They filled storage containers with leftovers and placed the dirty dishes in the washer. Then they wiped down the countertops as if they had been working in concert for years. Tucker brought the coffee pot to the table and served each mug while Whitney placed the dessert on the table and went to the refrigerator for the clotted cream to serve over the piping hot dessert. Tucker brought the dessert plates and silverware.

"So, I'll be in Paris for a week," Fenster was saying, "and then in London for a week."

"This time I'm going with him," Anna announced and smiled at her husband.

"You'll be performing for the King and Queen and Royal Court?" JeNelle asked.

"Only one command performance and then two performances at London's Royal National Theatre. I'll be working with Trey Kennard while I'm there. He's an extremely talented producer and rumor has it that he's being knighted."

"If so, he deserves it," JeNelle said, with Bill nodding in agreement.

Though Bill was Trey Kennard's attorney and handler, and knew for a fact that the King of England would knight Trey, he didn't comment.

"Have you performed there before?" Tucker asked Fenster.

"Yes, I have, but it will be the first time I'll play for my wife in the audience. She's been invited to sit in the Prime Minister's box in the theatre."

"Wow, Anna," JeNelle said. "You must be so excited."

"I could not do this if my *bebita* would not be there," the Peruvian woman said. "My Angelique, she will come with Gregory to Paris for a few days and to London with us. She was a high-fashion model because of *Señor* Bill and wants to take me to these exclusive fashion houses she goes to in Paris and in London to find dresses. I tell her I have many dresses in my closet *Señor* Bill, he buys for me. I wear only one time these dresses, but she say no, I need new clothes. This one," she said, pointedly looking at her husband of less than ten years, "he sides with her. Does he have to go shopping? No! He gives my Angelique his credit card and says he must practice for his performance with Mr. Kennard," she said and huffed without heat.

"I'm with you, Anna. I hate to shop," Whitney said.

"You are not my own true niece, Whitney Ivy Alexander. Shopping is a woman's birthright," JeNelle said.

"I can find anything I want or need online without leaving the house. I'm not brave enough to go to a shopping mall."

"*Oh!*" JeNelle exclaimed, making the sign of a cross with her fingers as if to ward off an evil demon.

Everyone laughed at her antics.

"So we'll be on our own for two weeks?" Whitney asked.

"I will bring my sister, Salina, to take care of you while I am away. She will house sit for us while we go to Europe."

"That's good, Anna. I don't know what we'd do around here without you to keep us on schedule," JeNelle commented. "I wish I could join you. I haven't been to Europe in years."

Chapter 7

"So, am I going to have the honor of your company tonight?" Tucker asked of Whitney.

"You only need to ask."

"Then, I'm asking. Say around four-thirty or five?"

"Could we make it a little later? Say around seven? I have a meeting at four."

"We can, yes, but today is one of the days I have evening rounds at the hospital."

"May I go with you?"

She couldn't see his face, but Ian and Mallorie could see his smile was a mile wide.

"I'd like it very much. Then maybe we'll make some dinner at your place after and then study."

"Maybe I should warn you I'm just learning to cook. I'm not very proficient yet."

"It's a good thing that, after we're married, we will have at least one person in our future Tucker-Alexander household who can cook."

"You know how to cook?"

He laughed. "My mother taught me at her knee how to read a recipe to the letter."

Whitney laughed, too. "Okay, so we'll go visit your hospital friends, go to the grocery store, cook dinner, and then study. Does that sound like a plan?"

"As long as we can steal kisses between each task," he said an octave below his normal speaking voice.

"That's always a part of the plan," she said quietly. "I'll meet you in the front lobby of the hospital at say, five o'clock?"

"Works for me. I'll see you at five."

He hung up and stood a moment, marveling at how lucky he was to have Whitney Alexander in his life and to be in hers. Then he noticed the quiet in the Armory. When he looked up and around, his fellow officers were all staring at him. "What?" he asked.

Someone began to applaud and then he got the three *"Ooh Rah!"* cheers.

"The baby has finally popped that cherry," someone called out. Tucker flushed.

"So who's the lady?" someone else asked as Tucker tried to quickly clear up his desk in preparation for departure.

"Yeah, Tucker; share the wealth."

He kept his head down and dismissed all questions with a dismissive flick of his wrist. It used to mortify him that everyone seemed to know he was a neophyte when it came to the ladies. It didn't bother him anymore; not since he finally met the woman who he believed would become his wife one day.

"Cavanaugh, you got the medical plan ready yet?" Captain Murray asked.

"Yes, Sir," he said, handing the folder to Ian and continuing to clear up the paperwork on his desk.

"Not good enough," Ian said, tossing the ten-page plan back on Tucker's desk. "I said I wanted six teams of medics; not four."

Tucker's brows beetled. "We only have personnel sufficient to staff four teams, Captain. Also, as I understand it, the exercise will only involve twenty people. Six teams would be overkill."

"Are you questioning my strategy, Marine?" Ian belligerently asked loud enough so it caused everyone in the large room to stop and stare.

Yes, he was questioning his plan, but Ian had been riding his back since he came to Washington as a medical student and particularly for the recent past. Tucker believed he knew the genesis of the enmity between them, but he wouldn't voice it.

"A clarification, Captain. Six teams will be prepped."

"I want a full report on my desk within the hour!"

"Hey, Tucker, there are some Secret Service dudes here who say they're from the White House and they want to speak with you," a soldier hailed across the room, his confusion evident.

Tucker's confusion was evident, too, until it dawned on him what this had to be about.

"Show them into my office," Ian instructed. "I'll see them."

"They want Lieutenant Cavanaugh, Captain. Only him."

Ian turned to Tucker, his face angry. "What have you done, Cavanaugh? Why are people from the White House here to see you and not me?"

"I don't know, Captain, but I should find out quickly so I can get the report redone for you, shouldn't I?"

Ian stared for long moments before he said, grudgingly, "Go on."

Tucker immediately went to the front of the Armory where two Secret Service agents, male and female, asked to see his credentials and then showed him theirs. They went into a small, glass-enclosed conference room where they took seats. The interview lasted over an hour. Finally, they rose from their seats and shook hands. The agents left and Tucker returned to his desk.

"What was that about?" Ian demanded.

"Oh, nothing much." He shrugged. "They were conducting a background check on someone I know from back home," he smoothly lied. He knew before he returned to his desk everyone would be watching, but he wasn't about to waste time when he had an hour's worth of work to complete and was scheduled to meet Whitney in thirty minutes.

"I still want the plan on my desk before you leave, Cavanaugh."

"On it, Sir," Tucker said, without looking up. He turned on his laptop and got to work as everyone else except Mallorie packed up to leave for the day.

After everyone else was gone, Mallorie sat in the chair beside Tucker's desk and dramatically crossed her legs in an effort to get his attention. "So, who was the friend the Secret Service was interviewing you about?"

Tucker kept his eyes on his computer screen as his fingers flew over the keys. "I'm not at liberty to say."

"They certainly asked a lot of questions about you and your history."

"Is the conference room bugged or something?" he asked.

"No, but I can read lips."

"Good, then read mine," he said and mouthed something she didn't particularly want to hear. She was up out of his side chair in a flash and out the door.

"Got it," Whitney said, then hung up her cell phone and went back to studying.

She was sitting tailor style, her favorite position, on a bench in the Georgetown Hospital lobby with her back against the wall, waiting for Tucker to arrive when someone sat down beside her. Ian Murray. She didn't even look up. She recognized his cologne and his footfalls as he approached. She was half expecting him to show up. He called her several times daily, wanting to chit-chat or asking to take her out. She blocked his number on her phone. He even stopped by her home uninvited a few times, but Anna, before she left the country with her husband, would not admit him into the house, telling him Whitney wasn't at home and was not expected.

After Anna left for Europe, her sister, Salina, took over the household duties. She was not familiar with Ian and admitted him into the house. When he arrived, Whitney was in her room talking with her cousin and BFF, the prima ballerina, Linda Lewis Montgomery. When Salina called her room to say a Captain Ian Murray was there to see her, Whitney quickly devised a plan and got her cousin to play along. They dressed and chatted as they descended the stairs.

"Captain Murray, what a surprise. I'm not able to take time to talk. My cousin and I are already running a little late."

"Oh, maybe I should join you lovely ladies."

"Not tonight, Captain, and please call if you need to speak with me instead of just showing up uninvited."

She and Linda left him standing in the vestibule as they got into her car and drove away. That was four days ago and here he was again.

"Fancy meeting you here," Ian said.

"That's happened quite a lot recently, Captain," Whitney said, without looking up at him.

"Apparently, you're stalking me or we're destined to be together. In either case, I'm flattered you're interested in wanting to be with me."

"Stalking? Oh, no, Captain," she said while continuing to study. "That's a crime punishable by five-to-ten in a penitentiary. Not my idea of something to do."

"You're a hard woman to get to know, Whitney. Since we're both free, single and disengaged, why don't I take you out on the town tonight?"

"I'm not free, single or disengaged. I'm waiting for Tucker."

"He's back at the Armory with Lieutenant Colbert. They probably had plans of their own, so destiny has put us together again."

"Again, you're mistaken, Captain," she said as she looked up, smiling broadly. She loved the way Tucker filled out his uniform. "My destiny just walked in the door. Hi, babe," she said and stood to accept her hug and kiss from Tucker.

He knew Ian was looking on, but he only had eyes for Whitney and her beautiful smile. She had her hair in one long, thick, braid down her back with a bow at the end.

"Cavanaugh, I told you to finish the report and have it on my desk before you left the office."

"That's correct, Sir. It's on your desk as ordered and a copy logged via e-mail to you in case you wanted to review it tonight."

"You'll go on report if it's your usual slap-dash work product," he said, fitting his cap on his head and stalking away.

"He can make trouble for you," Whitney said, standing in the circle of Tucker's arms.

"Not over this. He was angry to begin with and what he ordered me to do was unnecessary. I did it anyway, but documented the exchange." He kissed her again to erase the worry from her face.

"You made better time than you thought."

"I had to dislodge Mallorie or I would have been really late."

"She's not going to give up, you know?"

"Are we going to let her or Ian interfere in our relationship?"

She smiled brilliantly and kissed him before gathering her things. "Heck no." They headed for the elevators, hand-in-hand.

Neither noticed they were being watched.

"Come over here, young man," an elderly man said, sitting up in his hospital bed.

"Yes, Sir, Mr. Coombs," Tucker said, while picking up the man's hospital chart at the end of his bed. "How are you today, Sir?"

"I'm dying, ain't I?" he demanded.

"You've got more living to do."

"Don't try to fool me, son. I'm ninety-two years old and I've outlived three stupid wives and four of my stupid children."

"You're married to a wonderful woman, I hear," Tucker absently remarked while he read the chart.

"My Mary is seventy and too mean to die before me, but whatcha doin' with that Black gal over there? I saw you holding hands with her right out in public where everybody can see."

Tucker turned and smiled, looking at Whitney. She was reading a letter for another one of the patients who had bandages over the top half of his head and eyes. Then she took out a sheet of paper, a pen and started taking dictation. Tucker was so proud of how she just stepped up to help. She talked with the patients on the Senior Citizen's Ward as if they were old friends. She even made some of them laugh. A few of the older men made a pass at her, which she handled with aplomb. She also ingratiated herself with the nurses and doctors he introduced her to. However, Mr. Coombs was a difficult man to get to know or even to like.

Tucker turned back from looking at Whitney and continued reviewing the man's chart. He was, indeed, near the end of his life expectancy and should be in a hospice facility, but was kicked out of two places already because of his rudeness to the staff.

"Would you like for me to do anything for you, Mr. Coombs?"

"Boy, I may be old, but I'm not deaf, dumb, or blind. What'chu doin' with that Black gal?"

"If you mean Whitney Alexander, she's my friend."

"If you can't find no decent white girl to be your friend, I got some pure white great grandchildren you should meet."

Just then, Whitney walked up and stood beside Tucker. He took her hand in his.

"Thank you, Mr. Coombs. I appreciate that. I'm sure your great granddaughters are something special."

"Gal, don't you know your place yet?" he said to Whitney. "You need to find your own kind and leave decent, white folks alone. Dis here boy is gonna be a doctor. He don't need the likes of you hangin' around."

If she was offended, she didn't show it. "I guess it's really hard to watch the world change and you can't do anything to stop it. How old are you, Sir? You must have seen a lot of change in your lifetime."

Coombs huffed and shot daggers at her with his eyes. "In my day, Negra women knew their place. They was only good for cookin', cleanin', warmin' my bed and such."

"I'll bet you fathered some children with them, too. Is that who you wanted Dr. Cavanaugh to meet?"

"Hush up 'bout that, gal! Them babies was better off with me sleepin' in they mammies' bed than some no account lazy, shiftless field hand. Why, in my day, I had me a trade. We didn't need none of that 'firmative action foolishness. I was an electrician and made plenty money, too. Built me a nice business and I charged them Negras double the rate, too. They, like you, was too dumb to know you don't put a black wire and a white wire together," he said with an evil, satisfied smile.

"Yes, but you had to have both the black wire and the white wire in the same box with a ground wire to make the electricity work, didn't you?" Whitney said, grinning.

Mr. Coombs was nonplussed as Tucker took her hand in his, bid the old codger a good night, and led Whitney to the next patient on the hospital ward.

"Okay, I need canned tomatoes," Tucker said as they walked down the grocery store food aisle, picking up items from the shelves.

"Aren't we already going to use tomatoes in the salad?"

"Do you have allergies?" he asked as he stooped on his haunches to study the larger cans of tomatoes on the lower shelves.

Whitney surreptitiously peeked at his nice, high and tight backside. "No, no allergies I'm aware of."

"Good. We'll have fresh tomatoes for the salad with onions, asparagus, and field greens." He looked up and caught her checking him out. He stood up, grinning at her. "What's next?"

"Garlic bread," Whitney said, reading the text message Tucker's mother sent. "Then that's it."

"Okay," he said, placing two large cans of chopped tomatoes in the shopping cart, then critically surveying the contents. "Let's get a loaf of unsliced fresh French bread. We can slice it, butter it, and add garlic, chives, and cheese."

"With the onions and garlic, we won't be able to talk to each other the rest of the night."

He snapped his finger. "Fresh lemons for lemonade," he said and grinned at her.

She giggled at his resourcefulness.

"Whitney Alexander?" asked a tall, young man, coming up behind her.

She turned and smiled. "Yes?"

"Kaman," he said, extending his hand. "Kaman Brown? We met at Senator Alexander's conference on battered women?"

"Oh, yes, Kaman. Now I remember. Sorry I didn't place you at first. You're one of Senator Wellford's aides," she said, shaking his hand.

"Intern. I'm in graduate school at Howard University. I asked around. Someone mentioned you're in law school at Georgetown."

"I am, yes. This is First Lieutenant Tucker Cavanaugh. Tucker, Kaman Brown."

They nodded at each other.

"I heard your parents are in the military. Are they having you chaperoned?" he said and laughed.

Whitney laughed, too. "Chaperoned? Uh, no. Tucker and I are friends."

His brown face contorted with confusion. "Friends? As in boyfriend/girlfriend?"

"Well, yeah," she said, confused.

"I asked you out on a date, but you said you didn't have the time and that you weren't dating anyone. Yet, this white boy shows up and now you can make time?"

"Your point would be what?" she asked, annoyed.

"Well, if that just ain't the shit!" he huffed. "You high yellow chicks are all alike. You can't give a dark-skinned Black man the time of day! Obviously, you don't have respect for your heritage!" he angrily spouted off.

"I don't live in your Black and White world, Mr. Brown. My family prefers we live in a Colors-of-Benetton world."

"Yeah, right," he said derisively while looking Tucker up and down before he stalked away.

"Was it something I said?" Tucker asked.

She shook her head. "Racism comes in all colors, it seems," she said and pushed the cart toward the fresh bread aisle.

"Are you going to be okay with people making something ugly out of our relationship?"

"It's only the beginning, Tucker. We've got miles to go before we sleep."

He nodded his agreement and then kissed her before the white bread shelf.

Dinner was done and the kitchen set to right. They hadn't done a bad job of making a simple spaghetti and meat sauce dinner with a field-green salad and toasted garlic bread. There were even leftovers after some of the housemates joined them. Now Tucker sat in the grand, front salon with a roaring fire in the grate across the room. A reading light illuminated his textbook, but otherwise, besides the fire, it was the only light in the room.

Whitney leaned her back against his chest, reading and making notes while he played with her hair, lazily sifting it through his fingers. He looked at his watch on his left wrist.

"Lean up, babe. I've got to go," he said.

She did as requested and then sat watching him put his books away in his bag. "You have to go already?" Whitney asked.

"I wish I didn't, but I've got band practice in fifteen minutes."

Her brows bunched. "Band practice? It's almost ten-thirty."

"Yeah, I know. It's the only time we could all get together and get a practice studio." She pouted prettily and made him grin at her. He pulled her toward him and kissed her mutinous mouth. Then something dawned on him. "Why don't you grab your axe and come with?"

"Really?" she asked, all smiles.

"Yes, really, but don't sing, okay? I wouldn't want you to jeopardize your ability to stay here."

"I'll get my coat."

They were in one of the practice rooms on campus and had just finished a set. The sound died slowly and every band member stared at Whitney in wonder.

"*Dayum*, baby, you sure can roll!" Payton said, amazed.

"Scared me!" Mike said, expressively.

"That felt like more," another band member said and led them into another jam session of free-flowing rhythm.

Whitney played over their funk-reggae fusion with her lazy calypso staccato adding another layer and flavor to their sound on her electric guitar. Tucker was right with her, playing the hell out of his drums.

A half hour later, they were dripping with sweat and guzzling ice-cold water.

"Man, you got yourself something there," Mike said to Tucker, who was drenched, but grinning from ear to ear. "She is real, man! Could you talk to her about maybe playing with us sometime?"

Worry lodged in Tucker's chest, but he played it off and just shrugged. He didn't want anyone to discover Whitney's true identity. Though she hadn't played any of her own hit cuts or opened her mouth to sing, her skill on the guitar was enormous and unmistakable. He would talk with her about it, but didn't really want to take the chance they might let slip her identity. Nevertheless, he liked including her in this part of his life.

She was definitely talented as witnessed by the number of pats on her back and the top of her head by his band members. They truly enjoyed her and when she released that polar-ice-melting smile of hers, he fell even more in love with her as he expected his band members had, too.

She approached him, still smiling. "That was fun," she said. "Why are you just sitting there grinning at me?"

"Because you are absolutely everything I ever wanted as my best friend, a wife, and mother of our children." Then he frowned. "Uh, we are going to have children, right? I mean, other than the ones we are going to adopt?"

She chuckled. "Yes, Tucker, I plan to keep you barefoot, pregnant, and living on the outskirts of town in a one-room bungalow with only a mattress on the floor. When I finally get my hands on your terrific body, we'll have to use your medical training to treat the bed sores on your back," she said, grinning.

He swallowed convulsively and grinned. "Yes, please."

She laughed at his sexy expression.

"How long did you say we had to wait to get married?" he asked.

She chuckled again. "At least two years. I want to graduate from law school and then pass the bar exam. Maybe even work in a career for a year."

"I'll be starting my residency before then. It's going to take a lot of my time away from you. I hear a residency program is hard on a relationship. Is it going to be okay with you?"

"It is, yes."

"Good. Let's pack up and get out of here. I need to kiss you, but not in front of all the guys and Trisha."

She laughed, helped pack up his drums, accessories, and loaded them into the van.

Across the street in another van, someone took pictures of the band members, particularly of Tucker and Whitney.

"Okay, so this is going to be the last kiss, okay?" Tucker asked.

"You said that four kisses ago," Whitney said and sighed, leaning her forehead against his broad, firm chest.

They both took deep breaths, trying to get their rapidly beating hearts and runaway hormones under control.

"No, I didn't—well, maybe," Tucker confessed. "I lose count when I'm kissing you."

She grinned. "I like that you like to kiss me. I like kissing you, too, but we have to stop kissing each other or we won't get any sleep tonight."

"Okay, if you insist. Do you want to run in the morning?"

"Uh, no. I can't. I have to save my legs. I have a game tomorrow."

"A game?"

"Basketball," she said, hugging him as they walked to the front door.

"You didn't mention that, did you?" Tucker asked.

"I was going to, but you kept kissing me. I can't think straight when you do that. Would you like to come to my game?"

"I would, yes. When and where?"

"Meet me here at one o'clock."

"Okay. The band has a gig at nine tomorrow night. Do you want to come?"

"I can't promise. After the game, I was planning to go out to the ranch to see the new baby and have dinner. Would you come with?"

"I would, yes. Now kiss me good night, so I can go."

She did and a while later he left.

"You two are so cute," KiLi said, with tongue planted firmly in cheek. "You're like the living version of the Ken and Barbie dolls."

Whitney chuckled. "Why are you still up?"

"Unlike you, some of us mere mortals have to study."

Whitney noticed the surliness in KiLi's tone. "What's up, KiLi?"

She huffed out a frustrated breath. "Probably just PMS. I've got cramps and I'm not acing my Poli Sci class. American government confuses me."

"Okay, what is it you don't understand?"

For the next hour, Whitney helped KiLi study.

"So why didn't Professor White explain it like you did?" she asked rhetorically. "Now it makes complete sense. Oh, by the way, I forgot to tell you that guy, Captain Murray, stopped by to see you. He saw your truck outside and didn't believe me when

I told him you weren't home. He's kinda cute in an over-thirty-something kinda way. Is he Greek or something? He's got that Mediterranean look going for him."

"I don't know anything about his ancestry. What did he want?"

"He said he wanted to take you out to dinner or a movie. I thought it strange he would want to take you out so late at night. He asked a lot of questions about your schedule, but I didn't tell him anything. I know how you are about your privacy. He wanted me to call him when I knew you'd be home. I told him I wasn't going to spy on you for him or anyone else. What's with this guy anyway? Is he like stalking you or something? If so, your mother is going to freak. She scares me how careful she is about your security. Running background checks on everyone who lives here. That's out there, ya know?"

"KiLi?"

"Okay. Okay. I know. I'm talking too much."

"Sometimes."

"May I ask you one more question, though?"

She sighed. "Okay. What is it?"

"Is Tucker a really good kisser? He looks like he could really lock—. Where are you going, Whitney?"

"To bed. Good night."

"Gees, Whitney. Can't a girl live vicariously sometime?"

"No!"

Chapter 8

"The game is here?" Tucker asked as Whitney parked her older model Pathfinder SUV in a lot behind a high school gymnasium amid an array of expensive, imported cars. The neighborhood was dilapidated, rundown, and looked dangerous, even in broad daylight. The expensive cars juxtaposed against the surrounding neighborhood seemed such an anomaly to him. He had been in tough neighborhoods in Harlem, Little Italy, Spanish Harlem, Bedford–Stuyvesant, Benson Hurst, etc., many times, but this place seemed somehow different. Still, he moved closer to her, carefully checking the area for any sign of a threat.

"Yes," Whitney said as she pulled her gym bag out of the back. "Don't worry about the neighborhood. It looks rough, but this school is 'hallowed ground' for lack of a better term. Basketball rules in this area and is sacrosanct. It's been like that for generations. Some great basketball games were played here under the auspices of the Urban Coalition. No one wants it to end because of a spate of vandalism or muggings. Games go on here year-round and pros and amateurs alike come here to play. It's all about the game the same way it is in New York City's Harlem. Here, in DC, it's the Urban Coalition League and in the Georgetown area, it's the Kenner League. Final Justice, the team I play with, plays in both leagues. You'll see," she said as she led him up the wide, concrete back steps of Dunbar High School. "I'm in this neighborhood all the time. Georgetown's law school is just on the other side of New York Avenue."

When she opened the gym door, the noise and heat immediately crushed them. They managed to snake their way through the mass of humanity to the edge of the basketball court and then stood watching a game in progress.

"That's your Uncle Chuck," Tucker commented, leaning down over her shoulder to speak directly into Whitney's ear.

"Yeah, it is. He plays with a team of doctors, nurses, and other hospital personnel called The Body Snatchers. The other guy, number forty-four for the Wrecking Crew, is JRock Baylor," she said, leaning up on tiptoes and pointing as she named other former pro and talented amateur players on the team.

When play momentarily ceased for a time out, Whitney led the way to center court behind the two teams and began to climb up into the packed bleachers.

"*Tuc-ker!*" Vivian and Chuck's children chorused in welcome. He exchanged knuckle bumps as he and Whitney squeezed into limited space. Then hand-over-hand, a small, tightly wrapped bundle was carefully passed to Whitney.

Whitney took the alert, little, baby boy and cuddled him, sharing the view of him with Tucker. "Hello, Alexander Montgomery. I'm your cousin, Whitney Ivy, and this handsome guy, next to me, Tucker Duncan Cavanaugh. We're grooming him to be your cousin, too. Aren't you a sweet boy?" she continued talking to him while the game resumed.

Tucker was mesmerized by the baby swaddled in a mint-green blanket with a matching skull cap. He could see the evidence of the recent surgery to correct his cleft lip and palate, but the infant, with bright eyes, did what passed for a smile at Whitney's caressing voice. Tucker was itching to get his hands on the little guy when Whitney kissed the baby, then him, and handed

Alexander over to Tucker before she stood up. She wiggled her way to the stairs and then with her gym bag over her shoulder, followed her Aunt Vivian out of sight.

"I guess it's just you and me, pal," Tucker said and continued to talk to the baby who watched his face and moved his little features as if he was trying to answer Tucker. Moments later, his small face clouded and his new little lips quivered. Before Alexander let loose with a wail, a bottle was passed into Tucker's hand by Ryan or Roger; he couldn't tell them apart yet. He put the bottle to Alexander's lips and the infant greedily latched on.

One day, Tucker mused, *I will hold my own child…children with Whitney.* A little girl with her beautiful, light, crystal-brown eyes and long hair she could almost sit on like her mama's hair. Or sons they would name for his grandfather and hers. He wanted a family with Whitney Ivy Alexander and a lifetime of loving her.

They had good role models in his parents and, apparently, in hers back many generations. He had seen pictures of her family all over her bedroom. It was in and of itself a rainbow coalition. Interracial marriages seemed commonplace in Whitney's family. He need only look as far as her Uncle Chuck and Aunt Vivian to see a life with Whitney was going to be a happy one, despite the Coombs or the Browns of the world. He continued to look at the baby in his arms as he sucked the last of the bottled milk dry. Someone behind him placed a towel over his left shoulder. He passed the empty bottle to one of the twins and leaned Alexander up over his left shoulder to rub his little back. The loud burps that escaped the baby had people close by giggling.

When Tucker again had the baby nestled in his arms, despite the noisy gym, the little guy was fast asleep.

Final Justice, the team Vivian and Whitney played for, was up by only two points at half time. Tucker was surprised to see Maria Rossi played for the other team of females, Three Martini.

It certainly was exciting watching a group of high-powered attorneys, local, state, and federal court judges, and law school women streak up and down the basketball court and score. The rotation included all eleven women on each team. The younger women played longer minutes than the older ones it seemed, but they all held their own.

Whitney was playing a good, solid game as the swing player at the third position. Her aunt was a shooting guard. Whitney had maybe an inch or two on the US Supreme Court Justice, but it was clear aunt and niece often played together. They had a rhythm about their moves with smooth handoffs, quick dribbling, and deadly accurate shots. Everyone on the Final Justine team put points on the board, but Vivian was killing the other team with three-pointers. They would try to double team her, but she would always pass off the ball and break free to receive the ball again to score or provide an assist. She also had a built-in defense: not one of the attorneys or judges wanted to foul a sitting Supreme Court Judge. Besides, she rarely missed foul shots.

She also had a boisterous cheering squad with her husband and children in attendance.

At the buzzer, Final Justice only won by two points.

The two teams, Final Justice and Three Martini, quickly passed one another, shaking hands with or hugging members and then cleared the court for the next team to take the floor to warm up. At the end of the game, Vivian and Chuck's family cleared the bleachers and headed to the exit. They waited there until Vivian and Whitney came out of the locker room and cheered the victors. When they walked out of the heat and noise, the cold air slapped them in their faces. A big, bus-like, recreational vehicle idled in the parking lot. The Montgomerys climbed aboard while Whitney and Tucker climbed into her SUV.

"Thank goodness for heated seats," Whitney said as she followed the big RV out of the parking lot and along New York Avenue East to Route 50 toward Annapolis, Maryland.

"You had a great game, Whitney," Tucker complimented.

"Thank you, but I was dragging a bit. I stayed up late last night after you left and studied with KiLi. She told me Ian stopped by again and tried to get her to spy on me for him."

"This guy can't seem to buy a clue. I know you don't want me to get involved, but if this keeps up, we may have to bring it to the attention of his commanding officer."

"That could lead to charges of behavior unbecoming and I don't want to go down that road if we can avoid it. All I have is a suspicion he stole my purse, but then returned it to me. I checked. The purse was turned in by a waiter and Ian went to the club desk to claim it. I haven't interviewed the waiter yet, but I will. The only thing Ian's done is to ask me out on dates or shown up unannounced. Not exactly actionable behavior of the criminal kind."

"The fact he's at least fifteen years your senior probably doesn't rise to the level of a pedophile either."

Whitney laughed. "I'm young, babe, but I'm legal."

They continued to talk while following the big RV through the ranch gates to the huge, antebellum-style White Mansion. Whitney parked on one of the gravel parking spaces in front of the mansion while the Montgomerys poured out of the RV bus and headed for the tall, front, glass, wrought iron, and mahogany double doors. The children scattered to their bedrooms up dual staircases as Whitney hung her coat and Tucker's in the walk-around closet at the entrance. She guided Tucker into what, to him, resembled a high-end hotel lounge in the center of a great room. Above his head was a high ceiling with skylights and huge, modern chandeliers illuminating the space. He turned slowly in a complete circle, noting the large ceiling fans circulating the air and the breeze swaying the tall palm fronds. Two levels of balconies squared the circumference of the space with live, potted greenery draping over the banister's edge in long, narrow flower boxes. The dark woodwork gleamed and the upstairs hall carpet muffled the sounds of pounding feet.

"Don't just stand there," Whitney said, smiling and grabbing his hand.

"I can't help it. This place is huge. It looks like a hotel or posh country club lounge. I've been in hotels where you can look up in the interior to several floors, but I've never seen this in a private home before. It's hard to take it all in."

"It is, yes, but Uncle Chuck and Aunt Vivian need the space."

"They've got it and then some."

"Hey, look what I found," JeNelle Alexander hailed, leading her husband and children into the great room.

"Uncle Kenneth!" Whitney screamed and launched herself into her uncle's open arms.

He caught her on the fly and swung her around. "How is my first favorite niece?" he asked, squeezing her tightly.

"I'm great. What are you doing here?"

"I came to see my latest favorite nephew."

"Oh, I'm so glad to see you. I want you to meet my friend, First Lieutenant Tucker Duncan Cavanaugh, US Marines," she said, introducing him to her uncle.

"Governor, it is a pleasure to meet you," Tucker said, extending his hand.

"You, too, Lieutenant," Kenneth said, accepting Tucker's hand for a shake.

"These are my cousins," Whitney proudly said and continued, "Kenneth, Junior, Kevin, Jeffrey and Jarrett, Marcella and Michelle, and Kendra, Kirkland, and Kristy."

"Three sets of twins and one set of triplets? Awesome," remarked Tucker of the picture-perfect family. The boys were tall for their ages, handsome, with an athletic build and expressive, intelligent eyes. The girls were also tall, the spitting image of their beautiful mother, with intellectual bearing.

"Wow, Whitney, he's really cute," Kristy, the youngest of the triplets said.

"Don't start, Kristy. You're seven, but way too pretty. I don't need the competition," she said, laughing as she hugged her. "When did you get in?" she asked her uncle.

"A little while ago. We didn't make it in time to see my sister and brother-in-law's games, but we knew where we could get a decent meal."

"Good. We'll have time to talk over dinner. I'm going to leave Tucker with you while I take a shower and change my clothes." She turned to Tucker. "Keep your eye on that one," she said, referring to Kristy. "She may look young and innocent, but believe me, she's wise beyond her years. She's a real operator, too, so don't play poker with her."

"I'm forewarned," Tucker said and then settled in to lounge with Whitney's Uncle Kenneth and Aunt JeNelle. However, the Alexanders' children chose to scatter to parts unknown.

Kenneth Alexander, Tucker knew, was the former lieutenant governor and then the successful two-term governor of California. He was now the head of the monolith CompuCorrect Global, an information database, computer design, development, security, and telecommunications company with offices in Santa Barbara and San Francisco, California.

After his stint as governor was over where, for the first time in decades, he put the California economy firmly in the black, he settled back into public service as the chief of staff and local public face of his wife's senatorial offices in San Diego, Santa

Barbara, and San Francisco. He did all of the constituent contacts for her at meetings and speaking engagements. He was the perfect political husband just as his wife was for him when he decided to accept a public office first as the Lieutenant Governor and then as the Governor for two terms. She campaigned for and with him when he ran for Governor just as he did when she ran for the US House of Representatives and then for the US Senate office. Neither Kenneth nor JeNelle lost a campaign. They were the California power couple, but despite their wealth and influence, they lived modestly in an oceanfront home on the Pacific Ocean in Santa Barbara, with a second home in Marin County outside San Francisco, and a third home in Goodwill, Summer County, South Carolina.

They were grass-roots people who worked hard for their constituencies. Kenneth's legacy as governor was to finance educational programs that worked while still balancing the state budget and paired that with a statewide health insurance program that substantially brought down the costs of health care and medicine. Californians experienced near full employment during his time in office.

Tucker was impressed with the man and understood why people wanted him to run for the presidency. However, Kenneth begged off, stating his desire to spend more time with his family. That's exactly what he did with their nine children by becoming the primary caregiver. Fortunately, JeNelle's parents, Harvey and Canty Towson, also lived in Santa Barbara and owned and operated a small fashion house clothing store, but were always available to lend a hand with childcare.

"JeNelle told me you and Whitney performed like a well-choreographed team, making dinner the other night," Kenneth commented.

"We had help from my mom. She texted the menu and the ingredients to us while we were in the grocery store. It's a recipe my Nana Felicia likes to make. It's great for cold weather and is even better for leftovers."

"Except we didn't have any leftovers," JeNelle supplied, laughing. "Some of Vivian and Chuck's children stopped in after school and the housemates swooped in, so that was that. Tucker and Whitney were making enough so we wouldn't wear Salina out."

"Gregory says Anna is having a wonderful time in Europe, by the way," JeNelle told Tucker.

"Gregory is your younger brother, correct?" Tucker asked Kenneth.

"Youngest brother, but not the youngest child. My sister, Aretha Grace, is the youngest child of our parents."

"Gregory is the stockbroker and Aretha is at Harvard, right?" Tucker affirmed.

"You're getting the lineup down pat. Whitney is the first grandchild born in the family followed by our twin sons, Kenny and Kevin. Then there's Vivian's daughter, Linda," he said and continued with the lineup by age or entry into the Alexander family. "And now the newest addition, Alexander Montgomery."

"Whitney said there will be a baby-naming ceremony?" Tucker asked.

"Yes, at the closest holiday when the family will gather. That will be at Thanksgiving in Goodwill, South Carolina. We will officially name Alexander and name his godparents."

"Whitney told me that then your big annual reunion will be held during the Juneteenth celebration."

"Well, actually, before that, Chuck and Vivian host a Christmas Eve party here, but essentially, that's right. You and Whitney must talk a lot, if you've already learned the basics about our family traditions."

"We do, talk a lot, yes. We talk every day and usually try to find time to spend together. We want to get to know each other well."

"My brother, Whitney's father, tells me she intends to marry you."

"Yes, and I have every intention of marrying her, too, even though her parents aren't thrilled I'm a Marine instead of a Navy or Air Force man."

"I understand the First Lady wasn't too thrilled with your military status either," Kenneth said, laughing.

"She made that abundantly clear when she invited us, Bill Chandler, and the Senator to dinner in the residence. She said she had plans to marry Whitney off to one of her sons, but it was somehow worse Whitney chose a Marine instead of an Army Ranger, like her or one of her sons."

Kenneth and JeNelle both laughed at Tucker's confused expression.

"For a highly intelligent General, she didn't seem to grasp the idea the Marines are the best the American military has to offer the world," Tucker declared.

"Oh, there are going to be some lively and interesting times around the dinner table in the future," Kenneth said, laughing.

"*Ooh Rah!*" said Tucker and grinned.

Dinner was another enlightening experience for Tucker. The dining hall was enormous and consisted of round tables and buffets the likes of which he hadn't even seen in a military mess hall. There were rows of piping hot dishes and others of cold salads, loaves of bread of every type and description. The array of entrées was staggering. He noticed Chuck and Vivian's children took on tasks in preparation for dinner and were aided by Kenneth and JeNelle's children. Whitney pitched in by spreading the crisp white table cloths on the tables. She was quickly followed by another cousin placing a fresh floral centerpiece on the round tables and someone else following with ice-filled, goblets of water. Napkins and silverware were added by yet other cousins or siblings until the tables were beautifully dressed.

What struck Tucker was this well-ordered teamwork didn't seem out of the ordinary for the family members. No one seemed to have an assigned task. They all seemed to do whatever came next until everything was done and the grace was said.

Then Tucker noticed that the older children helped the younger ones fill their plates while the adults relaxed. He and Whitney were joined at their round table for twelve by her uncles and aunts and some of their eldest children. The table fairly bubbled with interesting and lively conversation often punctuated with laughter.

When the time came to clean up, it was accomplished with the same precision as the setup had been.

After the meal ended, Chuck and Tucker had their heads together, talking shop about the medical field as they played a lively game of pool in the game room. Whitney sat on the floor with Kristy between her knees and braided her long, thick hair. Linda sat on the sofa behind Whitney, braiding Whitney's hair. JeNelle held baby Alexander while she and Vivian talked with Kristy, Whitney, and Linda. The other family members were sprawled here or there most touching each other or in energetic games not necessarily electronic. Ryan and Roger were in a spelling contest with six other family members while little Eden Ann, no more than five years old, sat cuddled in her Uncle Kenneth's arms, looking on with avid interest.

Not yet two-year-old Teresa Angelique squealed and giggled as she played hide and seek with her big brother Craig.

While Chuck lined up his next shot, Tucker leaned on his pool cue and surveyed what clearly looked like a Norman Rockwell scene which could easily have been titled "Happy Family Afternoon." It was such an idyllic scene; he longed for his own family to be sitting among this group of loving family members. Most of the children may not have been born into the family, but they were each clearly comfortable in their own skin and pleasingly ensconced in their family milieu. They epitomized the gold chains they each wore around their necks that read FAMILY.

Chuck came to quietly stand beside Tucker as Tucker continued to survey the dynamics in the games room. They watched Whitney lean forward, while still sitting on the floor, to listen more closely to something Kristy was saying. Then she wrapped her arms around the younger girl, swaying from side to side before she kissed her on the cheek, making Kristy giggle. Vivian, Linda, and JeNelle grinned down at whatever Kristy was saying. Ryan missed a word and had to put a chip in the pot. Four people were playing doubles Wii tennis and sending up a racket that didn't seem to disturb the chess match between the cousins, Kevin and Geneviève. Her twin brother, Vincent, was pouring small cups of lemonade for his younger siblings. Bryan Jackson Montgomery, the second oldest of Chuck and Vivian's children, was on his knees helping Marcella and Michele set up an electric train set complete with miniature scenery, landscape, and houses that their grandfather, Bernard Alexander, had built for them out of wood. There were energetic ping-pong and air hockey games underway as well.

Chuck put his hand on Tucker's shoulder. "How does all of this make you feel?"

At that moment, Whitney looked up at him and smiled. He returned her smile with one of his own. "Like words are inadequate to describe it."

"Exactly right," Chuck said, patting him on the shoulder before they returned to their game of pool.

"He's so cute and smart, too, Whitney," little Kristy was saying as she continued refining a picture that bore a striking resemblance to Tucker without looking up at him.

"I know you're right and that picture looks just like him, Kristy," she said as she continued to braid the little girl's hair to resemble hers. "You are so talented. You could be an artist just like Uncle Russell and Nana Helen."

"Do you think so? Do you really think I could be an artist?" Kristy enthusiastically asked.

"I do, yes. You are really good. Tucker is going to be so happy when you show the picture to him."

Later, Whitney leaned her head on her Uncle Kenneth's strong, muscled shoulder, and sighed. His arm automatically enclosed her and then he kissed the top of her head.

"He's some kind of wonderful," she declared while watching Tucker and Ryan competing in a Wii baseball game. Others stood or sat around cheering and waiting their turn at bat. Tucker was just a few years older than her cousins and fit in so easily with her family. That fact alone let her fall just a little bit more in love with him.

The first test would come from her Uncle Kenneth, though. He was the eldest of the five Alexander siblings and every one of them looked up to him, including her dad, the second born after Kenneth. She looked around the room. Uncle Chuck was feeding Alexander and carrying on a conversation with the baby while Aunt Vivian looked on with their youngest daughter, Teresa Angelique, cuddled in her lap and arms. Aunt JeNelle was helping Preston, Reed, and Micah dish up the home-made ice cream fresh from the churn onto warm sponge cake straight from the oven. It was a typical Sunday afternoon and early evening in the Montgomery-Alexander household, which somehow made it so much more special because Tucker was there with her; with them.

"Did Dad ask you to come to check him out?" Whitney asked her uncle.

"No, your mother did," Kenneth said honestly and squeezed her briefly.

"I thought as much. It's not like you to take my cousins out of school on the spur of the moment like that and fly here just to see the new arrival. We Skype each other all the time, especially on Sundays. You've already seen Alexander in virtual reality. Besides, Thanksgiving is right around the corner. You could have waited to see Alexander then."

"Maybe you don't already know this, but let me tell you I love you so much your mother really didn't have to ask me to come to check out 'the love of your life.' I was already planning to come when your dad told me that bit of news. Don't think your Uncle Gregory and Aunt Aretha aren't going to be the next ones to pop up on your doorstep to check out this potential new addition."

"It will depend a great deal on what you think, Uncle Kenneth. Nana Sylvia and Pop Bernie will ask you what you think. So will Nana Helen, Popi Willis, and Uncle Russell. What will you tell them and Mom?"

"That I trust you and your judgment about who you fall in love with. So far, I think Tucker Cavanaugh may be the type of man who may aspire to deserve your time and attention. He's clearly crazy about you to put up with the beatdown Ryan is about to give him. Wasn't Ryan state baseball MVP at the Nationals last season?"

Whitney chuckled. "He was, yes, a fact I failed to mention to Tucker. Ooops! Ryan just struck him out."

Tucker threw up his hands in surrender and bowed several times while Ryan jumped around, pumping his arms in the air like he was Rocky. Tucker came and sat next to Whitney and Kenneth.

He shook his head and sighed. "Kids these days," he said and had Kenneth and Whitney hooting with laughter. "There's entirely too much talent in this family. I have to step up my game."

"Whitney tells me you're pretty talented, too. Care to give us a demonstration?"

"I wouldn't mind, but I don't have..."

"Hey, folks, let's grab dessert and head to the music room," Kenneth hailed, interrupting Tucker.

"Music room? There's a music room in here?" Tucker asked, surprised.

"You have no idea what's tucked between the walls of this house," Whitney sagely said.

Sure enough, in another part of the mansion's lower level, there was a soundproof music studio space large enough to seat an orchestra, with lounge-like ample sofa seating and floor pillows. They all piled in while Whitney slid open a door where instruments hung in protective cases on the walls. There were several types of guitars, some were electric.

"*Voila!*" Whitney said, indicating the instruments.

"*Man!*" Tucker said and selected a beautiful smooth teakwood guitar.

Whitney selected another one and they took their seats on tall stools and tuned the instruments. Other family members flooded the room and grabbed various instruments to add to the ones already on the stage.

Roger set up microphones and held an earphone to his head while Ryan maneuvered levers and dials on a soundboard mixing console and tape-to-CD converter. "Give me a sound check, Whitney."

She did and he gave her a thumbs-up signal.

"What do you want to do?" Tucker asked.

"'When You Know It's Right,' of course," she said with a warm smile, referring to the piece she started writing on the day they met and they finished together that same night before their impromptu flight to Maine.

"Is it okay for you to sing here?" he asked, concerned.

She nodded and started the intro. He picked up the beat.

You can look for a lifetime and never really find that special
Someone who fits into your life just right that tight
But when I met you, I knew in an instant you were my Mr. Right
The man who would light up my life.
You held me and kissed me just right.

I knew, at first sight, you would be my Mrs. Right. Because
When that feeling grabs you in your heart, with might, that's when
You know it's right.
You will put an end to my lonely nights.
You will hold me tight and I will always love you just right.
Love isn't a game for us. It's what we'll have for the rest of our
lives.

They went on singing the reggae-funk-calypso duet to each other as if no one else was in the room. The lights were lowered and a spotlight shined only on them. Three minutes later, they played the final chord to rousing applause and cheers.

They were grinning at each other like idiots.

"More! More!" the crowd called. Others took up instruments; a jam session ensued and recorded on audio and video for posterity.

"I have to go, Whitney, or I'll be late meeting the band to perform at a club at Harbor Place tonight," Tucker said, aggrieved and kissed her again.

"I know," she said and hugged him tightly. "Alahandro is going to drop you off at your dormitory."

"I know. He's been waiting for me for ten minutes, so you have to kiss me again so I can leave."

"I already did that," she said and grinned, "ten minutes ago."

"So you're going to stay here tonight?"

"I am, yes. I'll come back to town tomorrow morning with this crew. My first class isn't until later in the morning."

"Okay, I'll call you before you go to bed tonight. I'm going to miss you."

"Maybe we'll find some time tomorrow?"

"I've got labs all day and class prep to do. Then I'm in the Armory tomorrow night for a lecture series until late."

"This may be the first time we won't see each other for a whole day since we met."

"If you can come back to town early, we'll make time for coffee." He kissed her again and was gone.

Chapter 9

Changelings took a well-deserved break and turned on a recorded disk of their music for the crowd. The place, though large, was packed.

"You want to take the lead, Tucker?" Mike asked.

"Not tonight."

"You sound a little hoarse."

Tucker didn't want to mention he and Whitney did two hours of music with her family. Her cousins, many of them, were excellent singers and musicians and he enjoyed performing with them. Her Aunt JeNelle was an incredible pianist. Everyone sang with varying degrees of proficiency, but they enjoyed every minute of the impromptu show they put on. Not once, however, did they sing any of Ivy's hit songs. Apparently, her family was attempting to protect Whitney's identity, unaware he knew her secret. He didn't let on he knew and neither did Whitney.

"So, where's your little friend tonight." Mallorie ambushed him as soon as he came out of the men's room.

"Oh, hello, Mallorie. I didn't know you were here. This crowd is very large."

"Your bookings are on Changelings' website. I usually check to see when and where you're playing."

"I see. I didn't know that. Enjoy the rest of your evening," he said, as he started to pass by her, but she stepped into his way, blocking his attempt to return to the club stage.

"I guess your young, junior high school girlfriend isn't old enough to be out late at night or in a club that serves alcohol."

"If you mean, Whitney Alexander, then you're mistaken."

"You should be careful, Tucker. Your career severely would be damaged if she screams statutory rape."

"As you're aware, she's in law school, so she's over the age of consent. However, speaking of age, it confuses me why a woman who is obviously nearly or over thirty would want to compete with a woman at least ten years her junior."

"You simply don't know what you're missing."

"I haven't had jock itch either, but I don't miss it," he said and finally stepped past her.

The band was reassembling on stage for the final set.

She watched him head back to the stage and pulled the little recorder from her pocket. She believed there was enough of his voice print to put together a conversation of a very different kind and play it for his little girlfriend. She intended to have Tucker Cavanaugh before the end of the semester. After the first of the year, she had to resume her position as a Communications Officer at the Pentagon on the Latin America Desk. She was not happy about that probability. Still, she had time to put her skills to work and manufacture a conversation that would have little Ms. Whitney Alexander go running and screaming away from Tucker.

During the final set, when Tucker took time to actually look out on the dance floor, he noticed KiLi waving at him and trying to get his attention. He nodded to her, acknowledging her presence. She was showing up more and more with his band member, Payton Bradshere. She was an attractive young woman and he didn't want to see her hurt. Payton wasn't the faithful type. He dated all types of women like some ate multi-colored jelly beans; one after the other or sometimes more than two at a time.

He hoped KiLi was mature enough to know what she was in for with Payton. It was none of his business, but he would mention it to Whitney the next time they spoke. It wouldn't be tonight, though. The band was scheduled to gig until one o'clock in the morning. He was going to have to sleep fast and be up for lab work by seven o'clock.

It was one-thirty when Tucker left the men's room of the club and headed toward the empty main room. The club closed at one, but they were delayed in leaving by a bunch of women who wanted autographs and much more. Fortunately, he and his band members already packed up their equipment, preparing for departure. If some of the guys hooked up, that was on them. He wasn't interested in what the women were offering. He was ready to get some sleep after a full day of classes, hospital duty, and with Whitney at her game and then at her family's ranch. As he walked the corridor, he heard someone crying. Stepping back into the hall, he noticed Mike holding Trisha as she wept on her husband's shoulder.

"Wash your face, babe," Mike said, sending Trisha into the ladies' room.

"What's wrong?" Tucker asked, joining Mike in the narrow offshoot of the corridor as he watched Trisha leave.

Mike shook his head. "Trisha's family found out we're married and they're furious. They threatened bodily harm to me if we didn't divorce immediately. They have some old guy they promised her to and they intend for her to marry him. Trisha is afraid they're serious and would put a hit out on me."

"Seriously?" Tucker asked incredulously. "What is this feud all about?"

"Something from the old country about my great, great-grandfather who killed Trisha's great, great-grandfather in order to take his wife. Folklore says that the woman in question was young and stunningly beautiful. My ancestor was older, wealthy, and wanted her, but she loved someone else and refused the demand from her family to wed someone she didn't love. Instead, she eloped with the young man she loved and stayed away from her family and village for many years.

"When she was informed her father died and her mother's life was threatened because she no longer had a husband to protect her, she returned with her husband and children. My ancestor killed her husband and threatened to kill her sons and her mother if she didn't marry him. She sent her children away and threatened to commit suicide if my ancestor harmed another of her relatives.

"However, even though her husband and father were dead, she had no patron to protect her; she still refused to marry him. He abducted her, kept her under constant guard and, after a year for her to mourn her husband's murder, my relative married her against her will. Because she fought him, he killed every one of the remaining family members he could find. Many escaped to America and other parts of the world, but the vendetta remained in place."

"That's what this feud is all about?"

"Oh, there's more. Over the years, her family and mine have killed off some faction of the other's family members. Several years ago, my family was accused of killing one of Trisha's cousins, Millos Santangelo, on a street in New York City's Little Italy. Privately, my family said they didn't do it, but they took credit for it. Several years later, my family was nearly decimated by the governments of several countries, including the US. My family believes remaining factions of the Santangelos were behind it. You see, my three times great-grandfather is Tommaso Cascioferro."

"Don Tomas?" Tucker asked, incredulous. "He's the godfather's godfather. He's the head of one of the largest Italian syndicates."

"Exactly. Translated to be the top Mafia Don and a lunatic. Believe it or not, he's still alive."

"That's longevity."

"In my family and hers, girls become brides before they're out of puberty. If they make it out of their teens unmarried, it's a rare thing. Trisha was betrothed to some Mafioso when she was ten, but her father believes in education for girls, so she was allowed to finish high school and college. In order to finish grad school, she had to agree to marry immediately after she graduated. Her wedding was scheduled for May of next year. In both of our families, a selected husband wants assurances the girl he marries is a virgin and both of our families make that guarantee when they agree to the marriage bands. Don Tomas' reputation rides on it. My mother was fifteen when I was born. My grandparents married her to my father, who was twenty years her senior. They never met before their wedding. She was not his first wife, but, somehow, that wife mysteriously died. My mother said she probably would have met the same fate, if she hadn't given my father sons. Apparently, the first wife couldn't have children."

"What about you? Are you betrothed to be married?"

"I am, yes, but my fiancé is seven years old as we speak. I'm allowed to 'sow my wild oats,'" he said, using his fingers as quote marks, "but I'm being groomed to take over one of my family's businesses when I leave here in the spring. Something I have no intention of doing."

Tucker just shook his head in sympathy. "Don Tomas has got to be up there in age. Where is he now?"

"He's over one hundred years old and lives in Palermo, Italy. He still rules what's left of our family through his six sons. One of his sons, Diego Valachi Cascioferro, is my great-grandfather. When the governments arrested and convicted most of the men in my family, they blamed Trisha's family for providing the evidence that got my family incarcerated or killed. My cousin, Francisco 'Frank' Delaware, was also blamed for the governments' ability to gain incriminating evidence against us. Don Tomas killed him before the feds could get their hands on him. Frank's son, David Delaware, was gunned down at a resort in Atlantic Beach, South Carolina, by a government agent. So, follow this logic. It's okay for the Don to kill his own, but not a government official he believes is a tool for an enemy, like Trisha's family. He's still hunting for the agent who shot David. Consider this: David was gunned down while trying to kill Justin McCoy and his family."

"The hotelier?"

"The same," Mike confirmed.

"I remember reading about that. I thought it was the FBI, CIA, DEA, Interpol and other nations' enforcement agencies who banded together and formed a strike force."

"A Tiger Team, yes, but my family still believes it was Trisha's family who put the authorities onto them. Neither family seems capable of grasping the simple fact that what they do and the shady businesses they own are against the law and would be investigated by the government."

"What are you and Trisha going to do?"

"Because of the baby, Trisha's Aunt Maria wants us to lay low for a while until she can figure out how to protect us from her family's threats. We're going away for a while."

Tucker's brows furrowed in confusion and concern. "What about your classes and hers? How are you going to manage to fulfill your requirements for your master's? We're only a month or so away from the end of the semester and then you've got another semester to go."

"Thank God for cyberspace. I'm a cyber geek, remember? We'll video monitor our classes and send in assignments through a secure server for as long as we have to. I know this super geek who can channel us through a lot of places in cyberspace to protect us and our location. I've worked with him before and I trust him. We'll be fine as long as Trish and I are together.

"However, I'd appreciate it if you would try to keep the band going as much as you can. I know you have a heavy course load and military obligations, but Changelings is very important to all of us. I've sent a couple of our demo CDs to Trey Kennard and I think he's interested. He's out of the country now, but when he comes back, he says he'll take a meeting."

"I'll do what I can," Tucker said, but immediately thought that if Whitney and her sisters could write enough music, they were also scheduled to work with Trey Kennard over the coming summer. He planned to mention to Whitney that Kennard may also be working with Changelings at the same time. This could prove problematic.

"Great! Take my van and park it somewhere safe. I don't want anyone, namely her family, to get their hands on our equipment. It would be just like them to destroy it."

"Sure, not a problem. I think I know a safe place to hide it."

"Good. Here are the keys," he said just as Trisha came out of the ladies' room. "You and the rest of Changelings can finish out our remaining gigs, but I didn't schedule anything for after the beginning of the New Year. You or Payton might want to talk to KiLi about filling in for Trisha or interview someone else to take her place for now. Don't forget about the holiday extravaganza at the university."

"Okay, I'll talk with the band at our next rehearsal about what we should do. You be safe," he said, giving Trisha a warm embrace and Mike a clasped-hand, shoulder bump in parting.

Tucker watched them go, surrounded by five behemoths all carrying more weapons fully visible than a SEAL team.

"So, you're sure it's all right?" Tucker asked Whitney.

"Yes, I'm sure. I'll alert security that you're expected. Do you remember how to get here?"

"I do, yes. I take that turn off from Route 301 before it becomes Route 3."

"That's right. When you get to the ranch, I'll meet you and we'll put the van into one of the stalls in the barn garage. There's plenty of space and no one will bother it there. Then you can spend the rest of the night here and ride into town with me early in the morning."

"Thanks, Whitney. I hate to ask, but I didn't know of a place where our equipment would be more secure. I apologize for waking you up. I'm on my way, though. I should be there shortly. Ten to fifteen minutes tops."

"Okay, I'll see you soon."

When they disconnected, Tucker adjusted his rearview mirror. An eighteen-wheeler was dogging his tail for the last five miles since he turned off I-95 onto Route 50 Eastbound toward Annapolis. The truck's high beams were making it difficult for him to see the road with the lights reflecting off his rearview and side-view mirrors.

Tucker changed lanes in an effort to let the tractor trailer pass, but the truck changed lanes, too, and stayed on his tail.

"This is ridiculous," Tucker said aloud and switched lanes again. Before the truck could get behind him, he slowed down to let it pass.

He thought the maneuver worked until the trailer started drifting into his lane crowding him. He blasted the van's horn, but the truck kept coming. He slowed, even more, trying to avoid a collision. Suddenly, the trailer slammed into the left side of the van, forcing it completely off the road. Tucker fought to maintain control of the van, but before he knew it, the van was airborne and tumbling down an embankment into thick vegetation. When it finally landed, the van was upside down in a deep ravine where it could not be seen from the highway and Tucker was unconscious with the band's equipment piled atop him.

"I don't know what happened," Whitney complained, yet concerned. "When I spoke with Tucker, he said he would arrive in about fifteen minutes."

"Maybe he changed his mind," Vivian said, as they sat at the breakfast table. It was seven in the morning and everyone was preparing to head out to school or work. JeNelle was taking her husband and children to the small municipal airport for their flight back to California before she went to Capitol Hill to begin her day.

Whitney wasn't sure what to do at this point. She was awake, waiting for Tucker since he called and woke her. As time passed, the more worried she became.

"Did you hear me, Whitney?"

"I did, yes, Aunt Vivian, but if he changed his mind, I think he would have called me to let me know. He's not an inconsiderate person."

"Well, Chuck checked with the highway patrol. There have been no reports of accidents involving a panel truck anywhere on the route he would have taken from the club at Harbor Place. He would most likely come here via the I-95 and I-495 Beltway to Route 50 East and then to Route 301. He knows where the turn off is from Route 301, doesn't he?"

"He does, yes, but maybe he took Route 295, Kenilworth Avenue," she said, hopefully.

Vivian shook her head. "Not likely. It's a little out of the way. Moreover, if he had, and something happened, the van he was driving would have been spotted by now. Route 301 is mostly rural, but Route 295 is urban."

Whitney threw up her hands in frustration. "I don't know what to think."

"Since he hasn't answered his cell phone, get in touch with the other band members. Or go to his dorm room and determine whether he's been there. Keep checking with Highway Patrol." She rose from her seat, kissed Whitney's troubled brow, and prepared to leave with the rest of her family. "Don't sit and worry, okay? You'll feel better if you're doing something to find him. Plan your steps and then work your plan."

"You're right. Thanks, Aunt Vivian."

"You're welcome. My schedule is light leading up to the Thanksgiving holiday. Call me if you need me."

"I will," Whitney agreed.

It was nine o'clock in the morning when Whitney left the club at Harbor Place in southern Prince George's County, Maryland. She checked with the staff who were on duty the night before about whether there were any incidents involving the band. No one knew of anything, but two guys offered to help her look if she would stick around and have lunch and breakfast at their place with them. She declined their invitations and took the most likely route Tucker would have taken to the ranch.

She spoke with KiLi and Payton Bradshere, Tucker's friend and fellow band member, on the way while she drove. KiLi posted pictures on several social media sites about the club's event and pictures of herself with the band members, including Tucker. According to them, Tucker was driving the van instead of Mike and Trisha, but they didn't know where Tucker went after he left the club with the equipment. They said that Mallorie Colbert was there, trying, as usual, to snag his attention. They assumed he was heading to his dormitory sans Mallorie.

Whitney didn't want to alarm Tucker's friends unnecessarily, so she didn't share her concerns with them.

Morning traffic was heavy and crawled on I-495, the Washington Beltway, so she had time to call his dorm and have someone check his room. His motorcycle was in his parking spot, but no one had seen him. She knew a missing person's report couldn't be submitted for, at least, twenty-four hours and likely wouldn't be given much credibility by the police if submitted by a girlfriend instead of his family. She wasn't ready to call his parents until she knew something more definitive, but she did know who she could call to expedite the process and she didn't waste time making that contact.

"Mom," she said when Stacy answered.

"Hi, babe."

"How far behind me are you?"

Stacy hesitated only a split second. "Three cars."

"Okay, I'm going to turn onto Route 50 East toward Annapolis. Stay with me. I need your eyes to spot anything unusual."

"Will do. How long have you known I was here?"

"I didn't know for sure, but KiLi talks with her parents daily and her father is on your staff. I knew you would find out about Tucker and perform your usual due diligence. The minute I reported my purse was stolen, I figured you'd go to DefCon Four. Also, when I talked with Dad, you were never with him. If you had been deployed, he or my sibs would have mentioned it. Otherwise, I talked with him at times when you would have been at home. That's when I realized you were either on your way or already stateside. The dead giveaway was running into the President jogging through Rock Creek Park. You taught me not to trust coincidences. Don't trust, verify.

"When Tucker and I had dinner with the President, Mrs. Gordon said how fortuitous it was for him to jog a trail he never ran before and to bump into me. That's when I knew the President changed his route so that he could get an up-close-and-personal look at Tucker and have a legitimate reason to have him vetted. Regardless of the fact I'm his goddaughter, President Gordon wouldn't go to that much trouble for just anyone, but for you; it was a no-brainer. Finally, Aunt Vivian wouldn't have left me to my own devices if she didn't already know you or Dad were here."

"I'm so enormously proud of you, babe. You're not only beautiful and smart, but you're good under pressure and a methodical thinker. You're going to need all of your positive traits going forward. Right now, I want you to pull your SUV to the side of the road and walk back to my car."

It seemed like a non-sequitur, but Whitney didn't hesitate. While she was speaking with her mother, she was checking the roadside, but had not noticed anything. Apparently, her mother had. Whitney parked, cut the engine, and jogged back to a black, custom-built SUV. Two people stood sentry by the road, but her mother was squatting on the embankment talking into a cell phone. She picked up what looked like a sliver of red glass.

"No, I want Beta Team to turn out in road repair gear. No local LEOs unless they're ours. I'll give the order when I need more." Then she stood up, ended her call, and faced Whitney. "Okay, babe," she said, leading Whitney back to her open rear car door where so much equipment was in operation in the back seat, it resembled the cockpit of a space shuttle. She pointed to two scenes which appeared to be shot from far above the Earth's atmosphere. Whitney looked up for a drone, but saw none. "See this, it's going to be hard, but a satellite has picked up the signature of Tucker Cavanaugh's cell phone at this location. There is a truck at the bottom of this ravine, with one heat signature inside. No, don't look or react..." she cautioned her daughter.

"Mom," Whitney pleaded, aggrieved. "He's not moving. He's got to be hurt. I have to get to him."

"His body heat says he's alive, so what you have to do is keep him that way. Right now, you're a motorist who has a flat tire you stopped on the road to fix. We stopped to help you. So, go back to your SUV and change your tire as your father taught you to do."

Whitney learned long ago that when her parents told her and her siblings to do something, their directives were not considered to be requests. So, reluctantly, Whitney walked back to her SUV and, sure enough, her right rear tire was as flat as a pancake. While she began to unload the jack and spare tire while surreptitiously looking into the thick underbrush, a road crew arrived and began roadwork diverting the traffic around the point where her mother's team was standing. In the interim, her mother's custom-equipped SUV with satellite video access was snuggled up to her bumper, providing a shield from the view of passing motorists.

It has to be the record for the slowest tire change, thought Stacy Alexander. However, her daughter had a stubborn streak a mile wide like Benny and she couldn't convince her to leave before Tucker was removed from the van and on his way to the closest hospital. Thankfully, it happened to be Physician's Hospital, owned and operated by her brother-in-law, Dr. Chuck Montgomery.

Arrangements were made for Tucker to arrive at the hospital by what looked like a commercial utility truck, but was, in actuality, a government ambulance.

Once the tire was changed, Whitney got into her SUV and drove with haste to her aunt's and uncle's ranch. When she parked in the barn garage, she quickly transferred into Chuck's extended cab truck and sat on the floor out of sight. Anyone watching would assume Whitney was in the house and, as instructed, she left her cell phone in her car. Chuck drove out of the garage and to his hospital.

There were a lot of moving parts to this operation and Stacy was juggling them all. Tucker's parents were notified and secretly flown to a municipal airport near Annapolis, Maryland. Then they were driven to the hospital and given immediate access to Tucker in a secured, intensive care section of the hospital. Whitney was already there, holding Tucker's hand.

"What can you tell me?" Benjamin 'Benny' Alexander asked of his wife, Stacy, via secured sat-phone.

"Tucker Cavanaugh was forced off the road and was still unconscious when he was located this morning. Our daughter had the right instincts. She knew something was wrong and proceeded logically to find out what happened to him."

"You taught her that," Benny said.

"*We* taught her," Stacy affirmed.

"I hear the pride in your voice," Benny said, warmly.

"That's because she figured out I was tailing her. As I said, she has good instincts," Stacy said.

"She knows we would never let anyone into her life who wasn't investigated six ways to Sunday," Benny averred.

Stacy laughed. "You're right, she does, and I'm pleased that she doesn't complain about it."

"I don't want to jump to any conclusions. What have you learned about Cavanaugh and why he was forced off the road?" Benny asked.

Stacy shook her head. "Nothing I've learned about him or his family sends up any warning signals. Tucker hasn't had so much as a parking ticket in his twenty-one years of life. He seems to be an incredibly smart young man just as Whitney said. He comes from a small, tightly-knit family. I haven't completed my review of his friends and acquaintances, but I will.

"I looked at satellite images for a couple of hours before Whitney tagged me. The Grade A contour of a three-hundred-mile radius around ground zero confirms the truck never stopped after hitting the van, but got off Route 50 onto Route 301 and on to Route 3 North to Baltimore. It ended up at Patapsco Shipyard where the trailer was dumped. I have someone surreptitiously checking for fingerprints on the trailer. The tractor disappeared from sight inside a warehouse full of tractors. At the time, we didn't know we had to tag the tractor. If I had known, it would light up like a Christmas tree. We don't have eyes inside the warehouse yet and we can't legally go in without a warrant. What's worse, there are more than eighty tractors parked there that would need to be checked.

"The one lead we have is that no one seems to know where Mike and Trisha Rossi Giaconni are."

"Who are they and why are they significant?"

"The van Tucker was driving is registered to Mike Giaconni. Tucker and Giaconni are friends and band members. The van is generally used to transport the band's equipment. From what Whitney told me, Tucker asked her whether he could leave the van at Vivian's and Chuck's ranch. Tucker is still in a coma, so we haven't been able to establish why he asked for the favor and why Mike and Trisha weren't driving or riding in the van as they usually do after a gig. Both Mike and Trisha come from a long line of Italian Mafia. In fact, Mike is related to the Santangelo branch of the family. The same family JeNelle was once a member of through her marriage to Michel Santangelo before he was murdered."

"Should I be worried?"

Stacy laughed without humor. "As if you aren't already. I can feel your anxiety from here, babe. You probably have a jet on standby in Japan ready to bring our children here."

"You know me too well," Benny said sagely.

"There is no such thing as knowing you too well, but I love you fiercely and I love our children. I know what not being here is doing to you. For now, stand down, big guy. I've got this. Trust and believe I will get you here the moment it appears necessary. You've got six of our babies to take care of there. I've got Whitney."

Benny sighed. "I trust you, but I want regular reports."

"Done."

"I love you more, Stacy."

"I know."

Chapter 10

"Come on, Cavanaugh," Whitney fussed as she crisscrossed his large, private, intensive-care, hospital room. "Open those pretty blue eyes of yours and look at me. If you do that, I'll do the Dance of the Seven Veils for you. It's no time for sleeping on the job. We've got plans to make for our future. We haven't decided how many children we're going to have or how many we're going to adopt. Then there's the question of what we're going to name them. Come to think of it, where are we going to live with all of our children? I haven't been to Maine for more than a few hours and that was at night time. So, I couldn't see very much, even at thirty thousand feet. Maybe we should consider putting down roots there. It will be a little tough for me because I won't be able to see my family very often. I'll have to Skype them a lot. Still, no matter where we live, I'll have to take the multistate bar exam so that I will be permitted to practice law in every state, but, then again, you could be stationed anywhere in the world.

"Aunt Vivian practiced law before the World Court in The Hague. That's why she was selected for the US Supreme Court, because she was the only contender, other than Thomas Ashton Marshall, who had World Court experience and we live in a global society. Mr. Marshall wasn't interested in a judgeship and no one else on the court had the type of background in law she does. I'll have to talk with her and Thomas Marshall about that.

"Maybe Uncle Bill would be the best place to start, but I'm not sure I want to practice sports and entertainment law the way he does. His career involves a lot of travel and we want to have a family so we'll have to find a way for you to be assigned somewhere near Maine so I can practice law there for a while.

"Okay, Tucker, it's time for you to wake up. I've been talking in a stream of consciousness and non sequiturs for a long time and I'm a little punchy with fatigue. You've been sleeping all this time and haven't said a word. That's not the best way to keep our relationship—."

"It gets too cold there sometimes for you to do the Dance of the Seven Veils," Tucker croaked out, causing Whitney to skid to a stop and then attack the emergency call button.

"Well, if you hold me real tight through the coldest nights, I think I can cope and give you a performance you won't forget," she sang some of the words to their song, her eyes misty as medical personnel flooded into the room.

He smiled at her and winked groggily. It was a fight to stay lucid, but looking into her beautiful light, crystal-brown eyes when she kissed him, revved his engines.

His parents came in, surrounding her as her Uncle Chuck, other doctors, and nurses attended to him.

"You said he just started talking?" Leland Cavanaugh, Tucker's father, asked. His mother, Aurora, was on her cell phone, calling Tucker's grandparents with the good news.

"That's right. I was talking out loud to him and getting on his case, reminding him that we still have plans to make and he, without opening his eyes, answered me. He must have been coming awake for a long time because he responded to something I said earlier in my harangue." She wouldn't mention the seven veils part of the conversation.

Tucker could see Whitney and his father holding onto each other as Chuck asked questions, checking his faculties and ordering specialized lab tests to be performed. He was a bit foggy still, but he knew and understood what was going on around him. Yet, his focus was riveted on Whitney and the affection she and his parents were sharing with each other. It warmed his heart to see it.

Then, in walked an incredibly beautiful woman with light, crystal-brown eyes exactly like Whitney's. Tucker knew, without question, the woman had to be Admiral Stacy Greene Alexander, Whitney's mother. Except for a slight height difference, Whitney being taller, mother and daughter looked as if they were twins. She had hair the shade of warm honey, like Whitney's, but short, almost a crew cut, but she did not have to wear a uniform to determine she knew how to wield power and command. He witnessed those traits in Marine Corps officers, but there was something of an edge, beyond control and power, about Whitney's mom that said there was much more to her below the surface.

Tucker watched as Whitney introduced the woman to his parents and they hugged instead of shaking hands. That gesture indicated to Tucker that Admiral Alexander, despite her military rank, was approachable. He wasn't at all sure what to expect from a woman who climbed the ranks of the military to the station she attained as an Admiral. He momentarily lost sight of them as Chuck flashed a penlight in his eyes, checking to determine whether his pupils were even and reacting to light stimulation.

When he could again focus, Whitney, his parents, and the woman he believed to be Whitney's mother, were no longer in the room. So, he settled back and let the medical personnel check him out. It was a little strange being on this side of a stethoscope.

"I have to admit, my wife, mother, and father-in-law have fallen in love with your daughter. It's a distinct honor to meet you, Admiral Alexander," Leland said.

"Thank you, Mr. Cavanaugh, but please call me Stacy. According to my daughter, she's fallen in love with your son and all of you, too. Your son, apparently, told my brothers-in-law, Kenneth Alexander and Chuck Montgomery, that he's in love with Whitney."

"Stacy, I'm Leland or Lee and my wife is Aurora. I believe we will probably have a long relationship if our two young people have anything to say about it."

"We also want to thank you for getting us here so quickly," Aurora interjected. "I must say, I've never flown on a private jet before."

"You're welcome. I apologize for all of the secrecy, but we weren't sure what precipitated Tucker's accident."

"He was probably tired and fell asleep at the wheel," Lee said, concerned. "He tends to burn the candle at both ends. He's very studious that way. Then he enjoys being in the band as an outlet and hobby."

Stacy looked meaningfully at her daughter who nodded imperceptively before she regarded Tucker's parents.

They must have sensed something because they both looked back and forth between mother and daughter. "Is something wrong?" Lee asked, concerned before he and his wife reached for each other's hand.

Stacy nodded. "Lee, Aurora, what happened to Tucker was not an accident."

Aurora shook her head, her pretty blond, chin-length Pageboy hairstyle swinging attractively around her gamine face. "You mean someone intentionally tried to hurt our son?" At Stacy's nod of agreement, Aurora asked, "Why would someone do that? Tucker doesn't make enemies. He hasn't had so much as an argument with anyone."

"I don't have an answer for you, yet, but I will have one before this is over."

"Shouldn't we alert the authorities?" Lee asked. "If someone wants to harm our son, he needs protection."

"I've taken care of that," Stacy said.

"That's why you arranged to have us brought here via private transport. Do you know what's going on? If so, please tell us," Lee asked.

Stacy shook her head. "At this point, no, I don't know, but an investigation is underway. In the interim, Tucker is in this hospital incognito. I'm having him protected under security watch twenty-four-seven. I'm also bringing your parents into protective custody here with you."

"This is very serious, isn't it?" Lee questioned.

"It is, yes. However, I'm working as quickly as possible to see to his protection and yours."

"Mr. and Mrs. Cavanaugh, I know this is alarming, but, right now, Tucker is in the best care possible. My mother, my family, will not allow anyone to harm Tucker. For now, I hope you'll continue to be patient and trust us," offered Whitney.

His parents reached for her hand.

"I'm not sure what to make of this, but I do trust you'll keep your word, Stacy. You couldn't have risen to the rank of Admiral in the US Navy without knowing what you're doing, but why would you do this for Tucker and for us?" Lee asked.

"Military families are identified as high-value targets by terrorists and by association, anyone who may come in close contact with the family. As parents of a Marine, you probably already know the risks. Tucker has likely discussed with you that once he becomes a full-fledged physician, he could be deployed to some very dangerous places around the globe. Although I don't know for sure whether that's the case here, that his military status has anything to do with it, in an abundance of caution, I'm ensuring your family's protection, until a determination can be made."

"You mean some terrorist organization could be out to hurt our family?"

"I am unwilling to jump to conclusions until I know all of the facts."

Lee and Aurora simultaneously wrapped their arms around Whitney. "These young people deserve to live a life unaffected by criminals," Lee said, forcefully.

"Thank you. I agree. However, for now, my daughter is going to leave us and go about her routine as if nothing has happened," Stacy advised.

"Mom? Really? Can't I stay with Tucker and his parents?"

"No, babe." She looked at her watch. "You have just enough time to get to your next class. Then, after class, pack a bag for Tucker and come back to the ranch. By then, your father and siblings should have arrived."

"Dad?" Whitney asked, frowning. "I've talked with him. He didn't say anything to me about coming here."

"That's because he was already in the air at the time he talked with you and me. You know your father as well as I do. He wouldn't stay put for two seconds if he thought you were in harm's way. He drafted a couple of his pilots out of Hawaii to fly with him."

Whitney smiled. "I'll bet one of the pilots is his Top Gun, Shawn Baxter Rodgers."

"See what I mean? You know your dad. Now scoot or you'll be late."

Whitney hugged the Cavanaughs and then her mother. "I love you, Mom. Thanks for doing this."

"Back at ya, babe," Stacy said before Whitney left.

"Now, Lee and Aurora, I'll take you back to Tucker's room. When your parents arrive, we'll get everyone, including Tucker, loaded up and moved to a more secure location where we can relax."

Later, after the Cavanaugh's and his grandparents left Tucker's room, Stacy stayed to question him.

"So you know nothing about why you were run off the road? You haven't made any enemies recently?"

"No, ma'am, I haven't. Not that I'm aware of."

"What were you doing in the twenty-four hours before the incident?"

"I got up at four-hundred hours for my usual run. Because of the icy conditions, I used the gym. I showered after, ate breakfast, and went to the lab until nine-hundred. Then I was on the hospital floor for rounds with the other doctors. Lunch at twelve-hundred, reviewing patient charts, and then, when I went off duty, I met Whitney at her place," he continued.

Stacy already knew most of what Tucker was telling her. Her people learned it from the investigation that was underway. It tracked with what the Secret Service learned through its vetting process to give Tucker White House clearance. The kid was squeaky clean, well-liked, and well-respected. She sent in two undercover Marine operatives under Captain Ian Murray's command who looked young enough to still be wet behind the ears. Actually, they were both seasoned agents who, given their youthful appearance, looked like they were just out of high school. They were stepping up their undercover operation due to what they learned from Ian Murray about his interest in Whitney

Alexander. He bragged that he was seeing her behind Tucker's back. The agents knew nothing could be further from the truth, but their directive was gathering information and they were good at it.

A female doctor and male nurse were deployed by Stacy at Georgetown Medical to ascertain whether there was Intel that might prove useful among the medical staff Tucker was a part of. That was made easier since her brother-in-law, Chuck Montgomery, was once the chief of the emergency room and was still on the hospital's board. What was more problematic was inserting someone in the band Changelings. The best she could do there was to put a couple of operatives in the Holiday Pageant with the university's entertainment department. She employed one of her best operatives, the White Stallion, to ensure the best covert agents were selected.

When Tucker hesitated in his delivery, Stacy noticed. "What? You thought of something?"

He shrugged. "Well, not really."

"Any little detail might prove useful," she prompted.

His brows drew together in thought. "I don't think it's significant, but I've been having problems with a female officer for a while. She doesn't seem to get the idea that I'm not into her, but I don't think she'd want me injured or dead. She'd rather have me alive and in her bed," he said, the color rising in his embarrassment.

"Who is she?"

"First Lieutenant Mallorie Colbert. She's a ComSpec assigned to the Pentagon. She shows up a lot when Changelings is gigging. She was at the club the night this happened. As I said," he hastened on, "I'm not interested in her that way, but I don't think she'd have someone attack me."

"Does Whitney know about her?"

"Yes, ma'am, she does. We don't have secrets."

"I'll look into it. Was there anyone else at the club that night you recognized?"

"Yes, I mean, not anyone I know personally…" he paused in thought a moment. "Well, actually, KiLi Hakamora was there in the audience, but I think she's seeing one of the other band members, Payton Bradshere. She's been coming to a lot of our gigs lately."

"Okay, anyone else?" Stacy asked. She already had background data on KiLi. The girl considered Whitney to be her best friend and confidant. She virtually grew up in their home in Japan. So, she didn't think there was a connection, but she'd take a second look. She would also have a detailed dossier prepared on First Lieutenant Mallorie Colbert. "I'll look into what you've told me so far. If Lieutenant Colbert is not involved, the matter will be dropped and you and Whitney can deal with it as you see fit. Now, did anything unusual happen at the club?"

He shook his head, mentally running through the events of the evening. "It was a typical, four-hour gig. We've played this club several times, particularly during the summer. I was a little tired, but I torqued it up because it was a good crowd; maybe two hundred people. We used our CD while we shut down, posed for pictures, and signed autographs. Nothing unusual."

The next question Stacy posed carefully and closely monitored his reaction. "What about your band members. Anything unusual happen with any of them?"

He thought about it and mentally his brain skidded to a stop on Mike's and Trisha's family issues, but thought little of it. What was going on with them had nothing to do with him.

She sensed when Tucker's memory was engaged. This kid was completely guileless. No wonder Whitney had such confidence in him. "What? You've thought of something."

"Nothing really. Mike and Trisha Rossi Giaconni are band members. They have some family issue, but it has nothing to do with me other than I was driving their van."

"What type of family issue?"

"They're both grad students and were recently married. They're pregnant with their first child and..." he went on, telling her what Mike had told him.

Although Stacy didn't let on that she had up-close-and-personal interaction with factions of both Mike's and Trisha's families, she had another line to tug. The couple's disappearance was indication there was more to this situation than what was on the surface.

"I'll look into everything you've told me, Tucker. Now, it's time for you to get some rest." She ended her questioning with the young man who would, she believed, become her son-in-law and the father of her grandchildren one day. She was enormously proud of her daughter who, so like her father, recognized the best in people. Benny saved Whitney's life before she was even born when he insisted that they go through with her pregnancy many years ago. She was around Tucker's age when she made that fateful decision and now, as she looked at Tucker as he slept, she was very glad she and Benny made that decision. Her life now was full of love beyond belief. They had seven children now and were seriously considering having more, at least one more, before time ran out on her ability to conceive. She was living a dream with the only man she could ever love, Benjamin Staton Alexander.

Chapter 11

Whitney had to admit her mother's strategy was right. She needed to let the medical personnel tend to Tucker's needs, while she pretended nothing was amiss. All she could add, at that point, was moral support for Tucker and his family. Having his parents and grandparents with him would help him get better faster. Still, she would be there for him when he woke up in the morning.

In the interim, her task was to surreptitiously pack up some of his things so he would have something to wear for the next few days and his books to study. Fortunately, she found a parking space near his dormitory and hustled into the building through the stinging cold wind and rain. If she wasn't mistaken, there was the scent of snow in the air. Her mother taught her and her siblings to be aware of such things. Never rely on only her sight, but employ all of her sensory perceptions to ensure her safety.

She took the elevator up to his floor and, although she hadn't been there before, she easily found his room. She timed her arrival so very few students were around. She calculated most dormitory residents would probably be in one of the dining halls at that hour. With his keys in hand, she quickly opened the door, but immediately sensed she was not alone in his room. Before she went further, she flipped on the ceiling light and prepared to defend herself against attack. She was surprised to find Mallorie Colbert waking up in Tucker's bed.

"What are you doing here?" Mallorie demanded.

"I should ask you the same question," Whitney parried.

"Tucker and I are lovers. He expects me to be here. We spent the night together making love. We didn't sleep much, so I told him I would meet him here after his lab classes and hospital rounds today. We have duty tonight at the Armory and we'll spend the night together again."

"Tucker spent the night here with you, you say?"

"Of course he did. We sleep together all—."

Whitney broke into hysterical laughter.

"Why are you laughing? Look, little girl, you should stop trying to insinuate yourself into his life. You're a child. He wants and needs a woman, like me, not you!" She waited a bit before declaring, "I don't see what you find so funny about Tucker and me being lovers."

Whitney finally got control of her laughter and just shook her head. She must be punch drunk at this point because she was weary beyond belief. She'd been running on pure adrenaline since Tucker called to wake her shortly before two o'clock in the morning to say he was on his way. She knew from the satellite images that he was run off the road shortly thereafter until they found him at ten that morning. KiLi's web page contained scads of pictures of the band at the club and, although Mallorie was in attendance, Tucker would not have spent the night with her.

She sat down tailor style in a chair by his desk. "We'll just wait for Tucker to get here and he can tell you and me his preference." She took out her cell phone and dialed. "I'll just call and hurry him along..."

"Don't do that! If he's in class or making rounds at the hospital, he doesn't like to be disturbed. I'll tell him you were here."

"You're right. He probably has the ringtone turned off." She took a picture of Mallorie in Tucker's bed. "I'll just send a text message to him with your picture attached. If he's so eager to be with you, that picture should be enough to get him here quick, fast, and in a hurry, wouldn't you say?"

Huffing in agitation and frustration, Mallorie climbed her naked body out of bed and began to dress. Whitney took several additional pictures. When finally dressed and without a backward glance, Mallorie stormed out of Tucker's room, slamming the door behind her. Whitney sent a text message and the pictures to her mother, adding Mallorie's name to a list of people who should be investigated.

Once Whitney was sure no one was in the hallway to see her, she escaped down the stairs with a duffel bag full of books, clothes, and toiletries she believed Tucker would need. Then she drove to her home to pack a bag for herself. She kept clothes at the ranch for the times she stayed over, so she didn't need much. No sooner had she parked in the driveway and exited her car, than Ian climbed out of his car and joined her on the porch just as she unlocked the door.

"I thought you should be coming in soon. Your last class for the day ended over an hour ago. Where have you been?"

"Why are you here, Captain?" she asked as she entered the house and put her keys in her pants pocket. She wasn't about to leave her keys anywhere he might pick them up. At this point, she didn't want to have the locks changed again on the house the way she did after her purse with her keys inside went missing.

As she started to take off her coat, he trapped her arms at her sides. "I wanted to do this," he said, snatching her into his tight embrace and kissing her.

Whitney remained stone still, eyes open while he tried to arouse her. When he smiled and stepped back, he met the frown on her face. His smile faded by degrees. Mentally, she counted out the moments until she heard the footfalls she knew to expect.

"Hey, babe," Bill Chandler said, coming up behind her in the vestibule. He wore a Velcro towel around his trim waist and nothing else. He was drying his hair with another towel. Leaning down over her left shoulder, he kissed her cheek. "I didn't know we were expecting company. Who's our visitor?"

"Captain Ian Murray, who thought, for some insane reason, I would welcome a kiss from him and the feel of his engorged phallus against my body."

"Enough said. Hello and goodbye, Captain."

"Who is this, Whitney?"

"Someone who lives here and knows you don't."

The man is built like a Greek god, thought Ian and his face was movie-idol perfection, and familiar. He looked like the actor Matt Bomer but not exactly. Something in Bill's tone or demeanor alerted Ian that his continued presence could be detrimental to his health.

"Another time," Ian said significantly to Whitney before he left.

"Thanks, Uncle Bill. I wasn't sure you had the security cameras on in the exercise room.

"I heard and saw the alarm flashing when you pulled into the driveway. You pressed the alert button on your key fob. The cameras activated immediately. Are you all right?"

"I'm fine, but I admit I'm tired of having to dodge Ian Murray. He snuck up behind me before I realized he was there."

"I think the Captain is going to get a come-to-Benny or Stacy lecture if he keeps up this pursuit."

"Yeah, I know. Mom is already here and she thinks Dad is on his way."

"Oh, hell, buckle up, babe. With Benny and Stacy in town, it's going to be a bumpy ride."

Whitney turned around and regarded his nearly nude body. "You know, Uncle Bill, Margo and Angelique told me you were hot in the buff, but wow."

Bill shook his head and sighed. "Don't listen to those delinquents."

"I didn't until now, but they had pictures of you, which pale by comparison to the real thing…" She laughed at his pained expression as she started up the long, wide staircase. "Be still my heart."

They flooded into his hospital room and the guards and nurses let them. School was out for the day and the Montgomery posse was everywhere and had his parents laughing with tears leaking from their eyes. If Tucker wasn't aching all over, he would have been doubled over laughing, too, at their antics. They were a bunch of comics. Every last one of them. They gave him a scrapbook full of hand-made, get-well-soon cards that were also funny. The picture on the front of the scrapbook was a caricature of him that was extremely well done and signed by Kristy Alexander, Kenneth and JeNelle's youngest daughter. Although the little girl had returned to California with her father and siblings, the gesture warmed his heart.

When the transporters came and rolled him out of his hospital room, his parents and entourage accompanied him. His gurney folded up like a chair, he was lifted onto the big bus the Montgomery kids used for transport to and from school and other events. He was strapped into place before his parents boarded and then the Montgomery children and teens piled on. It dawned on him that the means of transport was a camouflage. Should anyone be watching the ranch, it would appear the Montgomery children were just returning from visiting their father at the hospital or from school. He was convinced of that when the bus pulled into the barn-sized garage beside the mansion. Generally, the bus unloaded the family in front of the small castle, which was how Tucker thought of it.

Whitney's family was taking extraordinary measures to keep him and his family safe. He was grateful for everything they were doing; however, he was more worried about Whitney and her safety.

Medical personnel took him off the bus and rolled him right into the house through a wide mudroom door. A short trip down one hallway and then a left turn to another brought him into what resembled a well-equipped, hospital room full of medical emergency and monitoring equipment. A very attractive, middle-aged woman waited there for the orderlies to transfer him to one of the beds before she smiled at him and began attaching various monitoring devices to his body and hanging his saline drip.

"Hello, Tucker, I'm Sylvia Benson Alexander, Whitney's maternal grandmother," she said and then turned to shake hands with his parents. Turning back to Tucker, she said, "I understand my grandchildren descended on you at the hospital and, fortunately, you survived the onslaught. Shortly, your grandparents will be in to see you, Tucker, and then I'm sending your family out of your room for you and them to get some well-deserved rest before dinner.

"Now that you're all hooked up so I can monitor your vitals on this little, cell phone device, I'll go bring your grandparents to see you."

So saying, she left the room.

"How are you doing, son?" his dad asked as he and his mother each took one of his hands and stood on opposite sides of the bed.

"Just a little achy, but Dr. Montgomery has me on mild pain meds and antibiotics for the cuts and abrasions. I'll be fine. I'm in good hands. Dr. Montgomery is one of the finest Emergency Room doctors on the east coast. He's a real technician when it comes to instant diagnosis."

"We're in his debt for taking care of your Nana and now you. I really don't know how we will ever repay his kindness," Lee said, worried. "He and Dr. Stone wouldn't accept payment for taking care of your grandmother. So we sent them each a fruit basket and a thank-you note. It still seems so insignificant considering all the trouble they've gone to."

"Don't worry, Dad. They don't operate that way. Just like Nana wouldn't sue the City of Poland Springs for the tumble she took on the icy steps at City Hall, the Montgomerys don't take advantage of people. They simply do what comes next."

"Yes, but to bring us here to their home and to arrange for your grandparents to join us? Son, I've never met more kind people than them in my life. To think, Vivian Alexander-Montgomery is a Supreme Court Justice. I've read and cited many of her opinions. I'm both nervous and excited to actually meet her."

"If the situations were reversed, what would you do?"

Lee smiled and nodded. "Point taken."

"I'm fascinated with the thought that Whitney's father is an astronaut," Aurora said.

Tucker nodded in acknowledgment, but he was drowsy and suspected Mrs. Alexander added a mild sedative to the saline cocktail solution slowly dripping into his vein, along with pain meds. When his grandparents came in, he was nearly nodding off to sleep. They were chatting when he heard his grandfather say, "When Mrs. Alexander introduced herself, I could have sworn she was the vocalist Phyllis Hyman reincarnate."

"I agree," Lee said. "I felt the same way. She doesn't look old enough to be the mother of five adults and the grandmother of so many. I was having a hard time making the distinction between her and Phyllis Hyman."

Just then, Sylvia stepped back into the room and checked on her patient, waking him. While she methodically went about her duties, she didn't acknowledge the four pairs of eyes studying her. This wasn't the first time it happened. She and her sister, Mariah, looked a lot like the songstress Phyllis Hyman and had been mistaken for her many times. At least in her sister's case, she also had a strong singing voice like Ms. Hyman. Her sister was known worldwide as the actress and songstress the French Mariah and Ms. Hyman's voice was compared to hers.

Oh, well, she silently sighed. Her sister would be back in the United States for the holidays. It appeared Tucker's family would be around long enough for them to meet her sister. In the interim, she had to nurse this young man back to good health so he could someday marry her granddaughter. "Tucker, wake up for me."

"You're beautiful... ," he groggily slurred.

Sylvia chuckled. "Thank you. You're beautiful, too. Now, I need you to answer questions for me."

"You're beautiful, but so is Whitney and I'm in love with her."

Sylvia and his parents chuckled.

"That's good to know. So, what year is it?" she began and asked a series of questions to ensure that his faculties were still intact. He correctly answered each one, but then nodded off to sleep again. As a result, he didn't hear Mrs. Alexander shepherd his family out of the hospital room.

Each hour, she woke him and asked him a different set of questions, which he continued to answer correctly before drifting off to sleep again.

Whitney sat tailor-style in a lounge chair recliner beside Tucker's bed while she studied and prepared an assignment for her Torts' class. She'd come in when dinner started and made the introductions when her Aunt Vivian came home. When she began to make the introduction for Tucker's parents and grandparents, to her cousins, she learned they already introduced themselves at the hospital. So she introduced her grandfather, Bernard Alexander, and Chuck and Vivian's toddlers to Tucker's family while they ate dinner. Then she left and came to Tucker's hospital room to relieve her grandmother so she, too, could eat with the family.

She was wearing earbuds and so ensconced in the lecture she was listening to she didn't immediately notice the tall, well-built man leaning against the door jamb with his hands in his pockets and his feet crossed at the ankles. When she stretched her neck from side to side to work out the kinks and then her arms above her head, she spotted him and a smile grew bright on her face, lighting her eyes. "Hi, Dad."

"Hi, babe," he said, as he came forward, lifted her off the lounger, and sat with her on his lap, with his arms tightly around her.

She tilted her head onto his broad shoulder, got comfortable, and just breathed him in. "Did you just get here?"

"About half an hour ago."

"Did Mom give you grief?"

He shrugged. "It wasn't as bad as it could have been, but she was so happy to see our babies, she couldn't fuss much."

"She knew you were coming."

"I know. I've been in love with your mother for a very long time and she knows me completely. However, this time it wasn't only because I missed her and you. I've been asked to pilot another flight to SPACEHOME."

Whitney leaned up so she could look into her father's eyes when she asked, "Are you going to do it?"

"I'm considering it, but I have someone else in mind to fly the bird."

"Captain Shawn Baxter Rodgers, Code Name: HOT ROD," Whitney guessed.

Surprise showed on her father's handsome face. "Yes. How did you know?"

"He's one of your best jet fighter pilots and you like his acumen, courage, and tenacity. You've trained him for a very long time. I think you see yourself in him. If you don't, I certainly do. Plus, he has a baby girl he's raising alone because the little girl's mother is in the military and disappeared just like Mom did when I was a baby. I think he reminds you of the time it was just the two of us when we lived in San Diego and you were raising me alone. There seem to be a number of similarities between the two of you." She circled her arms around his neck and laid her head on her father's shoulder again. "I think you were sizing him up as a potential mate for me," she said, laughing.

"You can't convince me that your mother didn't keep inviting young Navy lieutenants to have dinner with us because we lacked for company. She was trying to gauge your level of interest with each young man under her command."

Whitney laughed. "You did the same thing by inviting Sean and his daughter over to have play dates with my little brothers."

His arms closed in around his firstborn as he marveled at how perceptive she was and how lucky he felt to have her as his daughter. Stacy felt the same way, but she still anguished over the fact she initially wanted to have an abortion when she learned she was pregnant with Whitney. He and Stacy were lovers, but not married at the time. They were career-oriented and ambitious. Stacy felt having a child would derail their military careers. He disagreed. Because she didn't believe they were in love with one another, she proposed the abortion. Although he talked her out of it, immediately after Whitney's birth, Stacy disappeared from their lives without seeing their daughter for five years.

It probably would have been for life if Stacy hadn't stopped by his parents' home for a short visit before she redeployed. She hadn't expected to find him and Whitney there visiting his family, too, and probably wouldn't have stopped by if she had known they were there. When she finally met her daughter for the first time, it was instant love. Stacy refused to forgive herself for deserting them without a trace for so long. She was still trying to make up for her earlier mistakes ever since.

Although it took Stacy another year to admit she loved Benny and agreed to marry, she was now fiercely protective of him and their seven children. She was still ambitious, having gained the rank of Admiral in the US Navy during their time together as husband and wife. The medals and ribbons she wore on her uniform staggered his imagination for what she must have endured to earn them. The majority of what she did were covert operations and she never talked about them, not even to him. Sometimes she still deployed without warning to places where he sensed her life was in danger. Still, he couldn't and wouldn't ask her not to do her duty. He was still ambitious, too, but stayed home and took care of their family until she returned. He feared one day she might not be able to return and took care to appreciate every moment they had together as a family unit.

Stacy did the same for him when he took on the task of piloting a space shuttle for long periods of time. He loved to fly and being an astronaut was his dream from the first time, as a young boy, he gazed up at the nighttime heavens while swinging in a hammock he and his brother, Kenneth, built in the backyard of their home in Goodwill, Summer County, South Carolina. He could no more give up space flight or ask the love of his life to give up her dedication to duty. He hugged his daughter a little tighter. He didn't object to the extraordinary measure he and Stacy took to protect their family.

A photoflash brought his thoughts back to the present. His mother stood in the doorway and took another quick series of pictures of him with Whitney on his lap. He smiled at her, the woman who gave him life and an abundance of love.

"Hi, Mom," he said as she came forward for a hug and a kiss.

Whitney stood and moved aside so her father could gather his mother in his arms.

"Stacy said you'd come," Sylvia said, looking up at the second of her handsome sons.

"Here I am. How's your patient?"

"I think he's doing well for someone who was in a serious accident less than twenty-four hours ago. I saw pictures of the van. It is so mangled it could end up as a paperweight on someone's desk. It's a total loss and so are the musical instruments. He has some contusions, abrasions, and severe bruising from where the seatbelt held him securely and the airbag deployed. However, all the musical instruments in the van battered him badly. He was unconscious for a very long time. We've done an MRI, with and without contrast, and a battery of other tests, but so far, we haven't found anything pivotal. His brain got knocked around in his skull, but we found no bleeding. He's coherent and his faculties are alert. For now, he's in fairly good condition, but he needs rest. I'll wake him every hour to check for a head injury, but Chuck believes his prognosis is good. So does Dr. Stone. He's read the head CTs and examined Tucker once today. He'll examine him again tomorrow unless I find something to be concerned about during the night.

"Tucker is resting so you two should go relax. You've both had a long day. Whitney, according to Vivian, you've been up since

Tucker called you early this morning. Go take a warm soak or swim, and get some rest."

"Yes, ma'am," Whitney said, hugging her grandmother and father before kissing Tucker's lips. She gathered her books and other paraphernalia before she trudged off to bed.

"Thanks, Mom. Whitney was dead on her feet," Benny said to his mother, Sylvia.

"She'll sleep for a while, but I know my grandchild. She'll be back sometime during the night to check on Tucker."

"Are you going to be all right?" Benny asked.

Sylvia smirked. "For Pete's sake, son. Many nights I sat up with you or one or more of your siblings and then went into the hospital to manage my staff of nurses. This is nothing new for me. Now, you go find your wife and introduce yourself to Tucker's family. They're good people and eager to meet you."

"I love you, Mom, for coming to Maryland to see to Tucker's care," Benny said.

"I love you more for being the man you are. You're a fine, thoughtful husband and father. Your father and I couldn't be more proud of you, Stacy, and our grands."

They embraced again before Benny left. Sylvia checked on Tucker's vitals again and then sat next to his bed in the seat her son and granddaughter vacated. Sighing contentedly, she took out her knitting to work. She always relaxed when she was knitting a sweater for someone in her family. Tucker was a tall, muscular young man, but she'd have this sweater ready for him for Christmas.

Tucker slowly woke after Whitney kissed him, but he couldn't quite get his eyes open. Still, he heard the conversation between Whitney's grandmother and her father, General Benjamin Alexander, the astronaut, and smiled. His mother had been right. Meeting an astronaut was pretty freakin' cool!

Chapter 12

The woman's face registered a certain amount of surprise when Whitney answered the front door at the Georgetown brownstone. "Hello, I'm Maria Rossi. Is this the home of Bill Chandler?"

"Yes, it is, Ms. Rossi. Please, come in out of the wet."

"Thank you." She stared intently. "I apologize for staring, but your face is familiar. I've seen you somewhere before. Are you and Chandler related?"

"Technically, no, but he's my surrogate uncle. I'm a friend of Tucker Cavanaugh." At her continued blank expression, Whitney said, "He's in the band Changelings. We weren't introduced, but I attended Trisha and Mike's wedding. I also play basketball with Final Justice."

Maria snapped her finger. "Ah, yes. You're related to Judge Vivian Alexander Montgomery."

"Yes, I'm one of her nieces," Whitney confirmed.

Maria nodded, holding Whitney's gaze. "As I recall, Vivian and Bill were in law school together and then in private practice at their law firm, Alexander, Carter, Chandler, Charles, Lightfoot, *et. al.* You look a little young to already be practicing law, so you must be in law school to be on the Final Justice team."

"That's correct. Is Bill expecting you?"

"No, I learned he lives here. He wasn't in his office and I know that he travels a lot. I didn't have his contact number, so I took a chance I'd find him at home."

"I see. Please, have a seat in the library. I'll see whether he's available."

Before she could go, JeNelle rushed in.

"Hi, Aunt JeNelle."

"Hello, Whitney. I hope you don't have to go out. It's an icy mix of rain and sleet out there today," she said, stripping off her outer layer coat, hat, gloves and boots and moving to place them in the walk-around closet at the entrance.

"No, I'm in for the day. Would you like something warm to drink?"

"Thanks, I would, yes," she said, speaking from inside the closet, "but don't bother yourself. I know you're probably studying so I'll get it myself. Would you like something, too?" she trailed off when she left the closet and spotted Maria, who looked on with avid interest. "Hello," JeNelle acknowledged, coming forward and extending her hand for a shake.

"Senator Alexander," Maria said, accepting JeNelle's hand. "This is a surprise."

"Oh? Why?" JeNelle asked.

"I was given to understand this is Bill Chandler's home. I didn't think you would know someone like him."

JeNelle nodded. "Yes, I do know him very well. He's a close, personal friend and this is his home. I gather that you're here to see him?"

"I am," Maria acknowledged.

"I was about to check...," Whitney began just as the front door opened again and KiLi came in with Roland Harrington, another Georgetown Law Advanced Scholars Program student, who also lived in the house.

"Hi, Whitney, Mrs. Alexander," they chorused and nodded to Maria, but didn't stop. They continued talking and moving toward the back of the house, chatting.

"Apparently quite a few people live here," Maria commented.

"I apologize, Ms. Rossi," Whitney said. "Please have a seat."

"Thank you," she said, moving from the double-glassed paneled doorway into the well-appointed library.

"I'll keep her company until you return," JeNelle said, following Maria into the library and taking a seat in one of the many wing-backed chairs. She, too, was cautious about unexpected guests left unattended in their home.

Maria sauntered around the room, looking up at the high, half-barrow-shaped ceiling with dark blue paint in the center, lime green borders, and contrasting complimentary beige walls with intricately designed crown molding. The lights were on low and the ceiling fans turned slowly, dispensing the heat from the ceiling down the walls to the Brazilian Cherry hardwood floors. Rich, solid wood bookcases, smelling of beeswax and lemon oil, held a multitude of books. The window seats offered pleasing views of Rock Creek Park and the fireplace centered one wall of the room. Whitney's study paraphernalia was spread out on one of the long, wide, highly polished library tables. A cup of tea, a bottled water, and wedges of cheese, crackers, and half a red apple sat next to her work on a tray.

"I don't mean to be indelicate, but are you and Bill Chandler lovers?"

JeNelle laughed. "Wouldn't that be interesting, but no, we're not. I'm married to Kenneth Alexander and we have nine children. Bill may be movie-idol perfection, but I don't have the time or inclination to take on a lover, Bill Chandler, or anyone else."

"Well, that's disappointing," Bill said, as he entered the library and noisily kissed JeNelle on the mouth, making her laugh. He was indeed a Matt Bomer clone with black hair and blue eyes.

Whitney followed him in to gather her study materials and snack.

"On that note, I'll leave you two alone," JeNelle said, preparing to leave the library. "I was about to make a snack, Bill. I'll bring some refreshments for you and Ms. Rossi in a moment."

"Thanks, JeNelle," he said and waited for her and Whitney to leave. Then he turned to the visitor. "Now, Ms. Rossi, I understand you're here to see me?"

"I am. You don't remember me, do you?"

"I know you're an attorney and lobbyist; a partner in the law firm, Simpson, Loma, and Rossi, PA. What else should I know?"

"We grew up in the same neighborhood in New York City's Little Italy."

He shrugged. "Okay? You're right. I don't remember you."

"I'm a little older than you and left the neighborhood when you were still just a kid. Your parents are Ike and Dolly Chandler. You also have a younger sister, Margo. Do you remember the Rossellini family?"

He nodded. "I do, yes. My family lived in the same tenement building." It was a painful period of his life he chose not to remember.

Maria looked up and around the impressive room. "You're a noted sports and entertainment attorney; owner of the magazines *Stallion* and *Risqué*; and an actor and supermodel. Just last season, you were featured on the cover of several high-fashion magazines. I understand you give your fee for the magazine covers to charity. You're also involved in making movies. You've come a long way from your beginnings as a male prostitute."

Her assessment and knowledge of his background didn't surprise or faze him, but his curiosity was piqued. Everyone in their old neighborhood knew his parents pimped him when he was eight years old until he took over his own client base at age fourteen. One of his regular wealthy clients took him home to live with him and his wife to service them exclusively. They had him tutored by the best teachers money could buy to make him presentable around their wealthy friends. They called him their nephew in public, though there was no resemblance between him and them. Everyone knew what was going on, but no one stepped in to put an end to the sexual abuse subjected him to by his parents.

So, if this was an attempt at blackmail, she was SOL. Everyone he cared about already knew his story. Except, that is, what he did covertly as a member of The Nursery, an uber-secret G7 creation. "So have you, Ms. Rossi, if you've climbed out of the hellhole of your family's beginnings. If you're here to renew old acquaintances..."

She inclined her head in acknowledgment of his taunt. "I'm here in need of your help."

"What is it you want from me?"

"I need you to broker a deal between my family, the Santangelos, and the..."

The crash at the library door startled Bill and Maria. JeNelle stood there with the tray of coffee, cream, condiments, and snacks splattered at her feet; a look of stark terror on her beautiful face.

Whitney had resumed studying in the kitchen when she heard the crash. Immediately, she rose quickly, making her way to the front of the house. There she found Bill shepherding JeNelle out of the library and across the wide vestibule and into the front parlor.

"Whitney, please sit with your aunt a moment while I tend to this mishap," he said as he began to slide the pocket doors closed.

"Sure," she said, walking JeNelle to a comfortable seat. She added more wood to the fire that burned in the grate and then sat down on an ottoman at her aunt's feet. She sat quietly for a while and then asked. "How may I help, Aunt JeNelle?"

Her vision seemed unfocused, but then her eyes strayed to her niece. "I'm all right, Whitney. I promise. I just had a shock. That's all. It's nothing to concern yourself with."

"I don't mean to be rude or to pry, but you seemed more than shocked. That's totally out of character for you. You're usually unflappable."

JeNelle cupped her niece's pretty face and smiled slightly. "You're sweet to be concerned, but I'll be fine. There's no need for the worry I see in your eyes."

"Okay," Whitney reluctantly said, backing off a bit. "How about some coffee?"

"I'd much prefer wine," JeNelle distractedly said.

Whitney rose to go to the wet bar concealed in one of the cabinets her Uncle Kenneth built many years ago. While she poured wine into a goblet, she wondered whether she should contact her Uncle Kenneth about the incident. She decided she'd ask her parents first. She handed the wine to her aunt and then sat quietly watching the fire devour the logs in the grate until Bill came in to talk with JeNelle.

To give them privacy, Whitney left them alone. She noted Maria Rossi was gone. So, she returned to the kitchen to resume her studies.

"I'm not sure what I should do, Mom," Whitney said sometime later over the phone.

"It's okay, really, Whitney. Bill will handle it, but you say a Maria Rossi came to the house?"

"Yes, she came to see Uncle Bill. She's an attorney, a lobbyist here in DC."

"Did she say why she was there?"

"Not to me, she didn't. Why? Is something wrong?"

"No, not necessarily. Bill usually doesn't want people coming to the house uninvited."

"I know. She claimed she didn't have his contact information and just took a chance and stopped by. It did seem a little strange, but since I know who Ms. Rossi is, I didn't perceive her as a threat."

"No, no, you're right. Okay, babe. By the way, are you coming out to the ranch?"

She noted her mother's abrupt change of the topic of their conversation. Something was going on, and her mother wasn't telling her. For now, she'd let it pass, but she loved her aunt too much to drop it completely.

"Not tonight. The roads are pretty bad and I have early classes tomorrow. If the weather improves, I'll come after my last class. What did Uncle Chuck say about Tucker's condition?"

"He's making progress. If your sisters, brothers, and cousins would let him rest, he'd probably recuperate more quickly," she said, laughing.

Whitney laughed, too. "According to Tucker, the Munchkins are keeping him sane and entertained during what he considers his forced confinement. He's unaccustomed to being idle for any long period of time."

"So he's said...repeatedly," Stacy deadpanned.

"He's right, but, Mom, he's not a complainer."

"I know. He's just a little frustrated with the inactivity. However, he's planning to be a doctor, so it's good to know how his potential patients feel. Chuck is keeping him busy with his course work and he will let him get some exercise soon. His parents, grandparents, your father, and I have been in the swimming pool off and on today. Chuck may let Tucker join us tomorrow for a swim. Don't worry."

"I'll be okay once we find out why this incident happened."

"I'm working on it."

"I know, Mom, and we appreciate it. By the way, what are we going to do for Thanksgiving?"

"We're going home to Goodwill as originally planned. Your dad and I spoke with Tucker and his family. They've agreed to join us."

Whitney sighed deeply. "That's great. I hoped you'd do that. I didn't want to leave Tucker and his family here while we were away. Thanks for extending the invitation."

"You're welcome, but it was your grandparents' idea. We'll see you tomorrow after class?"

"Yes, and I'll be done with classes until after Thanksgiving."

"Good Love you, babe."

"Love you more, Mom." Whitney disconnected the call and fired up her laptop. She Googled JeNelle Towson and found quite a bit of information about her aunt before she married her Uncle Kenneth, then she found a link to a JeNelle San Angelo. When she clicked on the link, her eyes widened in surprise. She never knew her aunt was married before when she was seventeen. What was even more shocking was that she was the bride of a multibillionaire of Italian descent who was suspected of being a member of the Mafia.

There was much more to be learned in court records, so she switched from Google to LexisNexis, the world's largest electronic database for legal and public records and related information. She avoided using her Uncle Kenneth's database, CompuCorrect, because, although it was nearly as large as LexisNexis, her searches might be flagged. If they were, her uncle would certainly hear about it and wonder why she was searching for information on his wife. She didn't want that to happen. CompuCorrect was her Internet provider, but because of the amount of legal research she had to do for her classes, no one questioned her Internet research. She wanted to keep her discovery about her aunt a secret.

Stacy was on the hunt for information, too. Especially since Bill told her Trisha's aunt, Maria Rossi, visited him to enlist his help as a neutral party known in the old neighborhood. She wanted him to broker a deal between Trisha's and Mike's families. To Stacy, that information was surprising, but so much was when it came to people she cared about. She didn't know Tucker, except for what she learned from the deep dossiers she had run on him and his family. He was important to her daughter and he was close to Mike and Trisha. Anyone who may be in contact with her family would be subjected to an in-depth review. So, she had no qualms about doing deep background checks on both Mike's and Trisha's families.

Still, she didn't believe in coincidences. Maria's visit to the Georgetown house her husband, Benny, owned; a place where their daughter lived with one of Stacy's operatives, Bill Chandler, Code name: The White Stallion, seemed a bit too close for comfort for Stacy.

It was especially true because Mike Giaconni's family had an open contract hit out on another one of Stacy's operatives, Code name: Mata Hari, for the death of Don Tomas' four-time great-grandson, David Delaware. If these incidents were related to Italian Mafia criminals rather than terrorists, she had to shift her thinking.

"Delta, this is Explorer One. How do you read?"
"I read you five by five, E One."
"Copy that. Has the Stallion checked in?"

"That's an affirmative, E One. Sitrep."

"Investigation ongoing. Possible connections between pizza deliveries."

"Affirmative. The baby bird is stretching wings. Watch your six. Sandbaggers authorized and deployed."

"Copy that, Delta. It was to be expected. E One over and out."

Chapter 13

The weekend before Thanksgiving, the Montgomery family and the Cavanaughs flew to Goodwill, Summer County, South Carolina. It was primarily an agricultural county and mostly rural with small, picturesque municipalities interwoven into the countryside. People were more apt to ride horses rather than drive cars across the vast open fields and meadows.

The Harvest Festival was in full swing when Bernard and Sylvia drove the Cavanaugh family in a horse-drawn buggy to the fairgrounds. Whitney, her parents, aunts, uncles, and cousins rode horses to the event where live bands played country music. A multitude of tents dotted the grounds and people offered a wide variety of produce, like fresh fruits and vegetables, jams, jellies, and preserves and other fresh foods for sale . Tented venues sold a great deal of diverse offerings from livestock at auction to farm equipment and from fine art to specialty herbs and seasonings. Popular fresh-canned items were on display produced by the Alexander-Dixon Food Court under a huge tent where full meals were served and seating was provided.

Next to the food pavilion, Gregory Alexander and Willis Greene, Whitney's uncle and maternal grandfather, also had a big tent with antique cars for sale. The amusement part of the festival had games with prizes, Ferris wheel rides, bumper cars, a merry-go-round, and a haunted house. Visitors of a wide range of ages danced late into the evening.

The Cavanaughs stayed at Benny and Stacy's farm and spent much of their time meeting various branches of Whitney's family who stopped in to say hello. They already met Whitney's paternal grandparents, Bernard and Sylvia Benson Alexander, when they came to Maryland, but when they arrived in South Carolina, Stacy's parents, Willis and Helen Greene, and her younger brother, Russell, warmly greeted the Cavanaughs.

"You're Russell Greene, the artist?" Felicia Cavanaugh asked in awe.

Russell ruefully smiled and shrugged, his light, crystal brown eyes alight. "I am, yes, but I'm still a work in progress," he joked and slung an arm around his niece's shoulder.

"Uncle Russell is a phenomenal painter," agreed Whitney, hugging him around his narrow waist. "He just had an art exhibit in Tokyo, Japan, that completely sold out all of his Asian Impression Collection."

"Not quite all. I managed to save one for your Christmas present."

"Please tell me it's the landscape of the water reflection of the Tokyo Crystal Palace."

"I'm not telling you that. You'll have to wait for Christmas morning."

"Are you going to have an exhibit any time soon in the states?" Aurora asked.

"Not for a few years," Russell said, "but my mother has some art you should see while you're here. She has a pink tent on the second row over from here. You can't miss it."

The Cavanaughs turned to the pretty, middle-aged woman with the blond hair and blue eyes.

"You're a painter, too?" Todd asked.

"I do paint, yes, but I'm not as talented as my son," Helen Greene said.

"Don't believe that for one moment," her husband, Willis, chided good-naturedly. "My Helen paints beautiful pictures. Let me show you," he said, leading them to her tent where lights illuminated her beautifully displayed art.

"Wow," they each said, moving from one painting to the next.

"Do you have art shows?" Felicia asked.

"I have some on display at Summer County Academy. I've sold all of the first set of those I've exhibited here at the Harvest Festival. This is the second set, but I have more in the panel truck if you would like to see them."

"I love the ones you have here on display, but I would really like to see more," Aurora said.

"Me, too," Todd said.

"We can do that tomorrow," Whitney suggested, "while Uncle Chuck takes Tucker with him for rounds at Summer County General. Nana Helen and Uncle Russell can set up a display at the Summer House. Then on Thanksgiving Day, you should come to the hospital in the morning to see the murals Nana Helen and her students are painting for the hospital wards. They're really quite spectacular."

"That sounds like a plan," Todd said.

All were in general agreement.

"All right, Cavanaugh, you're cleared to accompany me for another day on rounds this morning," Chuck said as he passed an ID badge to Tucker. It was six-thirty in the morning on Thanksgiving Day. Each day, Chuck checked Tucker's vitals before he let him accompany him on hospital rounds. The shifts were about to change at Summer County General Hospital in Goodwill, South Carolina. "If you begin to feel weak..."

"I understand. I passed the stress test Dr. Stone administered before we left Maryland to come here. So far, so good, since we arrived here over the weekend. I don't relish the idea of doing a face plant. I'll immediately let you know if I begin to feel any symptoms."

"Okay, let's go to work."

On every floor of the four-floor facility, Chuck consulted with other doctors on cases where he was asked to offer medical opinions. As a financial backer to the hospital, a hospital board member, and a physician with hospital privileges, Chuck's advice was often sought on a number of issues. He even made time to see his own patients who came to the hospital just to see him. Though he wasn't a pediatrician like his best friend, Derrick Jackson, had been, during an emergency snow storm, Chuck had taken care of young Donovan Johnson, the adolescent son of the Summer County Fire Chief, Douglas Johnson. Donovan was in a serious school bus accident and in a coma for quite a while. Although Donovan was now a teenager, Chuck still took care of him and still monitored his health.

"So how are you doing in school, Donovan?" Chucked asked as he began his routine examination with Tucker looking on and reading the boy's medical chart on an iPad.

Donovan shrugged a typical teenager's response. "Fine."

"Your mom says you're a Dean's List student, strong in math and science and you're interested in going into medicine."

"Maybe. Mama Satarah used to be an Emergency Room nurse. She saved my life and didn't even know me then. You did, too, and you let me be your daughter's godbrother. Where did you go to medical school?"

"Georgetown in Washington, DC."

"That's where Whitney Ivy goes to law school," acknowledged Donovan.

"It is and so does my assistant today, Dr. Tucker Cavanaugh."

"You're Whitney's male friend," Donovan said, studying Tucker.

"I am, yes, and although I'm a First Lieutenant in the Marines, I'm in my last year of medical school at Georgetown Medical Center. If you come up to visit this summer, let me know. I'll take you on a tour."

"We go to classes at Summer County Academy all year. We don't take summer breaks. We go to class for six weeks and then we're out of class for two weeks. So I'll ask my parents whether I can come after my next rotation. Sometimes, my parents, brothers, and sisters go visit our godsister, Eden Ann Montgomery, Dr. Chuck and Cousin Vivian's daughter."

Surprised, Tucker held his questions until after Donovan's exam was finished and the tall, gangly teen left before he could ask Chuck about the school system.

"That's correct. Students at the academy study one subject for six weeks and then after a two-week break, on the next rotation they study a different subject. Some classes are for eight or more hours per day; sometimes six days a week. They have breaks during the day, but get more accomplished and rise according to their level of proficiency. It's a unique system of education, but it's highly effective. My children prefer this system and, if Vivian and I didn't have careers which keep us tied to the Washington, DC, area, we'd move here for the school system."

"I think Whitney mentioned this to me. Isn't there another program like this in Washington?"

"There is and they have a website you may want to visit. However, we'd need to move into the Baylor Plaza Park community. The school doesn't take students from outside the community at this time. With an ever-increasing number of children, we need the space living on the ranch provides. Our children love living where we are. However, our friend, Tina Justice Collins, is testing a prototype of the curriculum on one of her satellite channels. Vivian is considering chartering a school in the county where we live and using Tina's channel for class work. If she does, then we'll give the children the option of staying in Georgetown Academy, the school where they are enrolled now or attending the new charter school somewhere in the county where we live. Vivian wants to look for land to purchase and build a campus. We'll do that after the first of the year.

"Dr. Jefferson Logan is the Dean of the flagship academy here. He's planning to expand the academy's curriculum and reach via a new satellite delivery system he's working on with my father-in-law, Dr. Bernard Alexander and Ambassador Jake Hawkins."

"Wasn't Dr. Logan a diplomat at one time?" Tucker asked.

"He was, and from time-to-time, he's called up to intercede to resolve difficult international issues. Most recently, he was in Africa at the request of Ambassador Hawkins."

"I've read about Jake Hawkins' BlackHawk Industries," Tucker said as he and Chuck walked through the hospital's wide hallway to their next medical task.

Chuck nodded. "He has a foundation, a part of BlackHawk Global, which is headed by one of his sons, Adam Hawkins. As a non-government organization, an NGO, Jake and Adam use the foundation to help African countries improve their standard of living. They, along with Dr. Logan, are planning to institute an international academy built on the program devised by the flagship school that Whitney's grandfather conceived and implemented years ago. Dr. Logan has taken it up another level and beyond by making it a national academic institution. With the help of Tina Justice Collins, it will become the first international academy based on the unique program Dr. Alexander devised. If it brings the scholastic aptitude of the students in the program up to the stellar levels we've seen in the two academies already in existence, it will be an incredible success."

"I'll take a look at the website. The academic concept alone sounds intriguing. When Whitney and I start a family, I don't know where we'll be stationed. We'll want our children in the best scholastic atmosphere we can find. This international program may be a solution to how we will educate our children."

"Planning for a large family, are you?" Chuck asked, smiling.

"Oh, yes. In addition to having our own, we want to adopt children who need a good home just like you do."

Chuck nodded his approval. He really liked this young man.

While they continued to see patients, Whitney, her siblings, and cousins performed their usual hospital volunteer duties as Blue Teens under the direct supervision of their grandmother, Sylvia Benson Alexander, the head of nursing at Summer County General. She trained her grandchildren as volunteers in the same manner she trained her group of seniors, known as the Gray Ladies and Gentlemen, who wore light-gray uniforms. She encouraged her young, high school and college-aged volunteers, who wore light-blue vests, to sate their curiosity about the health care profession. It allowed those youngsters who had an interest in learning to be of service to a community to also satisfy community-service prerequisites as required by some colleges and universities.

"I met your guy, Tucker," Linda, Vivian's oldest daughter, said. "*Ooh la la*, as Grandaunt Mariah would say."

Whitney smiled. "He is just the right side of perfect, inside and out. What about you? Are you seeing anyone special?"

Linda slanted an incredulous look at her cousin. "Get real, Whitney. I'm on tour until next spring. Except for blocking out time to be with our family for the holidays, I don't even have time to date and I really wouldn't want to date anyone in the business."

Whitney laughed and joined arms with her cousin, one of her BFFs. They walked the hospital corridor and talked until they reached their destination, the children's ward.

Linda was the first one of the health-challenged and orphaned children adopted by Vivian and her first husband, Dr. Derrick Jackson, former basketball icon and a multibillionaire. Linda was in a fatal accident that claimed the life of her biological mother and younger brother. There was more tragedy in her young life. Linda's father died in Iraq, leaving Linda, at age six, a ward of the state, housed in a hospital and an orphanage. Derrick was her doctor; a pediatric surgeon who for years worked tirelessly to help restore Linda's ability to walk. The orphanage responsible for her care was balking at the spiraling health care costs to provide for one child when they had so many more to take care of.

Before Derrick married Vivian, she suggested they adopt Linda and, although as her father, he wouldn't be permitted to be her primary care physician, given Derrick's incredible wealth, he could continue to provide the medical care she needed through the other doctors who were in private practice with him. Her adoption led to the adoption of other orphaned and health-challenged children by Derrick and Vivian. Through some invention Derrick created, the world of pediatric medicine was revolutionized. Linda was the first patient to benefit from his efforts. She not only learned to walk again, but she also became a world-renowned, prima ballerina. She also scored Olympic gold several times as a figure skater while still in puberty. Now she toured the world, performing for standing-room-only crowds as the chief female dancer in a ballet.

"I thought that was you," Helen Greene, Whitney's maternal grandmother, commented.

"Hi, Nana Helen," Whitney enthused, giving her a tight squeeze as did Linda.

"Don't you two look beautiful," Helen said.

"I understand you had a hand in designing and making these Thanksgiving costumes," Linda said.

"Well, of course. It helps to be reminded why Americans celebrate Thanksgiving, so your Nana Sylvia and I thought it would be interesting if you and the other children and teens wore period clothing. The American tradition of Thanksgiving began with a three-day feast that took place in 1621 to celebrate a bountiful harvest. More than two hundred years later, it became cemented as an annual celebration in 1863, when President Lincoln declared a 'day of Thanksgiving' in the midst of the Civil War. So, we made costumes for all of you to wear to commemorate that timeframe."

"I think it's a great idea," Linda said. "Particularly since my brothers have to wear Indigenous American clothing, too." She laughed.

Gesturing and turning to the partially completed canvas attached to the hospital wall in the corridor, Whitney stepped back to admire what was shaping up to be a wall mural depicting a pastoral harvest scene. "This is beautiful, Nana Helen."

"Thank you, child. I must admit, I have a group of very talented, artistic students this year in my classes. I think this is going to be one of our best works of art."

"Except you say that every year, Nana Helen," Whitney teased.

"Well, it's true every year," she said, smiling, her green eyes shining with mirth. "Did the Cavanaughs see the murals here?"

"They did, yes. They bought several from my Golden Harvest series, too. Willis took the art to prepare it to be shipped."

"Where is Grandpop Willis?"

"Oh, you know your granddad. He's back at the ranch getting the wagons and horses ready for the hayrides. He is so excited about having his grandbabies home, he could barely sleep the week before all of you arrived. He'll be here before noon to take us all on hayrides to the Summer House for Thanksgiving dinner."

"Where is Uncle Russell? I haven't seen him today."

"Oh, he and your Aunt Aretha Grace are out with your grand uncles, Marvin, Melvin, Stanley, and Stuart, and their families, filling and delivering food baskets to the sick and shut-ins."

"Great-grandma Lula Belle Rae King is coming to dinner this year?" Whitney asked of her grandmother about her eighty-year-old mother, elated.

"Of course, she will. We all want to get a good look at your Marine Tucker Cavanaugh. Even your grandfather's brother, Wilton, who was in the Marines himself, and his family are coming. Did you think they wouldn't?"

Whitney blushed. "He's special, Nana Helen, and so are his parents and grandparents. They're a little awed by the sheer size of our family."

Helen laughed. "It's a good thing they're only going to meet *some* of our relatives. It will prepare them for the Juneteenth family reunion."

"Cousin Helen, nothing can prepare them for that," joked Linda. "It has to be experienced."

"You may have a point there, sweetheart. It's one thing to have a couple hundred to meet in a short period of time, like Thanksgiving, but the ten days we spend together with more than five hundred family members strains the imagination."

"You mean Whitney's grandmother painted these murals?" Tucker asked as he and Chuck slowly walked a hospital corridor to their next consultation.

"That's correct. She's an art counselor at Summer County Academy, the only combined high school and junior college here in the area."

"I was going to ask you about that. The academy is a public and private partnership, right?"

"Yes and the only one of its kind in the state. As I said before, the only other one is in Northeast, Washington, DC, in Baylor Plaza Park. Dr. Roselyn Hunter Greenfield operates it."

"I've heard of the academy, but I didn't make the connection. They produce talented musicians."

"They have several specialties there as they do here. You met my father-in-law, Whitney's grandfather, Dr. Bernard Alexander. As I said before, he's an educator who started the program here. When he was elected to the South Carolina Senate, he recruited Dr. Jefferson Logan to be the Dean of Summer County Academy."

"I read about him. He was an Ambassador who negotiated the peace accords between warring Arab factions."

"Although he is the Dean here, he still negotiates on behalf of the United States in difficult situations. Just a few years ago, he helped save twenty young African girls from the Boko Haram."

"Whitney said her parents were instrumental in protecting the girls by sheltering them on a US military base in Tokyo, Japan."

"I didn't know that part of the story, but it sounds like something Benny and Stacy would do."

Tucker stopped walking to look at a particularly striking piece of art. "Mrs. Greene and her students didn't do this one, did they?"

"You've got a good eye," Chuck said, nodding. "You're right. This one was painted by Mrs. Greene's son, Whitney's uncle, Stacy's younger brother, Russell Greene."

Surprise covered Tucker's face. "On our first date, Whitney said her uncle is Russell Greene, but I've only seen his work in magazines. I've never seen the real thing except in your home and here. His work reaches out and grabs you in. He's young and very talented."

"He's a tad older than you," Chuck said, laughing. "You'll see him again at dinner today along with additional members of Whitney's maternal family. I believe Russell is staying with his parents while he's here for the holidays because his maternal grandmother is there. His granduncles are here, too, with their families and they're staying at The Summer House where the dinner is being held. Believe me, we are a legion," Chuck said, slapping a hand on Tucker's back as they continued to walk the hospital corridor to their next consultation.

Chapter 14

"Look to your right! Look to your left! Look ahead of you! Look behind you! Everywhere you look, you see family. Thank the Ancestors and the Creator for this family!" the eldest member of the family said into a microphone on the raised platform.

"First Principle!" he stridently called out and then came the response from the family members assembled at tables in the ballroom -sized dining hall of The Summer House.

"We strive for and maintain unity in the family in our communities, in our nation and in the human race," family members said as they stood holding hands around the room.

"Second Principle."

"We define ourselves, create for ourselves, and speak for ourselves."

"Third Principle."

"We build and maintain our communities together, make our sisters' and brothers' problems our own, and we solve those problems together."

"Fourth Principle."

"We build and maintain our careers, stores, and industries, and profit from them together."

"Fifth Principle."

"We use our collective vocations to build and develop our communities in order to continue our ancestors' traditions."

"Sixth Principle."

"We leave our communities more beautiful and financially sound than when we inherited them."

"Seventh Principle."

"We believe in our family, our parents, our teachers, and the necessity to improve ourselves to reach higher levels of understanding."

"Eighth Principle."

"We honor ourselves and treat everyone with love, kindness, and respect, always learning to appreciate another point of view."

"Ninth Principle."

"We wear a never-ending gold chain as a symbol of what family stands for and what we are challenged to achieve."

"Tenth Principle."

"We honor and acknowledge our ancestors' struggles, which make a good life possible for all of us."

"Eleventh Principle."

"We stand for something or we'll fall for anything."

"Twelfth Principle."

"We are the links to an unbroken chain stretching back through the ages to the beginning. We will never falter or fail."

"No matter what we do in life, we're a family," the elder ended.

"Amen," the family members said and then hugged those around them. All in attendance for Thanksgiving were related by blood, love, marriage or friendship. They began to seat themselves at round tables of twelve. Trays of food were wheeled to each table and placed on the Lazy Susan that circumnavigated each table on rollers and tracks. With fresh, fall flowers and an array of scented lit candles, the tables were beautifully dressed with colorful Kente cloths and napkins, shining silverware, and sparkling crystal. Red and white wines graced each table as did bottles of water and sparkling cider manufactured in the Alexander-Dixon Industries' facility. Each person served him or herself from the aromatic dishes prepared by capable and professional hands.

"That was a powerful oration," commented Lee seated at the table next to Stacy and Benny on his right with his wife, Aurora, and their parents to their left. Stacy's parents, Willis and Helen Greene, and her maternal grandmother, Lula Belle Rae King, sat to her right. Tucker and Whitney filled the remaining seats, leaving one seat empty as a symbol of a missing family member, Lula Belle Rae King's long-deceased husband.

"It's tradition in our family," Benny said, in response to Lee's comment. "It is one of the first set of principles we learned as toddlers. It's like learning the Lord's Prayer or the Pledge of Allegiance."

"It must be. I noticed very few people used the printed version on the program and menu."

Todd Adamson, Aurora's father, activated the Lazy Susan and reached for the bowl of creamy mashed potatoes."

"Careful, Granddad, the trays are hot," Tucker said.

"He's right. The trays keep the food warm," Benny said.

"What a great idea," Felicia Cavanaugh, Lee's mother, said. "I haven't seen this on the market."

"It will be by Christmas. My brother, Kenneth, designed it at our mother's request. It operates on a twelve-hour battery which can be recharged."

"This will make a perfect Christmas gift. Does he manufacture them for different table sizes?" Felicia asked.

"He does, yes. It's built on the same principle as used by model electric train tracks. It's just a little wider to accommodate serving bowls and platters and warming elements."

"It certainly cuts down on the time it takes to serve a large crowd like this," remarked Todd, as he liberally ladled on steaming hot giblet gravy over his mound of mashed potatoes and turkey stuffing.

"I want to hear more about this ski trip," Lee said, as he helped himself to more succulent roasted beef and butter beans.

"Each year, following Thanksgiving Day, the men take the young children for a three-day ski trip to Vail, Colorado," Benny said.

"The women get to spend three days at the McCoy Oceans Inn Hotel and Resort Spa in Atlantic Beach, South Carolina, and shop to our heart's content at the outlet malls in Myrtle Beach," Stacy said.

"Have credit card, will travel," joked Felicia, holding up her goblet to toast with the other women at the table. The men laughed at the women's glee.

"I can forgo the shopping, but the full-body scrub, facial, and massages are the best!" Whitney exclaimed, joining the toast with her glass of sparkling cider.

"Spoken like a true daughter of mine," Stacy said, touching her glass of white wine to her daughter's.

"This ski trip promises to be an adventure," Todd said. "Lee and I ski every season, especially when Tucker was a youngster. Southern Maine's Sunday River is often one of the first ski areas to open for the season in the state. It has more than seven hundred skiable acres of terrain. Farther north, Sugarloaf is home to what I think is the most skiable terrain on the East Coast."

"Maine is also home to resorts like Saddleback, and their Kennebago Steeps," Lee said. "It's the largest steep skiing and riding facility in the east; or Mt. Abram, which recently partnered with the Mountain Rider's Alliance to create a model for sustainable, homegrown, local resorts."

"We've skied all over Maine, but we've never ventured west to ski places like Vale," Todd said. "We've heard how majestic the scenery is, so we're looking forward to this opportunity."

"It's a great experience," Benny said. "We'll stay at the family chalet. The kids sleep in sleeping bags on cots. The men share dormitory-like facilities all under the same roof. Fortunately, the breakfast is catered. Lunch and dinner, we're on our own and generally use one of the resort's all-you-can-eat buffets. The kids like the variety and we don't have to spend time in the kitchen. We also load up on snacks."

"Speaking of food, are they seriously bringing out more trays of food?" Aurora asked, astonished and wide-eyed.

"We're serious foodies here in the South," eighty-year-old Lula Belle Rae King said, laughing.

Later, after the meal, when the family members picked up their musical instruments and began the entertainment part of the evening in The Summer House's ballroom, Tucker and Whitney joined in. Groups or individuals performed dance routines, told jokes, did magic tricks, and various other expressions of the performing arts to the audience's enthusiastic delight and resounding applause. Linda was spectacular when she danced a scene from *The Nutcracker* to the enchantment of the little people.

The show closed out with songs performed by the incomparable French Mariah, Whitney's grandaunt, and her aunt, Aretha Grace. Whitney was pushed into joining Mariah and Aretha on stage, displaying three generations of family members with extraordinary musical talent. Whitney's voice as strong and true as her namesake, Whitney Houston, and the voices of her twelve-year-old triplet sisters, Shannon, Sharon, and Sierra, joined in. They even coaxed their grandmother, Sylvia, to join in.

As the hour grew late, the little ones were put to bed in The Summer House's big, rambling, four-story, bed and breakfast in preparation for their early morning departures for Vale, Colorado, while the other adults got down to some serious fun and frivolity.

Chuck led off the dancing with the line dance from *Footloose*. Lee and Todd tried keeping up with the energetic steps, but admitted to having two left feet. Aurora and Felicia succeeded, delighted and even got the hand-clapping portion right.

"Look at your father and grandfathers go!" Tucker exclaimed from the sidelines as he clapped to the beat.

"I know," Whitney said, grinning from ear to ear. "My dad loves to dance. So do my granddads, but Uncle Chuck kills it with line dances. My dad and mom like hand-dancing while my grands like to square dance. This is the first time I've seen my grand uncles on my mother's side of the family cut up like this!" She clapped to the beat, too, and shouted encouragement to the group of dancers.

Tucker slung an arm around Whitney's shoulder, causing her to look up at him. Tucker's pretty blue eyes were moist, she noticed.

Concern bunched Whitney's brow as she turned more fully into his embrace, searching his eyes for some sign of what may be causing his distress.

"What is it, Tucker? Are you feeling—?"

"Happy, Whitney. I'm feeling happy. The first time you took me to your family's ranch, I wanted my family there to witness what for me is an iconic event. For you, it's a routine occurrence. Then today, as I listened to and spoke your family's principles, it reaffirmed why I fell in love with you almost on first sight. I knew my parents and grandparents would love you, too, but to experience the boundless love you and your family share and offer us in return is so huge it's almost overwhelming."

She smiled up into his eyes, rose on her toes, and laid her lips on his. "The feelings are mutual, Tucker. I'm hopelessly in love with you. So I know exactly how you feel. I know someone my age can't know everything about married love." She turned, laying her head on his chest, and sighed, looking at row upon row of her family members now dancing the Down N Dirty line dance in the large ballroom. "I've been surrounded by this family's love all of my life." She looked up into his eyes again. "I know I'll be surrounded by your love, too, for the rest of my life. That makes me want to cry happy tears, too."

"I know it's only been a matter of months, but you make me very happy, Whitney Ivy Alexander, and secure in the love we'll bring our children into. I never want you to doubt what you mean to me. I want you to have the same smile on your face and sparkle in your eyes every day for the rest of our lives together." He leaned down and kissed her.

"You do know I have a likely high probability of multiple births, right? My great-grandmother has two sets of twins. They're dancing on the sixth row. My grandmother had a set of twins. My mother is a twin and has two sets of triplets. On my dad's side, my Grandfather Bernard is a twin and his twin sister, Olivia, has twin boys, Donald and James Dixon. That's them in the second row near the center. Both of them have a set of twins."

Tucker's mouth dropped open. *"Ooh Rah!"* he said while Lee and Todd finally got the footfalls of the Down N Dirty down pat.

Chapter 15

The ball caps Whitney found in the Broadway at the Beach novelty shop in Myrtle Beach, South Carolina, read *HIS* and *HERS*. The *HERS* cap would make a great gag Christmas gift for Tucker. He loved baseball. She would wear the cap with *HIS* on the brim. Her special gift to him would be one of her guitars; the one he enjoyed playing the most and the one they composed what became "their song" during their very first date. As she continued to shop, she found gifts for her parents and siblings. They gave group gifts to the grands and the uncles and aunts. They usually spent Christmas and New Years in Washington, DC, at their home in Georgetown. She hoped the threat against Tucker's life would be solved before then so they could spend an enjoyable time together as a couple.

For Tucker's parents and grands, she was giving complimentary, front-row center seats and tickets to her cousin's, Linda's, next ballet on Broadway in New York City. Linda would be the featured lead ballerina in the ballet *Don Quixote*. Tucker told her his mother and grandmother loved to see live ballet performances. They would also receive dinner reservations for her good friend's, Angelique's, restaurant for the same day as the show. Hopefully, she and Tucker would be able to join them for the outing.

She knew that Changelings was scheduled to perform in the Georgetown Holiday Pageant and other venues in and around the area. KiLi was filling in for Trisha and Whitney's cousin, Brian Montgomery, and her friend, Miguel Menendez-Gaza, Angelique's brother, was between movie roles and agreed to fill in for Mike Giaconni and Tucker. Brian was an excellent drummer and Miguel had mad skills on the guitar. Both also had very good strong voices.

Fortunately, Uncle Chuck was making sure Tucker could keep up with his classwork. Her parents pulled strings to cover Tucker's absence from his military obligations. So far, all of the bases were covered.

"Come on, Whitney," Linda said. "We have to hurry or we'll be late for Great-grandaunt Hannah Ivy's high tea."

Whitney quickly paid for her purchases and climbed aboard the bus to arrive by one o'clock for high tea at Point of View. The house in Atlantic Beach was a big Victorian surrounded by wide upper and lower wraparound verandas and sat on the sand, feet away from the Atlantic Ocean.

For late November, it was a surprisingly warm day. The windows were open, allowing the ocean breeze to billow the sheer curtains and the sunlight to stream into the tea room, Point of View. Round tables were set with charming, colorful tablecloths, antique lunch plates, and teacups. Four-teared plate trees centered each table, holding delectable finger foods. Each place setting had its own floral, porcelain teapot, steeping with one of many specialty hot teas.

Point of View offered apparel reminiscent of the eighteenth century to add to the old-fashion event. Ladies donned afternoon, broad-brimmed hats and colorful boas; some going so far as to wear laced gloves. A professional photographer moved from place to place, taking pictures as the women posed in revealing laced bodices and hooped skirts furnished by Point of View.

Hannah Ivy Benson, a woman in her eighties, along with her friend from Washington, DC, Alma Lewis, also in her eighties, decided to convert the first floor of Hannah's oceanfront home into a mid-eighteenth-century gift shop and tea room. In her youth, Hannah was a private duty nurse, but never owned a business before. However, Alma Lewis and her late husband owned a liquor store in Washington; one she still owned and her grandson, a former Marine, managed for her now that she lived year-round in the South.

Alma contributed valuable business guidance and financed the business while Hannah selected the décor and staged the tea room and gift shop. The house was equipped with a rising bench on a rail and the two senior women lived in the upstairs rooms and loved to have people around every day. They hired staff to prepare and serve the food to the customers while they chatted with other seniors who regularly frequented their establishment to sample or purchase a vast array of teas. In a separate room, visitors could experiment with different blends of teas. The different blends made great gifts.

Sofas and other comfortable seating in the main room were draped in pretty linens and crocheted cloths were placed inside the open-concept living and dining areas and on the lower veranda. Clear, plastic drapes were hung when inclement weather disturbed those who preferred to sit out on the deck to view the Atlantic Ocean while they drank their tea and had brunch. There wasn't a day that didn't have the tea room and gift shop filled to capacity with a line waiting to get in at appointed times.

With the beautiful view of the ocean and kitschy décor, Point of View was a throwback to the 1700s and 1800s. Sometimes, baby or bridal showers or small wedding receptions were held there.

For the Labor Day holiday, Hannah Ivy's grandnephews and nieces, and great-grands, who were still in school, congregated on the beach in tents and sleeping bags to enjoy the last vestiges of summer and rededicate themselves to the school year ahead. Hannah and Alma put the youngsters to work on various tasks around the house as a source of free labor in exchange for free food. All were pleased with the exchange.

However, on this day, Hannah and Alma closed the tea room and shop to the public to host Hannah's family's traditional Thanksgiving weekend visit.

"So you really like Tucker?" Geneviève asked, another one of Whitney's first cousins and BFFs, as they sat at a table for two drinking tea.

"Very much, yes. I don't know what happened. All of a sudden, he was just there, standing in front of me, introducing himself. I looked like crap and smelled worse. It wasn't that he's drop-dead gorgeous, but I read something special in his eyes and his smile was everything a smile should be, warm and open."

"When you know it's right, then it is what it is," Geneviève said and shrugged.

Whitney giggled.

"What's so funny?" Geneviève asked, perplexed.

"That's exactly what Tucker and I said and wrote a song with that title. 'When You Know.' From the first moment we met, we clicked. It's only been a couple of months, but we still have this intense feeling for each other. We don't get tired of talking with each other, either. We keep learning more and more from and about one another."

"You're going to give your relationship more time to grow and develop right?" Geneviève asked.

Whitney nodded. "We are, yes. A few years, in fact. We agree we're too young to marry now. I want to finish law school, pass the bar exam, and then begin a career. That should take two to three years. During that time, Tucker will still be in his residency program. He's a Marine and once he completes his medical training, he could be stationed anywhere. So we have that to consider."

"You're probably right about holding off on marriage, but how are you going to avoid making love?" Geneviève asked.

"I have absolutely no idea," admitted Whitney.

Friday ended with a great dinner show at The House of Blues in North Myrtle Beach in the Barefoot Landing open-air complex. Shops, like the Christmas Mouse, were doing a brisk business. The group of young girls, teens, and women took advantage of all of the shops in the complex before the show started and had to store their many purchases on the bus before they went to the dinner theatre. The show, which included saxophonist Paul Taylor, pianist Keiko Matsui, and vocalist Kem and his band Kemistry, rocked the House to its rafters with an array of smooth jazz selections. By the time the show ended at near midnight, everyone was ready to turn in.

After a full day of shopping on Friday, the next morning, Saturday, was slated as a spa day. The young girls, teens, and women were fed and pampered from head to toe.

"Oh, my, this is wonderful," Felicia Cavanaugh crooned.

"I'll say," Aurora moaned, delighted as they were treated to full-body scrubs and messages by talented staff hands at the Atlantic Beach McCoy Oceans Inn Spa Resort.

"I would move here just to enjoy this," Sylvia Alexander offered.

"I'd come with you," Helen Greene agreed. "I think we should do this at least once a month."

"I don't think I've had any man's hands on me that felt this good," Lula Belle Rae King offered.

"I heard that," Hannah Ivy and Alma Lewis agreed demonstratively in unison.

"Scandalous," Whitney mildly chided. "Young one here."

"She hasn't had any man's hands on her body yet," offered Vivian about her niece as she moaned at the hot, deep-tissue massage she received from her masseuse. "Neither have my daughters, Linda and Geneviève. They don't have anything to compare this to."

"*Ma!*" Linda and Geneviève wailed in unison, aggrieved.

Her masseuse chuckled while digging into Linda's tight calf muscles, making her moan in ecstasy.

"There are definite benefits to being female," Stacy Greene Alexander offered. "Tucker seems like the type of young man who will help you enjoy that aspect of your life, Whitney."

It was Whitney's turn to moan "Mom" in embarrassment.

"He's his father's son. He'll make every day memorable," Aurora offered.

"For sure," Felicia agreed about her son, Leland.

"TMI," Whitney groaned. "Help, Aunt Aretha."

"Sorry, kiddo, virgin here, but I'm having too much fun living vicariously through the lives of my experienced female family members and friends," she said, laughing.

"What do you think?" Tucker asked of his father and grandfather.

Lee nodded, his chest too full of emotion to speak.

His father-in-law's face showed the pride he felt. "A fine choice, Tucker. It's exactly right," Todd said, clamping a supportive hand on Lee's shoulder. He was as proud of his son-in-law as he was of his grandson.

The three men stood in the crowded Vail, Colorado, jeweler store admiring the simple, diamond engagement ring embedded in a titanium band. The young boys and teens were out on the ski slopes while other male family and friends were elsewhere in the store looking for sparkling, precious stone Christmas gifts.

Tucker looked up and around, spotting Whitney's father and two of her uncles.

"General," he called out.

Benny turned from looking at earrings to acknowledge Tucker. Together, with his older brother, Kenneth, and younger, but taller brother, Gregory, they moved toward Tucker to see the ring he held out.

"Well, hell, if this is an engagement ring for my daughter, you've captured exactly the right thing. Whitney's not the delicate type. This is perfect for her active life," Benny offered as he took the ring from Tucker's fingers. He looked up into Tucker's moist eyes and nodded. "I hoped I could interest Whitney in one of the jet fighter pilots under my command, but now I don't believe I could give my daughter's hand to a finer man, even though you are a Marine. You know, there's still time for you to join the Air Force."

The men laughed.

"The Air Force men and women don't get hurt, so they don't need doctors the way we do in the Marines," Tucker parred.

Benny hooted a laugh and handed the ring back to Tucker. "I hope you're prepared when you show this ring to the Admiral."

"I'll work on it, but I hope this necklace softens her up a bit," Tucker said, showing the group of men the birthstone necklace he selected for Stacy. He selected similar gifts for his mother and grandmother.

Leland whistled. "Nice job, son."

"Thanks, Dad."

"I think your approach is spot on," Kenneth said. "Where did you find that? A necklace like this would be perfect for my wife and daughters."

"Right over there," Tucker said, leading the way.

On Sunday afternoon, the family dispersed; some headed back home to Maryland while others returned to their homes in other places. Tucker and his family would continue to stay at the ranch in Maryland for the rest of the week. When they learned of Tucker's accident, his family dropped everything and came to Maryland from Maine. Although Todd, Felicia, and Aurora didn't have to work, Leland still actively represented clients and needed to arrange for another attorney to handle his law practice until the threat to Tucker's life was over.

Whitney came down the wide staircase in the Georgetown house, passing KiLi and Roland on their way up to their rooms on the second floor. Whitney and her family, including her Aunt JeNelle, occupied the third floor of bedrooms. Her parents and siblings were settling in, but would be down soon for dinner. Whitney was heading for the library to study when she noticed Bill in the front salon, feeding logs to the lit fireplace.

"Hi, Uncle Bill," Whitney said, entering the salon. She went into his open arms for a hug. "You were missed at Thanksgiving."

"I'm sorry I missed it."

"Where were you for the holiday?"

"I was in New York and had dinner with my sister. Where is everyone?"

"Dad and Mom are supervising the laundry brigade for the girls and the baths for the boys. They'll be down shortly for dinner."

"It should be ready soon," Bill said. "Anna's been at it for a while in the kitchen. I set up the buffet in the formal dining room. Did your uncles and aunts come back, too?"

"Uncle Kenneth and Aunt JeNelle flew back to California. Since the Congress is on break for the holidays until after New Year's, JeNelle had a host of constituent town hall meetings scheduled throughout the state."

Bill nodded in acknowledgment. "JeNelle's sister, Gloria, her husband, David, and their children will be in California for Christmas. They and their parents are going to their home in Lake Tahoe to ski."

"Yes, I heard Kenneth and David purchased land in Squaw Valley and built chalets there."

"They did, yes. So they plan to stay through New Year's Day. Aunt JeNelle said she'll be back early in January. Uncle Chuck and Aunt Vivian are at the ranch with Tucker and his family. Uncle Gregory stayed in South Carolina to monitor the progress of his semi-pro basketball league. His bank is having some big celebration because they reached some milestone and the renovations on his barn conversion are almost complete. Angelique flew back to New York City, and Miguel came back with us. He's next door with Fenster. They should be coming in here shortly for dinner. Aunt Aretha and Uncle Russell flew to England. She had to get back to school and he has a big art exhibit coming up in London."

"I saw the video of the holiday weekend Aretha posted online. It looked like a big crowd and everyone seemed to have had fun."

"It was. Although everyone was expecting you to join us, I'm glad you didn't spend the time working."

He did, but he didn't share that bit of trouble with her.

"Uncle Bill, you didn't work through the holiday, did you?" Something in his demeanor had her concerned.

He forced himself to smile brilliantly at her. "Any time I have to spend time with my family is work."

"You saw your parents?" Whitney asked, surprised. She knew Bill and his sister's, Margo's, parents weren't nice or good people.

Though she didn't know the whole story of his youth, she knew enough to not bring Ike and Dolly Chandler's names up in polite company. "I know you bought a house for them in The Catskills years ago, but I didn't know they still lived there."

"Margo and I spent the day in The Catskills with the parental units," Bill said.

That got a laugh out of Whitney as it was intended to do. He met with his parents, but only to interrogate them about the Rossellini family who used to live in the same tenement building in New York City's Little Italy neighborhood. His father drove a cab and was an illegal numbers runner for the Rossellini mob. His mother was a call girl, often servicing the men in the mob. His parents pimped him out to child pornographers until he wised up, kicked them to the curb, and handled his own clientele. He bought the house in The Catskills to get them out of the old Little Italy neighborhood and keep them from pimping his younger sister.

His parents had a wealth of information, particularly because their livelihood depended on staying in Bill's good graces. He paid all of their expenses and gave them a monthly allowance, which was more than adequate to keep them in style. So, as long as they stayed in the house he paid for and stayed out of trouble, he continued to see to their needs. Still, his parents kept tabs on what was going on in the old neighborhood.

According to his parents, at one time, the old Italian mobs would have nothing to do with drugs. Rather, their stock and trade were in alcohol, the trucking unions, and racketeering. However, when those industries dried up and went away, they gradually shifted into the sale of guns and the purchase of legitimate businesses where they could launder money from their drug and human trafficking trades. First, it was pot until it became legal, but less lucrative. They also migrated into designer drugs, but more recently they were buying cocaine from Afghanistan in exchange for the weapons and other artillery wanted by certain military dictators and renegades. They held their noises, recognizing that some of what they sold could and probably would end up in the hands of terrorists.

Most of this, Bill already knew. However, he didn't know the names of specific people involved. That information he learned from his parents in exchange for an all-expenses-paid vacation to Brazil or anywhere to get them out of the cold in the mountains for the winter. They were deplorable people, but they were getting old and they were his parents, so he acquiesced to their demands.

He learned from his parents who in each mob family was or wasn't involved in various illegal activities. He wasn't surprised to learn that Maria Rossi's name came up, but he was shocked to hear the name Antonio Santangelo aka Tony San Angelo.

Bill recalled that Antonio, Tony to his friends, was a student at the University of Virginia when Gregory Alexander was also a student there. At a toga party in the yard at Gregory's townhouse on campus he shared with three other male students, there was an incident involving his sister, Margo, and Tony San Angelo. His sister drove Angelique and Chuck's sister, Joyce, to Charlottesville for a weekend of parties, tailgates, and homecoming football game activities. Tony came to the party drunk and beat Margo badly for taunting and bullying him. Tony was the son of Michel Santangelo; a man who repeatedly raped his own mother behind his father's back. Tony was the result of those attacks on Christiania Santangelo. She committed suicide rather than contend with the monster her son, Michel, became.

Although Michel was killed by his half-sister, Maria Santangelo, and his uncle, Millo Santangelo, JeNelle still fearfully reacted to her former husband's name.

Tony held Don Dixon responsible for the death of Michel,

prompting him to kidnap Don's son, Donald Dixon Jordon. Little did Tony know that Don Dixon, Code Name: Delta Dawn, was the head of The Nursery; the most secret and elite law enforcement organization in the world. It was an entity created by the G7, with authority to act with impunity in any country in the world at its discretion.

Tony was pardoned for facilitating the kidnapping because, at the time years ago, Don and Cecile's six-year-old son instigated the act to get his parents, who were not married to each other, to marry so that Donald Junior would have a family and the siblings he wanted.

Bill hadn't kept tabs on Tony San Angelo, but since he had firsthand knowledge of Tony, he was searching for him now. He was also tracking Maria San Angelo, who took over Millos Santangelo's empire after his murder at the hands of Michel. He would also look into the current whereabouts of Milo Santangelo. He hoped, with their backing, he could convince the warring factions of Mike and Trisha Rossi Giaconni's families to resolve their differences and dissolve the threat to the young couple's lives.

Then he had to confer with his handlers in The Nursery concerning the information he discovered related to the guns-for-drugs connection between the old Italian mob and certain renegade countries, like Pakistan, Somalia, North Korea, and certain Russian oligarchs. His brain was clicking on all cylinders, but Whitney's question brought his thoughts to a screeching halt.

"Should I be worried about Aunt JeNelle?" Whitney asked.

"Why do you ask?" Bill asked neutrally.

"Aunt JeNelle had a reaction to something when Maria Rossi came here to see you. I was curious and did some research."

"What were you looking for?"

"Information so that I could help Aunt JeNelle."

"What did you find?"

"She was married at age seventeen to a Michel Santangelo and divorced when she was nineteen. Michel was the son of the mobster Millos Santangello who was killed in a drive-by shooting in New York City's Little Italy neighborhood. According to what I read, Michel was suspected of having arranged for the hit on his father. In addition to Michel, Millos had two other children, Maria and Antonio, but they didn't seem to be involved and they changed their names from Santangelo to San Angelo. Maria Rossi lived in the same neighborhood and changed her name from Rossellini to Rossi. You grew up in the same neighborhood with all of them, too, Uncle Bill."

"Have you discussed what you found with anyone else?"

"No, and I won't," Whitney affirmed.

"Good. Do you trust me?" Bill asked.

"Without question, but, although I'm still in law school, and you're a practicing attorney, I do recognize that you've not answered my question."

"You're going to be a great attorney, but leave it at that. Your aunt will be fine."

Whitney released a breath that she held in stasis and nodded. "Thanks, Uncle Bill."

"What are you and Bill hatching now?" Benny jovially asked as he and Stacy entered the salon with their two sets of triplets.

"I've given up on enticing your daughter to join me this summer as my dogsbody," Bill said, while giving Stacy a covert, nearly imperceptible shake of his head. He would provide a situation report, sitrep, to her later in a SCIF; a Sensitive Compartmented Information venue which could be accessed through his apartment in the lower level of this house.

"As far as I know, she still plans to come to Japan for a part of the summer."

"You're still coming right, Whitney?" Shannon asked, the oldest of her twelve-year-old triplet sisters.

"I am, yes. I have some ideas for the new CD."

"Good, because McDreamy, Trey Kennard, is planning to come," Sierra said, grinning.

"McDreamy?" Whitney questioned.

"Well, he's cute, but not as cute as Tucker," Sharon added.

"I think Miguel is the cutest. He has all that long, dark, curly hair and dark brown eyes," inserted Sierra, the youngest triplet. "Besides, he's a supermodel. He's on the cover of *GQ Magazine* this month and he has a new movie coming out soon."

While Sierra, Shannon, and Sharon debated degrees of cuteness with Whitney, Bill, Benny, and Stacy discussed the past holiday events.

Still, Bill's mind circled back to the tasks ahead of him. He still had primary responsibility for keeping Whitney safe. Stacy had taken more of the responsibility off his shoulders, but given him more tasks to resolve.

When Anna signaled, they all went into the dining hall.

Chapter 16

When Whitney woke, her hands and feet were bound with plastic zip ties. She was still disoriented from the pinprick, which obviously held some kind of sedative. One moment she was walking to her car after being in the public law library near school and the next she found herself here; wherever here was.

She knew she was in some type of shipping container because of the corrugated metal walls and wood flooring. It was a hollow sound, but she could hear the sound of tractors and trailers moving around. Faintly, she could also hear the weeping of other young women. If she had to guess, she'd bet she was in a shipyard. The closest one to Washington, DC, would likely be in Baltimore, Maryland.

She didn't have time to waste. Though her hands and feet were bound behind her back and looped in the ones on her ankles, she knew how to free herself. Her mother taught her and her siblings; actually drilling them on the techniques in case they were ever taken prisoner by terrorists.

Whitney didn't believe that she was taken in a terrorist attack. Rather, just before she lost consciousness, she smelled a distinctive cologne; one she had smelled before. She knew who her abductor was and concentrated on breaking the bounds on her wrists and ankles. It took three tries, but she finally got loose and scrambled up to work the blood flow back into her extremities.

The next task was how to get out of the box. It was dark inside, but she searched without success to find a lever or hand-hold to open the doors. There was only one alternative left to her and she didn't hesitate to use it. She broke the gold chain around her neck the read FAMILY.

Within the hour, she heard the sound of a Sikorsky UH-60 Black Hawk, a four-bladed, twin-engine, medium-lift military helicopter circling overhead and multiple voices calling out her name. She called out and banged on the metal walls in response until they acknowledged her. The next thing she saw was blade cutting through the top of the container and sparks flying while making a hole wide enough for her mother to fast-rope into the space. They caught each other up in a tight hug for long moments before they climbed the rope into the open air. The container she was in was stacked onto the four other containers amid sixty empty containers scheduled to be shipped out within the week.

However, they were able to find young girls in three other containers in the shipyard. According to her mother, the girls were kidnapped from different countries and made part of human trafficking schemes. Had they not been found, the girls and especially Whitney would have been forced into the sex trades. There were already pictures of her on the dark web and the bidding for her was intense. Had it not been for her resources and resourcefulness, she could have disappeared like so many others, never to be found again.

While the other girls were being processed and taken into protective custody, Whitney and her mother were in the military helicopter headed for a private airfield near Chuck and Vivian's. They agreed to keep the incident between the three of them, Whitney, Stacy, and Kenneth Alexander until the necessary arrests were made. It was Kenneth's CompuCorrect security system that received the distress signal from Whitney's family chain. It allowed hers and any other family members' whereabouts to be tracked in an emergency situation. That's why they were able to move so swiftly to trace her signal via telecommunication towers. The security system was accurate to within a matter of feet to locate and lock on as long as she had the chain on her body. Research by CompuCorrect was underway to perfect a security signal which could be inserted just under the skin in case anything happened to the necklace.

"Damn it! You did it again!" the woman fumed as she hastily uncoupled.

"I didn't do it intentionally!" the frustrated man declared.

"Why can't you get that little girl out of your head for one damn moment while we're having sex?" she vehemently argued.

"Oh, like you haven't screwed up more than once and called me by *his* name while you rode *me* like a damn jockey! At least I didn't make a big deal about it! I don't care what you have to do to get your rocks off!"

She flopped back against the damp pillow, her naked breasts and chest heaving with moisture and droplets, making a trail toward her indented navel. She looked over at him as he lazily stroked himself, his hairy body bare and flushed. No doubt he was still thinking about that twit again, she surmised. Well, he could have her as long as she got her hands on a young buck.

She admitted to herself that she fantasized about getting him naked. The man was built like a Greek God and a smile, his default expression, which did incredible, strange, and amazing things to her body's systems. She tried for such a long time to get him interested in her, but to no avail. He was younger than her, but he was shaping up to be a fine medical doctor. The fact he has a superb singing voice didn't hurt his sex appeal one bit. She wasn't getting any younger, so she had marriage on her mind. Marriage to a doctor, a younger man at that, could guarantee a comfortable future and a way to hide her ill-gotten gains.

Then, all of a sudden, in comes the young smart ass! She begrudgingly admitted to herself the child was gorgeous, but still, she's a child, about eighteen or nineteen years old, she surmised. The girl would have plenty of time and no trouble catching the eye of other men...including this one, who moaned her name periodically in his sleep or in her ear. How frustrating that was beginning to be!

Turning to his left side in bed, he began to play with her right nipple. He admitted to himself that she wasn't as well-endowed as the woman he wanted appeared to be, but, as second options went, she at least had experience.

She slapped his hand away, but he caught her wrist in a tight grip, yanking her until he could cover her body with his. He knew she enjoyed it rough, so he didn't spare his dominating tendencies on vanilla sex. He sheathed himself and drove into her with a vengeance. Though he continued to pretend she was someone else, he kept his mouth and eyes shut and rammed into her hard and fast until they both reach nirvana.

A while later, he asked, "Did you find out where that new shipment of AK47s is stored?"

"I did, yes. Stuttgart, Germany, in a warehouse near the Neckar River. It's an ammo depot. We could pick up other ordinance, but you've got to move fast. That shipment will only be there for a short time. They've got to be delivered in one week in order to get paid."

"I've worked out a plan to substitute what we've got in the warehouse and replace that stock with what we pick up in Germany."

"That's a good plan. By the time that ordinance arrives stateside, we'll be able to fill that order from the Italian Mafia." She grabbed the back of his head hard, guiding his head toward her open thighs.

He didn't have to have it spelled out what she wanted, but he wanted much of the same, so he maneuvered her into the time-honored 69 position. He couldn't wait to get back to his prize, though. He had her stored for the time being until he could return without drawing attention. He had others in the shipyard. He visited them as his time permitted, but they weren't nearly as intriguing as the pearl he had bound and waiting. He decided he'd keep her somewhere out of town until he had his fill of her and then put her back on the market for a tidy sum. He rammed harder, just thinking of when he would be able to do this to her.

"Go! Go! Go!" came the command and the elite force swung into action.

Each operative pulled the mask down over their face so that only the eyes shown through the night-vision goggles. A camera lens on a thin, black cable was inserted under the door, locating the targets in the midst of energetic sex. Hand signals silently counted down with those at the door while coordinating the attack via face mic with those stationed outside the bedroom window.

"Housekeeping!" came the loud announcement just before the door swung open.

It took moments for the ardent lovers to escape the sexual haze and realize the bedroom was full of ninja-clad figures, holding assault weapons trained on them.

"What the hell?" the man questioned.

"NCIS! Ian Murray. Mallorie Colbert! You're under arrest…" the speaker continued with a list of charges and then the Miranda Warning. "You have the right to remain silent…"

Later, in an interrogation room, Ian sat facing a mirror wall with his Judge Advocate General (JAG) lawyer at his side. Stacy stood watching the interview through the one-way mirror.

"Mr. Murray, you are charged with attempted murder by forcing Lieutenant Tucker Cavanaugh off the road in a van owned by the musicians he is connected with."

"You have no proof of that!" Ian vehemently spat.

"You're his Commanding Officer, yet you failed to report him as AWOL for more than three weeks. Can you explain why you failed to take notice of his absence?"

"He's in med school. I thought he was working and studying. So I cut the kid a break."

"Did you confirm your supposition with the medical school or otherwise try to contact him to confirm?"

"I'm not a babysitter," Ian testily spat.

"You are, however, responsible for the men and women under your command. You failed to report Lieutenant Cavanaugh because you ran his band's van off the road and then drove to Baltimore to deliver stolen armaments to Patapsco for shipment to Niger, Africa. According to the GPS equipment in your vehicle, you've made that trip many times. Each time corresponds with the date and time military ordinance went missing. There is also the fact we found young women in several shipping containers owned by you under various bogus corporate names. We don't attribute this action to coincidences, Mr. Murray."

"That's Captain Murray," the JAG lawyer said, "and all you have is circumstantial evidence."

"We have more than enough to charge him and bring him up before a military tribunal for multiple offenses, including behavior unbecoming an officer. He was, after all, found in the act, so to speak, with a woman under his command."

"That was nothing!" Ian spat. "It was consensual! I didn't force her!"

"Not as you forced the other young girls in the shipping container. By the way, they each identified you as their rapist."

Behind the glass partition, Stacy said, "Step into his past. I don't think he's American of Greek descent. I want to know everything about him from nine months before he was born, including DNA testing."

"Yes, ma'am," came the response from one of several aids quietly standing awaiting orders.

While Ian continued to protest the charges brought against him, Stacy turned to look through the one-way glass mirror at her back at Mallorie Colbert who sat with her JAG attorney. Her arms were folded tightly across her chest, an insolent expression on her face. She looked away and said nothing while her attorney carried on a spirited defense.

"Hampton..." Stacy began to another one of her aides.

"On it, ma'am," Hampton acknowledged. She didn't have to have her orders spelled out in detail. Hampton and the others knew what to do.

"Dismissed," Stacy said to the aids, but one remained. Once the darkroom cleared, Stacy sighed. "Benny and I have got to get back to Japan. North Korea is acting up again and we have to prepare for RIMPAC exercises. Benny is considering piloting another space flight. I know you already have your hands full..."

"I've got this. I don't have to be out of the country for anything any time soon, unless you have another assignment for me."

"You've also got a potentially volatile situation to handle that hits too close to home."

"If I need help, I'll activate..."

"I know," Stacy said wearily, "but we're spread pretty thin with many major missions on the horizon. When Benny takes this next space flight mission, I'll, of necessity, need to be stationary."

"You're going to have to consider activating The Songbird or Mata Hari. I know you don't want to do that at this juncture; however, it may be necessary."

"I know, but I'll only do it as a last resort."

The operative nodded, placed a comforting hand on Stacy's shoulder, and then departed the observation booth.

Stacy stood in the darkened room alone, reflecting on the danger that might have befallen her daughter had Whitney not been vigilant. Stacy had to trust her daughter and her other children would continue to be alert to possible dangers which could befall them...and now Tucker, too.

Chapter 17

It was five-thirty in the morning as Tucker stroked the length of the indoor portion of the pool in the ranch house. He was trying to burn off excess energy and the fear of what could have happened to Whitney. She was fine now and not in any immediate danger. Ian and Mallorie were both incarcerated and scheduled for court-martial. Ian would also face charges brought by the FBI. Tucker fervently hoped that Ian never breathed a free breath outside of the prison walls.

The Captain was cooling his heels in lockup, awaiting trial on attempted murder and a host of other charges involving the theft, illegal sale, and trafficking of US military ordinance and human trafficking. Mallorie was similarly incarcerated for her role in the thefts, but not the human trafficking. She claimed to have no knowledge of that.

Nevertheless, Ian and Mallory would have a long time to rue the day they tangled with a mother, as powerful as Admiral Alexander, who would go to any length to protect her child. The Admiral was ensuring that the prosecution had every scrap of evidence to convict and incarcerate both Ian and Mallorie for a very long time.

As he continued to swim laps to get his muscle tone back, his mind cleared of the worrisome thoughts of Ian and Mallorie and focused on his health. Though there had been weeks following the

Thanksgiving weekend ski trip, he still wasn't used to this much inactivity. Chuck and Dr. Stone were being very cautious about the steps and stages of his recovery regimen and he couldn't fault them for that. His equilibrium had been off a few times, but tests indicated his brain was still healing from being tossed around in his skull during the incident and battered by flying musical instruments in the tight confines of the van.

He was feeling better now and mindful of the latent effects of brain and spinal cord injuries. Getting back on his feet was his number one priority; for his sake and for Whitney's.

Whitney, he thought, as he often did while he continued to swim. Tonight would be the big Christmas Eve party here at the Alexander-Montgomery farm with scads of family and friends in attendance. Even the President, First Lady, and their sons were slated to be there. That was a lot of people to observe what he had in mind to do.

Changelings was scheduled to be the entertainment for the evening, which was going to be a big opportunity for them. The band was vetted by both the Secret Service and Richardson Security. Mike and Trisha were back from their forced hiatus and pleased that the feud between their warring families seemed to be settled—at least for now. According to Mike, someone outside the families intervened and forced a truce so that he and Trisha could plan a future together without fear of family reprisals. Their only requirement was that their child had to carry both names. They were happy with the outcome and looking forward to the birth of their son who they planned to name Ross Giaconni.

They were working with new musical instruments an insurance company paid for since the van and everything they previously had was a part of the evidence of a crime committed by his former CO, Captain Ian Murray.

Tucker executed a flip at the deep end of the pool and started back, doing a backstroke. About midway to the other end, Chuck

Montgomery passed, going in the opposite direction. Over the intervening weeks since being a patient in the Alexander-Montgomery household, the family shared many tidbits of information with him.

Since he was living in their home and in order to avoid any *faux pas*, Whitney shared that her Aunt Vivian's first husband, Derrick Jackson, also a stellar basketball icon and a pediatric surgeon, died less than a year into their marriage on the same day as their only biological son, Derrick, Junior, was born. Vivian shared that the whole adoption plan began when she and Derrick adopted five of his health challenged and orphaned patients before he died. After his death, Vivian continued to adopt abandoned children who were faced with serious and sometimes catastrophic injuries or diseases. Derrick "Dunk and Jam" Jackson was a multibillionaire when he died, leaving Vivian as one of the wealthiest women in the world. Chuck, Vivian's second husband, was best friends with Derrick since puberty; the Gale Sayers and Brian Piccolo of the basketball industry. Chuck also a very wealthy man with Vivian continued the family adoption plan and had no desire to stop helping children in need of special and costly medical care.

As a part of her aunt and uncle's backstory, Whitney explained to Tucker that the relationship between Vivian and Chuck also started in Washington, DC, and in the house in Georgetown. Vivian was a young law school student at Georgetown Law Center and Chuck was doing his residency program as an Emergency Room physician at Georgetown Medical Center. Unbeknownst to Vivian, Chuck was developing feelings for her even way back then, but hadn't made his intentions clear.

One night at a dance club, Chuck introduced Vivian to his best friend, Derrick Jackson. Unaware that Chuck was interested in Vivian, Derrick had no problem making his interest in Vivian crystal clear. That night, Chuck lost his unrequited love for Vivian to his best friend, Derrick Jackson.

While Vivian was still a law school student, she rented rooms in her brother's huge corner brownstone to others in the Georgetown Law Scholars Program. She was also volunteering at a family homeless shelter where she met Anna Menendez-Gaza and her minor children, Angelique and Miguel. Anna and her children came to America from Peru in search of her missing husband, but couldn't find him. They ended up, during a blizzard, as homeless, destitute immigrants at a shelter in danger of being rounded up by the INS and deported when they met Vivian and Alan Lightfoot, another scholar's student and full-blooded Navajo. Subsequently, Vivian persuaded her parents to sponsor Anna and her children. They agreed and Anna and her children moved into the Georgetown house with Vivian and her housemates to become their cook and housekeeper. Alan, a former Marine, and slightly older law school student, also moved into the house in Georgetown with his peers.

The relationship between Vivian and Anna led to the introduction of Vivian's youngest brother, Gregory Alexander, to Anna's daughter, Angelique Menendez-Gaza, while he was still in high school and college. After a successful academic and athletic college career, Gregory went on to an equally successful professional basketball career. Still at the top of his game, he ended his very lucrative career in favor of becoming a financial wizard on Wall Street.

During the time Gregory was becoming a famous athlete, Angelique became a highly-sought-after, high-fashion model, movie starlet, and later became a Gourmet Chef. Gregory and Angelique lived in New York City, where one of her restaurants and bars, Angelique's Place and The Run Way, were rated two of the top fifty in the city. She also opened her unique restaurant and bar in Washington, DC, Chicago, Los Angeles, and soon in Peru.

Anna learned, shortly after coming to Washington, DC, with Angelique and Miguel that her husband died in a rooming house fire. A widow for several years after that, Anna finally agreed to marry their next-door neighbor, bachelor Fenster Jones, a world-renowned concert violinist with the Washington Philharmonic Orchestra. By then, Anna's son, Miguel Menendez-Gaza, was a young Hollywood star with many awards under his belt and a high Q Rating because of his enormous talent and Latino good looks. He was also in demand, as was his sister, as high-fashion models. While he was now in college at Penn State, he was also embarking on a musical career to round out his talents as an entertainer. He often performed with Changelings as well as having a career as a soloist. He would be on stage with Changelings tonight.

Tonight, Tucker thought, *will be a very important night for me and I can't wait for it to begin.*

Whitney was dressing in one of the rooms behind the ballroom with the other women who would perform for the Christmas Eve party. Stephany Thomas, a waitress from one of the restaurants near campus, had an incredible voice and was added to Changelings while Mike and Trisha were away. Now that they were back, they made the decision to keep here on.

Trisha's costume was a little roomier due to her pregnancy, but otherwise the women wore identical dresses, each in a different traditional Christmas color.

"Whitney, what do you think of Payton Brasher?" KiLi asked.

Whitney shrugged. "I don't know him well enough to form an opinion. Why do you ask?"

"I've been going to his performances with Changelings. We've been out a few times on our own."

"Okay, so what do you think of him?" Whitney asked.

"I don't know. He seems nice enough, but I haven't had that much experience with men. He's from Australia, which intrigues me, and he's musically talented, but I'm not ready for sex yet. So, I've been holding him off as much as I can so that it doesn't get beyond a few kisses just like you're doing with Tucker."

That statement raised Whitney's curiosity. "Do you respect him?" Whitney asked.

KiLi frowned. "Well," she hedged on a long breath, "I never thought about that."

Whitney nodded. "Do you trust him?"

KiLi shrugged. "I don't know him well enough to say that I trust him."

"Then it's not like what's going on between Tucker and me. You see, we trust each other, respect each other and love each other. As a result, we've made a conscience decision to abstain from physical lovemaking until we're both mentally and emotionally ready to take that next step. We want to save that part of our relationship until we can make a commitment to one another when we marry. We don't want to rush into something and regret it because we were feeling the heat of the moment. We're in this for the long haul.

"I'm not suggesting that you should do with Payton what Tucker and I have decided to do with our relationship. However, if you haven't considered whether you respect, trust, and love someone, you may want to hold off on a committed relationship until you do. You want your time together to be a priority; not an afterthought, right?"

"I like him," KiLi admitted weakly, with a little shrug.

"I like strawberry ice cream, but I don't want a steady diet of it. Besides, there are so many other flavors to try which you might like as much if not more," Whitney said, laughing. Finished dressing, she applied a thin coat of lip gloss and smiled at KiLi in the mirror. She hoped that KiLi would benefit from their discussion. Tucker was concerned about the relationship between Payton and KiLi because Payton was not a man to trust with anything breakable, like KiLi's heart. Payton was not a one-woman man by any stretch of the imagination.

Together with Stephany, they left the dressing room headed for the stage. On her way, Whitney heard her name called out and slowed at the sound of her cousin's, Brian Montgomery's, voice. "Hi, handsome," she said, giving him a smile and a squeeze.

"Hi, pretty woman," he teased back. "I heard you had a little trouble. Are you okay?"

"Yes, I'm fine."

"Okay, let's rock in the holiday season," Brian said, slinging an arm around his cousin's shoulder.

Nearly midway through the party, the band was about to take a break when Tucker stepped up to the main microphone to get everyone's attention. When all was quiet, he knelt in front of Whitney and asked her to be his wife…in a few more years.

She laughed, stuck out her left hand, and yelled, "Yes!"

The room erupted in whistles and applause while Tucker and Whitney shared a kiss as an engaged couple.

Epilogue

Stacy finished her shower and sat smoothing lotion onto her body. She looked up at Benny, who sat up reading in bed. *When did he become more handsome than he was when we first met all those years ago?* she wondered. Back then, he was a chick magnet and rightfully so. Still, these days, she sometimes heard other women comment on what a stud he was. She couldn't argue that fact, but he was so much more than a handsome face and great physique. He hadn't changed much over time. He was still a good-looking man in and out of his uniform. His broad shoulders, solid pecs, and handsome face still thrilled her when she looked at him. Yet, the twinkle in his eyes never failed to excite her. She believed that their daughter, Whitney, and her fiancée would experience the same type of excitement in their relationship for many years to come.

"What's up?" Benny asked, not looking up from his reading. He sensed Stacy was studying him for some reason.

She smiled and stood, taking off her robe. He grinned at her as she climbed naked into bed. "I marvel at the fact that my husband is such a stud."

His grin widened as he pushed his papers aside and reached for her. She came easily into his arms and kissed him.

"Do you have any idea how much I love you?" she asked, palming his handsome face.

"I believe I do. You work tirelessly to protect our family and serve this nation."

That is right, so very right, she thought as she hugged him. She would sacrifice her life for Benny and their children.

"Why so introspective tonight, babe?" Benny asked.

"I suppose it hits me at odd times how truly fortunate I am to have you. When I was growing up, after my twin sister died when we were twelve, my mother deserted what was left of our family. I never expected I'd ever have a man like you in my life. I didn't believe in love or marriage or forming a family. Then, one day there you were, this tall, buff, and handsome man offering me a life I didn't know existed."

He smiled at her, palming her beautiful face and gazing into her distinctive, light-crystal-brown eyes. "It was kismet, Stacy. It took us long enough to realize we were meant to be and I thank the ancestors for their guidance in bringing us together. I love you in every way humanly possible. I also respect the woman you are. You're a phenomenal partner and mother and I couldn't be happier than to be your husband."

She smiled, misty-eyed and hugged him. "You're going to take on another mission, aren't you?" she asked, although she already knew the answer.

He nodded with her in his arms. "I am, yes. I may make this my last mission. I have someone in mind as my co-pilot."

"Captain Shawn Baxter Rodgers, Code Name: Hot Rod."

"See? You're not only beautiful with a slammin' sexy body, but you're bright, too."

She laughed at that. "It doesn't take a genius to figure out that you hold him in high esteem."

He nodded. "I do, yes. There are so many things about his skills and abilities that remind me of myself at his age. He's a natural pilot. His jet is an extension of him."

"He reminds you of yourself because he has a baby daughter he's raising alone because the mother of the child has been gone off the grid," she said somberly.

He looked into her eyes and nodded. "There is that." He reached for one of the papers he was reading before she came to bed and passed it to her.

Stacy read the missive and looked up into her husband's eyes. "This is another letter from Captain Rodger's daughter, Rosemary. She's what, four years old? How would she know to contact us?"

"He calls her Rosey because she always has such a great disposition. Shawn has brought her with him often enough when he was in Japan for meetings or training. She's four years old, soon to be five. You were already stateside the last time he had her with him in Japan. He doesn't like to leave her for long periods of time. The little girl and our sons had several play dates at the base's children's center. This recent letter showed up in our home office on my desk. I suspect our sons had a hand in helping her."

Stacy shook her head, concerned.

Benny recognized her dilemma. He wasn't positive, but he had every reason to believe that the little girl's mother was someone his wife knew and likely someone under her black-ops command. He knew when Stacy deployed, often without prior notice, she was on a covert mission. Though they both had the highest classified clearances, he knew and understood there were still things she couldn't talk about with him. There were aspects of his missions he couldn't share with her. Over the years, they learned to implicitly trust each other and work around any potential pitfalls in their marriage. This situation involving a pilot on his team she liked and trusted and the woman who was likely a member of Stacy's Special Operations Group could shape up to be a major pitfall with the life of a toddler in the balance.

Stacy had a lot to consider, but given the fact her husband was planning to go into outer space again, she had something else in mind. Moving the papers aside to the nightstand, she straddled Benny's lap, facing him. She began to move against him while her hands roamed across the hard planes of his chest to his raisin-like nipples; a particular erogenous zone for him. His arms came up around her, palming her narrow waist and moving her against his growing erection.

"Whatever it is you want, the answer is yes," he said, grinning at her.

"I've been thinking it's time to consider having another baby," she said, kissing her husband's face, tweaking his nipples, and riding his penis.

Benny stared into his wife's beautiful eyes, all merriment slipping from his face. "Seriously?"

She nodded and the smile that once again bloomed on his face was glorious.

He lay her on her back and slowly slipped in and out of her tight, wet portal. He had long wanted to add another baby to their family, but with seven children already to their credit, he wasn't sure she would agree. However, deep in his wife's loving embrace, everything except the love they shared left his conscious thoughts.

They had to return to their duties the following week. For now, it was just the two of them. He had more than twenty years in the Air Force. He was a five-star general and a member of the Joint Chiefs of Staff. His children were growing up so fast. Now, his and Stacy's firstborn was engaged to be married. He was an astronaut with years of missions under his belt. He and a friend, Dr. Tate Kennedy, started a company to collect space junk and return it to earth to be disposed of or reconditioned. Nicholas Collins, an industrialist and also a friend, asked to buy into the operation and he and Tate agreed to let him invest.

Nicholas, Nico to his friends, launched his second satellite geared to the distribution of data and entertainment programming, this one covering the western hemisphere and linked it to his satellite covering the eastern hemisphere.

Now his siblings, Kenneth, Vivian, and Gregory, also wanted to invest as did some of their friends. What began as an idea to clean up the building amount of human-made space debris that made trips to and from SPACEHOME more hazardous, now was turning into a consortium involving billions of dollars for the design of rockets and spacecraft needed to begin. He, Tate, and Kenneth were working on the design of a supersonic jet, which could circumnavigate the Earth and climb beyond the Earth's atmosphere without the need for booster rockets. With Tate's doctorate in aeronautical engineering, and Kenneth's masters in electronics, they had a good start on their project.

Dedicated to Duty

Dedication

To
My father
Sergeant William Turner Ward
United States Army
RIP

To
My husband
Sergeant Theodore Lee Jeffries, Sr.
United States Army
RIP

To
Active duty military and their families everywhere
Thank you for your service.

Chapter 1

Marry in haste; repent at leisure, thought an annoyed Commander Helen Marlowe, Code Name: Helen of Troy or HOT as her counterparts and pals chose to call her. Not because of the temperature or her disposition, but because of her extraordinarily attractive physical features. Assets her camouflage battle dress uniform (BDU) fatigues, Cammy hat, and aviator shades failed to disguise.

Absently, she stood with feet apart, arms folded, head up and back straight watching a new group of US Navy recruits going through combat diving exercises in the indoor/outdoor, lake-sized pool. The training was a part of Phase 2 of their Basic Underwater Demolition/SEAL (BUDs) regimen. The sun was scorching hot on the wide, forty-foot deep pool on the beach, making it much hotter than the ocean. She was fighting to keep her mind on the exercise and how her sergeants, many of whom were wounded warriors, representing an amalgamation of the military services, were handling their tasks with the new recruits. Evals were due before the end of the week.

Behind her, another military class was in Phase 3 of the seven-week land warfare activity. The master sergeants cordoned off areas of the beach and thick, rain forest, foliage over rocky terrain in one-mile segments each. They would begin to run their recruits through basic weaponry, demolition with live ammo, land navigation, patrolling, rappelling, marksmanship, and small-unit specialized training.

Still, others were scaling the perilous sheer rock face on the north shore. For them, Hell Week was on the horizon. Shortly, that class would be finished with BUDs courses and move on to the other side of the island for parachute jump school. Another class, further up the beach in the opposite direction, was navigating their inflated, motorized, watercraft through the rough surf in preparation for a six-mile, deep-sea, training exercise. They would learn to enter and exit a submarine through torpedo tubes underwater far out to sea and swim to shore using handheld, powered projectiles. Since Helen had seen it all many times and mastered it all with high honors, her concentration was drifting like the sands in high winds.

No matter how much activity surrounded her, *that wickedly handsome man*, whose face and physique had been created by the gods on a particularly good day, was stuck in her head, preventing her from operating at full capacity. US Air Force jet fighter pilot Captain Shawn Baxter Rodgers stood over six-four with the body of an Adonis, clever hands, and a grin on his too-handsome face that promised endless acts of naughtiness.

The first day, on a rest and relaxation (R&R) trip to Las Vegas, Nevada, they palled around the city and made some incredible memories along the way. Helen appreciated Shawn's drive and wisdom and willingness to do anything to please her, like adventures driving dune buggies at breakneck speeds in the desert.

He never met a stranger. Anyone he met became an instant friend. Shawn was a genuinely nice guy. He was one of a kind among eight of their friends in one of those impossibly long stretch limousines. They must have danced and lived it up at every high-end nightspot in the city. For a tall, solidly built man, Shawn proved to be quite agile and an exceptional dancer.

In the wee hours of the morning, and after having consumed far more ridiculously expensive champagne than was wise, she had woken naked in Shawn's bed with a beautiful, titanium wedding band on the third finger of her left hand and violently aroused.

Initially, she thought the whole wedding thing was a joke she vaguely remembered through a hazy wine-soaked mind and blurred vision. However, *that wickedly handsome man* convinced her that the wedding was real and no laughing matter. They were legally husband and wife. To prove his point, throughout the remaining days of R&R, he gave her endless hours of mind-blowing naughty, but neither rested nor relaxed. Though memory failed her about the wedding ceremony itself, she vividly recalled experiencing the pleasures of the body she previously knew nothing about. Her long-held and cherished status as a virgin was a thing of history. Now, every time she thought of Shawn, her blood warmed and certain parts of her anatomy came to rigid attention.

With supreme effort, Helen finally succeeded in blocking Shawn out of her thoughts, but not her heart. She had no doubt her effort to refocus on her tasks and keep him out of her head would be temporary. It always was, where he's concerned, she admitted to herself.

Still, it was her duty to ensure every Navy SEAL trainee passed each part of the rigorous, life-saving, and extensive training. They worked to earn the right to be among the elite group of warriors and wear the Trident Pin. That piece of metal was the Holy Grail of the US Navy recruits.

After three weeks of indoctrination (INDOC) in the island's Naval Special Warfare Operations Center, the novices were subjected to the physical training, obstacle courses, and other unique training aspects in preparation for the more rigorous conditioning during seven weeks of Phase 1.

It didn't matter that the trainees were all women who, for so many, barely exercised before they arrived. Helen personally picked each member of this class from a vast array of backgrounds and ethnicities. Some were high school or college athletes or ROTC members or military school graduates from all branches of service. They took to the grueling training more easily than the Rhodes Scholars, science specialists, computer geeks or engineering experts. Some who, but for her intervention, would have been guests of some local, state or federal detention facility, were blended in using their special talents as a guide. Having experienced life on the wrong side of the law, their daring gave them a leg up on some of the things they would be tasked to do. These women, most under the age of twenty-one, had rather high IQs, some bordering on the genius level. They were offered the opportunity by the court system to go to jail for some minor infraction of the law or into the US Navy with their slates clean. Their choice to enlist proved they were no dummies. Their re-education and attitude adjustment started the moment their signatures were on the non-disclosure documents.

Helen learned, at the outset of their training regimen, what the women initially lacked in covert skills and physical ability, along the way they more than made up for in a high level of dedication to duty, honor, and heart. Unlike some of her counterparts, she only picked women who had no or limited close family relations or orphans, like herself. To her, they seemed to be the ones who most needed kinship and desired to belong to something of substance. Before the yearlong training ended, new, lifelong friendships were forged and mutual support systems established. Each class became a tightly-knit, interdependent team with multiple, vital skill sets. They became a family closer than siblings.

Other teams, with the same makeup, had been molded into fierce fighting forces and smart operatives who infiltrated dangerous situations and carried out crucial missions often with their targets none the wiser. The teams accomplished with stealth, what other traditional military units attempted to do with brawn.

On long-term, embedded missions, where sex appeal and guile were required weapons, the women had an advantage over men and could reduce a target to a quivering mass of need. Similarly, when deadly force was required, these women, like their male counterparts, never failed to take decisive action. Those teams were temporarily deployed as officers, like her, and others as enlisted personnel, all making a difference in maintaining stability in the world.

Arms still akimbo, feet apart, head up, back straight, and eyes shielded from the strong Polynesian sunlight and blowing beach sand, Helen still wasn't completely focused on her tasks or teams. Rather, her thoughts strayed again to the man and newborn daughter she left behind in Louisiana, five years ago today. In the intervening years, secretly she had successfully trained women to be a combination of Mossad and SEAL operatives now deployed in both covert and overt missions. Class after class came through her rigorous twenty-four-week training program and command before moving on to a diverse group of specialties.

Another group scoured the country and some foreign lands looking for young women uniquely qualified to take on missions, which often meant the difference between life and death. In-depth dossiers were created to ensure that these women had the necessary skills and ability to invest in their futures over the long haul. Every six months a new group was brought on board. So far, their recruiting efforts were spot on.

As Helen predicted, her tasks weren't holding her undivided attention and her past with Shawn slipped back unbidden into her conscious thoughts. Helen hadn't seen him since she gave birth to his daughter. Even then, she hadn't seen or held the baby girl she bore him and didn't know the name he gave her. *She was so young back then; barely twenty*, thought Helen. She had no experience with men and certainly not with the out-of-control feelings Shawn caused her to experience. Craving him and his touch too damn much, she couldn't trust herself around him or hearing his melodic voice. So, during her pregnancy, she only communicated with him via text messages.

Checking out of the Navy Hospital in Louisiana before Shawn arrived from California to take them home was a juvenile act of cowardice. Still, her action should have convinced him, after she signed papers giving his child to him, there was nothing left between them...well, except the marriage. Yet, she learned today, that *Major* Rodgers was still trying to find her. That's what had him stuck in her mind.

Shawn, five years ago, at twenty-six, wanted them to move in together and live as a family. That would have required her to give up her commission and the career she worked so hard to establish and depend on him for her livelihood. She had absolutely no frame of reference about family life. From her perspective, with a relationship that was less than a month old before the pregnancy, they didn't even know each other well enough to consider that proposition. It certainly wasn't in her plan for her life back then to marry anyone.

Instead, she disappeared from his life and signed on to train secretly as a SEAL and Mossad. Now, she proudly wore her Trident pin around her neck with her dog tags...and a ring of diamond-encrusted titanium. However, although she had accomplished a lot, when she looked at the wedding band, she occasionally still wondered how it would be to share her life with a man; someone who wanted to make a family with her. Shawn and his daughter, she hoped, fared well. She wondered what might have been if she hadn't taken the road less traveled.

Nevertheless, though she was trying to block him out, she couldn't help but recall how they met in the Norfolk, Virginia, Navy Commissary. They had a whirlwind, one-month romance, and flew to Las Vegas on a lark during a four-day R&R break with other officers. They hadn't planned to marry. At least, she hadn't. Far from it, but after a magnum or two of top-shelf French champagne in the luxurious, penthouse suite of an exclusive McCoy Las Vegas Grand Hotel, she didn't know up from down. Although she had once worked in a high-end bar, she had never had champagne. The stuff was heavenly and went straight to her head. Couple that with a fabulous penthouse suite, the likes of which she never experienced before. They threw caution to the wind on every level.

For that one night, he caused her to lose herself so completely that he became all that mattered in the world. She was a trained warrior, but she had no defenses against Shawn. The next thing she knew, through her inebriated haze, a Justice of the Peace in some Off The Strip Las Vegas Wedding Chapel, no bigger than a hut, pronounced them husband and wife. Shawn was her first lover and, so far, her last. She wasn't planning to have sex and didn't take any form of contraceptive. Yet, that bit of insanity nine months later led to the birth of a baby girl. She told Shawn about the pregnancy, but refused to see him for the duration. She didn't even tell him when she went into labor. Rather, she had a nurse call him after the delivery when she was ready to leave the hospital. A contact alerted her when Shawn's private jet cleared California airspace. A few hours later, as she expected, he showed up. She hid in a coffee shop across the street and watched him arrive at the hospital. Less than an hour later, she watched him leave with his daughter. She still had no intention of being a wife or mother, so she left Shawn without so much as a by your leave.

She didn't understand why he was still searching for her. Initially, years earlier, when she received an intelligence report that

Shawn tried to hire Richardson Investigations and Security, a top firm, to find her, she considered filing for divorce as the ultimate *coup de grâce*. However, she couldn't stand the idea that the marriage was a failure. If she didn't make the effort, she couldn't be considered a failure. She had so many disappointments in her life, she never wanted to fail at anything again. It was just easier to ignore the whole marriage and family thing. It was a point of pride that she succeeded at everything she undertook once she left the foster home. So far, except for the marriage thing, once she entered the service, she had exceeded her own expectations.

She had no concern that Richardson Investigations would reveal her location to Shawn or anyone else. The company's owner, Slade Richardson, Code Name: Cobra Kahn, the actor Sendhil Ramamurthy's look-alike and she had partnered on several covert missions in countries with names that ended in *stan*. He was a sandbagger, a top-level member of the über secret organization known to only a few as The Nursery. Slade often brought his recruits to train on the otherwise uninhabited ring of Polynesian islands.

"Are you okay, Commander?" asked Admiral Stacy Greene Alexander, Code Name: Explorer One, the top brass of Operation: Explorers; this secret group in the Navy.

"Sir! Yes, Sir!" Helen replied sharply, coming to attention. She had forgotten for a moment the brass was on this particular remote, twenty-two-square-mile Polynesian Island that didn't even have a name. It was one of over a thousand uninhabited islands in the archipelagos, equal distance between Hawaii, New Zealand, and Easter Island. Secret training was conducted on this volcanic split in the Pacific Ocean and four others in a ring of islands. They formed a fiord avoided by outsiders because of the fierce trade winds and monsoons or typhoons that often battered and buffeted the islands and tall submerged mountain ranges.

However, from the beginning of the program many years ago, the group of five islands proved ideal for the secret SEAL and Mossad training programs. The harsher the terrain, the better for training recruits in adverse surroundings. There were underwater caves that catacomb the mountains with pockets of airlocks. The aboveground caves made excellent shelters against the elements. Some built their houses using the native vegetation and the gardens they grew for fruits and vegetables. They ate fresh seafood each day and had a variety of other foods flown in weekly.

It was the Admiral's theory that, because women were disregarded or devalued or, in many societies, simply not noticed, they had the ability to infiltrate and to hide in plain sight while wearing a burka or sarong that disguised their appearance. Modern warfare had changed to keep pace with the nature of the enemy. Admiral Alexander conceived and named the prototype, Operation: Mata Hari. Many terrorists simply weren't intimidated by women and underestimated a woman's skill and ability relaxing their guard to their detriment.

Male Navy SEALs trained at Coronado in California where they could be seen and possibly spied upon. Not so with the female group of warriors. The ring of islands was impervious to prying eyes.

The Admiral's theory had proven accurate. The fact they were lethal fighting forces, who successfully thought on their feet, was a bonus. Their unique strike forces launched from these islands and were redeployed whenever the need arose, which, in recent years, had been often and continuously.

Admiral Alexander, while still a lieutenant, fresh out of the Naval Academy in Annapolis, Maryland, convinced her then-boss, Admiral Clarence Gordon, to let her formulate Operation: Mata Hari; a secret group of initially twelve handpicked women who became warriors. Admiral Alexander was initially a First

Lieutenant and Admiral Gordon's Executive Officer (XO) and confidant. He had gambled on her plan to secretly train women as SEALs and Mossad operatives years before the Presidential edict declaring that women were to be permitted to be included in every aspect of military life, including combat.

As their first test, the women were challenged to extract a dangerous drug kingpin from his stronghold in a skyscraper hotel in a city in Central America. Two weeks before the planned extraction, a team of six women infiltrated the hotel as a cook, waitresses, housekeepers, and a desk clerk. Once established, a group of fashion models arrived to do a photo shoot for *Risqué*, a high-class magazine, and registered at the hotel. They made a spectacle of themselves poolside, purposefully drawing the kingpin's attention. When he invited two of the women to his penthouse where he expected a *ménage à trois*, a whiff of Devil's Breath put him into a deep sleep. The two women carried him to the balcony where ropes and harnesses dangled from a hovering stealth jet copter. Under the cover of darkness, they were hoisted aboard the hovering stealth craft and secreted away. The remaining women checked out of the hotel and the workers slowly resigned their positions so as not to draw any suspicion.

The criminal woke in a super-max prison somewhere in the American Midwest. The mission had taken two weeks from start to finish to plan and execute and netted a criminal the government heretofore spent years and many lost lives trying to capture.

When other missions proved to be equally as successful beyond belief, Admiral Gordon expanded the program to Operation: Explorers and authorized every secret agency, including the CIA, NSA, Homeland Security, especially the Defense Advanced Research Projects Agency (DARPA) and others, to secretly fund the program and use their resource.

More often than not, members of the female force were blended with male counterparts and deployed by The Nursery;

an über secret world organization created by the G7 and charged with global security. The Nursery included male and female multinational members who also trained as SEAL and Mossad agents on one or more of the Pacific islands in the group. Now, Admiral Gordon was the President of the United States. Admiral Alexander took his command and became the head of RIMPAC and the Rim of the Pacific Exercise. As it was the largest international maritime exercise held every two years in June and July, its operation was critical to military readiness. International military forces from the Pacific Rim countries were invited to participate. Admiral Alexander's US contingent included super nuclear aircraft carrier strike-force groups, submarines, over a hundred aircrafts, approximately twenty thousand Sailors, Marines, Coast Guardsmen, and their respective officers. Because it was a massive build up, it's an impressive show of strength to those renegade countries hell-bent on issuing antagonizing threatening behavior to otherwise peaceful, non-aggressive countries. Their tasks were essential to the continued stabilization of warring factions throughout the world.

"At ease, Commander. I've been reviewing the troops. This looks like a good class," the Admiral remarked.

"We're only into week sixteen of twenty-four."

"How did Phase 1 go?"

"Harder for some than others, Sir, which, as you know, is to be expected. However, my sergeants were able to carefully assess the candidates' physical conditioning, water competency, teamwork, and mental tenacity. As a result of their findings, they stepped up the twice daily runs, swimming, and calisthenics. Reports indicate they beat the four-mile timed runs in boots and the obstacle courses. Swimming exercises are up to at least two miles a day. However, surprisingly, they all survived. No one is ringing out. I've identified several natural leaders I plan to recommend for

Officer Candidate School. They got through Hell Week and are starting combat diving."

The Admiral nodded her approval of the precision sitrep she had come to expect from her young officer, but her keen insight sensed her top Commander for some reason wasn't on her game today. Stacy thought she knew the reason why.

She and Helen came from similar backgrounds with no real family structure to support her through adolescence and teen years. The US Navy became her refuge from the outside world. That was until she found her one true forever kind of love with Benjamin Staton Alexander, the family he came from, and the one they created together.

Helen Marlowe, barely eighteen at the time, put two men in the hospital for attacking her. It should have been a simple case of self-defense, but the two young men were wealthy and hired lawyers who made it appear Helen was a prostitute and had been the aggressor out to mug them for their wallets. Helen, an extremely attractive young woman, was convicted of solicitation and aggravated assault. In actuality, Helen wasn't at all what they made her appear to be. Rather, she was a waitress working in an upscale, exclusive men's club and paying her way through college on the above-minimum-wage job and generous tips she received from the patrons.

That's where the men spotted her and came back night after night, demanding to be seated in her section of the club. When she consistently refused the two young men's advances, one night after the club closed, they attempted to take what was not offered freely. Helen, having held a black belt in karate in high school, defended herself to her attackers' detriment. One man had a detached retina and the other would never father children.

Though it was not Judge Vivian Alexander Montgomery's case to adjudicate, law school students, from an advanced class where she lectured at Georgetown Law, brought Helen's situation to Judge Alexander's attention. She agreed with the students' assessment, that Helen Marlowe got a raw deal, and arranged for her sister-in-law and friend, Admiral Stacy Greene Alexander, to interview Helen as a potential recruit. On the recommendation of the Judge, after an extensive background check and exhaustive interview, Stacy lifted Helen Marlowe out of the court system, cleared her criminal record, and plopped her down in the US Navy's Officer Candidate School.

A former high school triathlon athlete, Helen blossomed in the Navy, breaking all records in the twenty-four-week BUDs training program and other specialized physical activity. She completed college, grad school, and worked harder and longer than her counterparts. Even her pregnancy didn't hamper her progress.

Stacy decided it was about time to introduce Helen to another phase in her life challenges before she burned herself out. Someone had done that for her when she was on the same exhausting track as Helen. In addition to her frequent covert missions, Helen had mastered the skills and abilities necessary to be a trainer for new female SEAL and Mossad recruits. Still, the Admiral knew Helen had so much more in her arsenal to give to the corps. Helen may not appreciate this upcoming change in her career, but she would do her duty. Of that, Admiral Alexander had no doubt.

"Gear up, Commander. We have a mission. Wheels up at 0100."

Chapter 2

"*Attention!*" Sergeant Higgins snapped, as five-star, US Air Force General Benjamin Alexander walked into the auditorium from stage left. As the head of the Pacific Air Force Command, and the Air Force attaché to the US Embassy in Tokyo, Japan, among other duties, the General oversaw the US Air Force's participation in RIMPAC or rim of the Pacific exercises from his duty station in Tokyo. Today, after the meeting, he was in Hawaii to meet and greet members of the twenty-two nations who were among the participants. His wife, Admiral Stacy Greene Alexander, the Navy's attaché to the US Ambassador to Japan, oversaw the Navy's role in the RIMPAC exercises as her husband did for the Air Force. She was away on a mission, but would join him and their children in a few days.

Immediately, jet fighter pilots jumped to their feet and sharply saluted the head man. The brass and colorful assortment of ribbons on the left side of the General's broad chest attested to the fact he had earned his position and their respect. He was a pilot's pilot; the sort of man each of the men and women in the auditorium aspired to be. Having flown successful missions in advanced, still classified spacecraft, he was also an extraordinary astronaut.

When General Alexander, Benny to his friends and close associates, returned the salute and smiled, the room erupted in applause, shouts, whistles, and stomping feet. The audience started singing the old Elton John song, "Benny and the Jets." The female pilots also swooned audibly, making the General laugh. Benjamin Alexander's command was the best of the best and their theme song was played each and every time they flew successful missions. It was also played at more than a few keg parties, too.

"Keep your day jobs," the General joked at the end of the serenade.

An affable man, thought US Air Force Major Shawn Baxter Rodgers, but a brilliant one, too, inspiring awe among all branches of the US Air Force. Married to a smokin' hot US Navy Admiral, they had seven children at last count. Shawn had met the Admiral's and General's children and introduced his daughter to them. The children had play dates whenever the Alexanders brought their children with them to Hawaii.

According to scuttlebutt, the General's eldest daughter, Whitney Ivy, a heart-stopper like her mother, the Admiral, was recently engaged to marry a Marine of all things. Shawn watched the General raise Whitney Ivy virtually alone for the first five years of her life. Now she was a law school student. He was emulating the General in that regard as well as raising his own smart and beautiful baby girl alone.

In earlier days, the Admiral's dedication to duty caused her to disappear from the General's life just as Helen had done. Shawn had hoped it would not take as long to find Helen. However, five years had already passed. He had no greater knowledge of where Helen was today than he did years ago when she disappeared. Helen was career Navy and Shawn hoped to find an opportunity during the RIMPAC exercises to speak with Admiral Alexander and request her help in locating Helen. He heard nothing but good things about Admiral Alexander and, according to her reputation, if anyone could cut through the red tape around

Helen's location, it would be the Admiral. He knew he was taking a big risk, but he had met the Admiral on several social occasions, including play dates between her children and his daughter. To his way of thinking, *Nothing beats a try, but a failure and failure was not in his vocabulary.*

Major Rodgers, Code Name: Hot Rod, one of the best airmen in the room of sixty or more, watched the General with a certain high level of awe and respect. He felt lucky to have been trained directly under the General's command years ago at March Air Force Base outside San Diego, California, and learned much from him in the intervening time. Now he was stationed at Joint Base Pearl Harbor-Hickam Air Force Base, Hawaii, home to the Pacific Command PACAF, Oahu, Hawaii. He had his own team of jet fighter pilots trained in the same high level of proficiency he learned from the General.

It was just last week, the General from his Fifth Air Force (5AF) Pacific headquarters at Yokota AFB ordered a roll out of his fighter jet squadrons in preparation for the RIMPAC war games. Shawn flew his stealth, twin red-tailed F-22 Raptor Eagle supersonic jet fighter from Hawaii to Japan while practicing midair, refueling over the vast Pacific Ocean. Later, he flew over the Euphrates and Tigris Rivers at airspeeds approaching Mach 2.25. AWACS confirmed enemy aircraft approaching at their three o'clock. Shawn took his pilots up to fifty thousand feet as they emulated a move created and executed by their World War II predecessors, the Tuskegee Airmen. They were honoring and imitating the famed airmen by having their aircrafts' twin tail fins painted a bright red in honor of their predecessors' superlative careers in World War II.

He armed his four Sidewinder, infrared heat-seeking missiles, four Sparrow radar-guided missiles, and nine hundred forty rounds of twenty-millimeter ammunition. Jettisoning his empty external fuel tanks, he prepared to fight. His pilots followed suit and pulled into a two-hundred-seventy-degree right turn to confront the targets. They had the element of surprise as they dive-bombed the enemy from above. A gutsy move he heard was praised by the General. As the enemy showed up inside the target box of his Heads-up Display projected on the windshield, he took them out. Each pilots' unique paint color on an enemy's fuselage would confirm each kill. They were one hundred percent successful at taking out the enemy drones without losing any of his pilots in the dogfight.

In addition to the Raptor Eagle, his pilots were qualified on all of the top fighter jets in the military: the F-35 Lightning II, F-15 Strike Eagle, F-16 Fighting Falcon, and the F-117 Nighthawk. They were the first to fly any supersonic jet that came off the military's assembly line for combat training against anything an enemy might send up against them. The Russians had their Mikoyan MiG 35, Sukhoi 27 and 35; the French the Dassault Rafale; the Chinese the Chengdu J-10; the Euro-fighter Typhoon used by the United Kingdom, Germany, Italy, and Spain; and Sweden's Saab JAS 39 Gripen. Still, leading the pack was his US manufactured F-22 Raptor.

In the last six months, he and his pilots flew thirty-five missions, logging over two hundred combat hours against live enemy aircraft. His team was the best and he was proud of each member. They demonstrated time and time again that no foreign air force in the world was superior to the United States of America.

However, Shawn recognized his was a dying breed. The government, particularly DARPA, was beginning to use more sophisticated, unmanned, far less expensive drones for targeted strikes like the ones used for the war games. Now a room full of war game geeks in undisclosed locations with joysticks and monitors could take out targets anywhere on the globe or in the air in a matter of minutes with precision and stealth. To date, his pilots beat the joystick jockeys, but it only took one team member to be off his or her game to change the odds of continued success. That's why he required that each person stay in a high state of readiness.

Though the brass was well aware that the computer geeks had yet to score against his team, the days of aerial dogfights were still rapidly coming to a close. He had to begin thinking about his future and that of his team who depended on his leadership on and off duty. Whatever the future held, he still wanted it to be with a home full of noisy children and Helen in the picture. He had to hold to the belief that he wasn't wrong and that Helen wanted the same things.

It was the life he witnessed in the General and Admiral's home when they entertained their top officers and their families for purely social events. That was the type of life he was putting his life on the line to guarantee each and every day. He often held social events at his estate in Hawaii for members of his team, both officers and enlisted personnel and their families. He only needed to find Helen to make his complete and put the plan for their future into action.

It wasn't often General Alexander toured the troops under his command, thought Shawn, but they were all the better for the experience. He trusted his pilots to perform over and above every other command in the US Air Force and make the General proud. They had certainly done that and earned more combat medals and ribbons as a result. Apparently, the General had more in store for him and his pilots soon.

That thought reminded Shawn his daughter was celebrating her fifth birthday today. With her teacher's help, he planned and executed the surprise catered birthday breakfast party for her in her classroom that morning. An outing, for just the two of them, was planned for later that day after her school let out for the day.

He couldn't believe the time had passed so swiftly. One moment a nurse in the hospital nursery handed a supremely pissed off newborn bundle to him and it seemed the next moment the same bundle of joy was off to kindergarten, telling him not to cry.

That morning, after her classroom party, his daughter wiped his tears at her classroom door with her little fingers. She palmed his face, gave him a big, sloppy kiss, a big, bright smile, and a snappy salute before sending him off to the Air Force base with her promise that *"every little thing would be all right,"* her favorite Bob Marley tune to sing.

He didn't know what she had up her sleeve, but with his precocious daughter, he learned to be prepared for anything. Shawn presumed her teacher was participating in his daughter's secret by the way they kept putting their heads together. He was so enormously proud she was such a wickedly smart kid for only five years old. She could read and write above her grade level and mastered her arithmetic and rudimentary Spanish, becoming quite a linguist. It amazed him every day while checking homework with her what she was capable of. His daughter was very bright and beautiful and meant the world to him.

There were so many fond memories he recorded of his daughter as she grew up over the last five years...and beyond to the day he met the woman who stole his heart and would become her mother—the stunningly attractive Helen Marlowe. He often talked with his daughter about her mother and showed pictures and videos of the times they spent together. His bundle of energy demanded to hear the story of how they met over and over again and look at the pictures and videos so often that he downloaded them to her iPad.

Nothing about Helen escaped his notice or memory. The day they met, they were in the Commissary at Norfolk Naval Base in Virginia, both in a rush when they rounded a corner and crashed their grocery carts in a head-on collision. When she looked up at him, her eyes sparkling, she said, "Oooops!" and grinned, he knew he had met the woman of his dreams. They were in Norfolk, at the largest US Navy Base on the eastern seaboard, for extensive training in their respective branches of the military and late for class. Both officers, that same day, they struck up a friendship that, in short order, became intense. They spent all their free time together, talking and getting to know one another. She even told him about her problem with the law. Although her slate was now clean, it still angered her that she was judged a prostitute, considering she was still a virgin. That was part of what intrigued him about her. She was incredibly open and honest, yet she had a kind of tough, city quick exterior, an edge about her that spelled danger. Still, there was a vulnerability about her she successfully hid from everyone except him.

A few weeks later, on a lark, Shawn and a few buddies took his private jet and flew a group of ten of their male and female officers and friends to Las Vegas for a few days of R&R. That first night, though he wasn't as inebriated as she or the rest of their friends, his relationship with Helen Marlowe went beyond the pale and off the charts. In the wee hours of the morning, the chauffeur took them to the first open wedding chapel he could find and helped Shawn make Helen his wife before she was completely coherent.

He was head over heels in love with her and couldn't believe he was so lucky to have found a woman who was so beautiful, intelligent, and in love with him, too. Once they got to his suite just before dawn, what she gave him, he treated as a gift. Still, he was in love and took full advantage of Helen, marrying her that same weekend before he laid a hand on her. When they woke, she thought he was joking when he reminded her they were legally married. Their relationship went downhill from there.

He knew she regretted what they had done and, after the Vegas trip, she severely limited contact with him to the point of being nonexistent. That's when he began to realize her feeling for him weren't as strong as his feelings for her. He had rushed her into a marriage he thought they both wanted, but learned she wasn't ready.

Training over, they went their separate ways back to their duty stations; him at March Air Force Base in California and her at the Naval Air Station Joint Reserve Base in New Orleans, Louisiana.

Grudgingly, six weeks later, she informed him of her pregnancy. She refused to let him see her or transfer to an air base in Louisiana. Through the months of text messages during her pregnancy, he hoped they would rekindle what they felt while in Norfolk, yet he felt she didn't understand what was between them was special. Maybe, just maybe, they could try to reawaken the magical weekend they shared in Las Vegas together before she gave up completely on their relationship and demanded a divorce.

Nine months later, after almost daily text messages that he initiated, when he hoped they would start their lives together as a family, she delivered their daughter, and promptly disappeared before he got to the hospital. Were it not for the beautiful gift Helen bore him, his heart would have been permanently on life support.

In subsequent years, he tried to forget her by dating other women; including one of his daughter's pre-school teachers. Still, he couldn't summon the interest to take another woman to his bed. Whenever he was home in New England for a visit, his parents, siblings, and his entire family took the opportunity to parade scads of bright, beautiful, eligible women past him. However, nothing worked or clicked for him. He still loved everything about Helen Marlowe and could not even psych himself up to make love with someone else.

Although his family accepted and loved his daughter, they didn't know about Helen or his status with her. Helen was stuck in his heart, brain, blood, refusing to be dislodged. He was conducting an exhaustive search...for his wife… and still had not found her. He hoped Admiral Alexander would help him find her.

He never considered divorce. His life had been stuck in neutral. As a result, his daughter the only joy in his world. He desperately wanted to find the love of his life, Helen Marlowe Rodgers...his wife of nearly six years and the mother of their daughter...again.

It worried him that he could not find her through normal military channels. So, he enlisted the help of a private investigation firm in case she had left the military. However, all indications were that she was still an officer because her duty station was classified. Still, it was almost as if she never existed. Shawn knew that only meant one thing: black or white ops. If what he suspected were true, Helen was repeatedly putting herself in dangerous situations, a prisoner of some renegade country or she was dead. No one would notify him if something happened to her. She refused to allow him to alter his official records to identify her as his wife and the beneficiary of his estate. Despite her refusal, his attorney had the details of his relationship with Helen and a copy of their marriage certificate. Should anything happen to him, Helen and their daughter were his only beneficiaries. He had to believe that she was still alive somewhere and that one day he would find her. If it took a lifetime, he would not give up until he did.

General Benjamin Alexander looked out into his audience and noticed he didn't have his best pilot's full attention. He never publicly played favorites among the hundreds of pilots who came under his command in the PACAF, but privately he believed Major Shawn Baxter Rodgers was a gift. The man was young, only thirty-one now, but he flew instinctively with an ease and skill unmatched among the squadron leaders Benny commanded.

He challenged Rodgers often and the man surpassed every test. He had absolutely no quit in him. That made Rodgers a standout among many top flyers, ideal for what he had in store. He was grooming Rodgers, a highly intelligent and strategic thinker with unmatched leadership skills, to take his place someday as a diplomat and as an astronaut. Benny recognized that in less than five years, he would be eligible for retirement. He and Stacy hadn't decided whether twenty years of service would be the right time to leave military service, but he believed Shawn Rodgers was made of the right stuff to, eventually, step into his shoes. Unbeknownst to Rodgers, after this year's RIMPAC exercise, he would earn his silver oak leaf and be known as Lieutenant Colonel Rodgers. In his view, the kid had more than earned the promotion with his dedication to duty.

Shawn reminded Benny of his own early days flying an old crop duster he and his brother, Kenneth, built back home in Goodwill, Summer County, South Carolina. Rodgers, however, grew up in the lap of luxury in New England, a member of the Fitch-Townsend pharmaceutical family. He came from a long and distinguished line of medical and academic doctors on both sides of his family tree and could have chosen any line of work.

He had a pilot's license at age thirteen and his own jet plane for his eighteenth birthday. Yet, he was no trust fund baby. Rather, in his spare time, Shawn played the stock market like a pro. As a result, despite his uber-wealthy family, the kid was filthy rich in his own right. However, rather than follow in his family's carefully planned footsteps into the medical field or sit on his laurels, Shawn chose the Air Force as a career and earned top honors in his graduating class at the academy as a student and pilot. He was well respected and liked, and, because of his skills and abilities, moved quickly through the Air Force ranks.

Benny understood what Shawn felt. He, too, graduated from the academy with top honors and climbed quickly through the ranks. Shawn seemed to be following in his footsteps professionally and privately, including raising a daughter alone without the benefit of having the baby's mother in his life. Benny generally didn't interfere in his pilots' lives, but his wife, Admiral Stacy Greene Alexander, made it clear this was one of those times when he should bend his rule somewhat. He surrendered to the theory that *if Mama ain't happy, nobody is happy*. He had learned over the years of their marriage that a happy wife made for a happy life. He was a happy man every day with a wife he loved and cherished and seven intellectual and rumbustious children who made his life a challenge, but complete. He hoped Shawn would one day enjoy the fruits of what every person in a military uniform put his or her life on the line to achieve...peace.

"... and the Ninety-ninth Red-tailed Fighter Squadron will meet me on the flight line, mission ready, at 0500," the General said, wrapping up.

Just then, Shawn clicked back into the discussion going on while his thoughts had veered to Helen Marlowe.

"That's us, Major," one of Shawn's captains commented. "Wonder what's up."

Shawn hadn't a clue. He shrugged and gathered his gear, hurrying out of the auditorium into the Hawaiian sun and sea breeze. He and his daughter would have to make it a quick high tea birthday celebration and an early night. He had to sleep fast to be ready for this deployment in the morning.

Chapter 3

The gunfire was sporadic, but persistent, with loud and deafening staccato sounds. The air was hot and heavy with the smell of blood and cordite that burned the nostrils.

Sick to their stomachs with fear and scared beyond terror, twenty young girls huddled tightly together in the small, dark, dank, smelly cellar with no way to know whether they would live or die from moment to moment. They had been there for hours, though it seemed like much longer, awaiting their fate.

Their parents, African royalty, sent them to the English-speaking, all-girls, prep school with the fervent hope they would be safe and learn to lead a better life through the benefit of education and exposure to a world outside of their villages. The girls were being trained and were expected to one day rule their countries. That was not going to happen if the militant Jihad terrorists got their hands on the girls who were between five and twelve years of age.

The Boko Haram respected no one's status in life. They would force the older girls into motherhood as child brides for the soldiers, hostages for ransom, and the younger ones would likely be sold into the perverted sex trade. Every girl at the school knew and understood what she was in for, if found. So they remained still and quiet, packed in like babes in the womb in the underground earthen tomb, while a war raged above their heads.

Little did they know, at that moment, a tightly-knit group of Ninja-clad operatives was there to search for and destroy the terrorists. The nighttime helo jump had been successful. Moving like ghosts through the thick forests, night vision goggles made them appear otherworldly, but they handily dispatched the last of the insurgents as the mission dictated. Now they were on a recon mission to tag and bag each Jihadist for posterity. Photos, fingerprints, and DNA samples were collected quickly and efficiently to add to a database of criminals when Commander Helen Marlowe discovered the hidden trapdoor in the floorboards in the school's kitchen storeroom.

Hand signals completed and guns drawn at the ready with laser sites engaged, the trap door was opened and twenty pairs of frightened young eyes looked up.

"Well, hell," the leader, Code Name: Explorer One, said in a decidedly female voice with an American Midwestern accent into a face mic. "Delta, we have a situation. How do you read?"

"Reading you five-by-five, Explorer One. SitRep."

"HOT found twenty little people, all female. Suspected missing royalty. They weren't kidnapped as originally reported."

"Breathing?"

"Affirmative."

"Execute: Gravedigger. Proceed with extraction. Secure for transport. Extra helos dispatched. Head 'em up and move 'em out, Explorer One. Let's see how quickly you can complete the forced recon part of your mission and make it to the landing zone. Your time is running out. Watch your six. You've got insurgents crawling all over the region. Other teams are going combat ready to replace you upon your return."

"Copy that, Delta. Mission complete. Asses on the move.

Thirty clicks from LZ. This is the Explorer One. Over and out."

As the girls were helped out of the space not much bigger than a Napa Valley wine barrel, one of the ninjas would step up and a child was secured by harness piggyback style to the human carrier. When the last child, a five-year-old, was aboard Helen's back, the dead Jihadists, who were not already buried, were dumped into the hole and the trapdoor secured, the squad triple-timed it through the thick woods without leaving so much as a leaf or a blade of grass out of place. Some of the Ninja-clad, recon-turned-rescuers took point while others spread out to cover both sides and protect the rear.

Not knowing their fate, but somehow trusting, the girls clung tightly to their personal carriers, not uttering a sound. The night was pitch-black, with no stars or moon to see their way, but somehow, they were moving swiftly and soundlessly through the dense forest.

Helen's gut clenched with the lightweight tethered to her back. Her own daughter was the same age as the child she carried. It momentarily scared her with Shawn's Air Force career taking him away often, their daughter could be at the mercy of people who did not love her, or criminals just like the child on her back suffered. She needed to find her daughter and ensure she was well taken care of...and, she realized, she wanted to see Shawn, her husband, again.

They were suddenly stilled by the sound of trucks up ahead, coming toward them through the woods in a space no wider than a goat path. The human carriers melted like mist into the foliage and the girls instinctively seemed to know they had to hold their collective breaths and remain still.

What the girls couldn't see, but the night-vision glasses revealed, was another group of about twenty to thirty militant Jihadists standing on the back of two open transport trucks with guns scanning the thick woods while the trucks slowly tried to navigate the narrow path. The girls also couldn't see the hand signals that could only be viewed with the specialized night-vision glasses or hear the voice commands that passed among their human carriers or the other Ninjas who had scrambled like silent monkeys up into the trees.

Yet, suddenly, what looked like fireflies centered on each terrorist, the trucks stopped moving as did the Jihadists who all seemed to collectively and, without a sound, simultaneously melt into the floorboards of the trucks. Not one terrorist sensed they were there or got off a shot. Each driver and his companion in the windowless front seats slouched down like melting goo. The headlights continued to glow in the dark and the engine ran, but that was the only sound that could be heard.

Quickly, another tag-and-bag operation took place, but with no time to bury the dead, they were quietly hoisted up into the tall trees and tied to thick branches with hanging twine where they could not be seen from below. The trucks were driven deeper into the woods, off the goat path, and camouflaged where they would not soon be found. In time, the jungle vegetation would take over and shield the trucks.

Then the ninjas were again off this time on a dead run to make up for the lost time.

Just before daybreak, the ninjas spread out in a circle around a clearing, facing the woods with weapons at the ready. They had not uttered a word, but meals ready to eat (MREs) and bottles of water were silently passed over their shoulders to each girl. The carriers never took their eyes off the woods and collected each scrap of debris after the girls had their fill. Remaining as still and quiet as a petrified tree trunk, the girls were still tethered securely in a harness to their carriers.

Chapter 4

"What's going on, Major?" one of Shawn's captains asked, as they were leaving a mission operations briefing session with the General. "I hear the General asked for us specifically."

Shawn heard the same thing, but was no better informed than the rest of the other officers selected for this mission. "He heard we're the best," he boasted for lack of a better explanation and heard his pilots' jubilant agreement as they strode across the aircraft carrier's deck to their individual stealth AV-8B Harrier II jump jet copters to mount up well before dawn. After this, they had orders to fly the jet copters with passengers to Japan and then to some top-secret base he never heard of in the Pacific Ocean. Whatever the mission, his team would do the job.

A huff of air signaled something and the ninjas went on heightened alert. Then, without otherwise hearing a sound, huge, black, bat-winged aircrafts were suddenly filling the clearing. The ninjas, with their charges intact, sprinted backward toward the crafts and were shortly airborne at treetop level. They were whisked across the land at dizzying speeds that made the lushly-green landscape blur below them. They were airborne for over an hour before land gave way to light-brown, sandy shores, a deep blue ocean, and what appeared to be specks on the vast, watery horizon. The crafts bulleted toward what soon became a super, nuclear-powered aircraft carrier surrounded by an armada of other battleships and submarines.

They all landed on the deck of the huge aircraft carrier long enough to transfer the twenty, young girls into the waiting hands of soldiers wearing the American flag and medical badges on their uniforms. Then another crew of Shawn's pilots, both male and female, took the refueled, bat-winged, stealth aircrafts and lifted off again, carrying a new contingent of Ninjas. At lightning speed, they moved off toward the place they had all just left as the sun came up over the Mediterranean and the far horizon.

It was unusual for Shawn's pilots to fly the jet copters. They generally flew the supersonic F-22 Raptor Eagle fighter jets. Their jets were stored below the massive carrier's deck. He figured the General was challenging him again to ensure his pilots were ready to mount up on any aircraft in military service. *Well*, thought Shawn, *if that is the case, the General has every reason to be pleased with me and my pilots' performance.*

Shawn held the heavy door open with both hands on the windy aircraft carrier's deck for others behind him to enter just as Helen pulled off her ninja skull cap and mask, revealing her face. When she looked up to thank the pilot for holding open the door, she and Shawn stood stark still and stared into each other's eyes.

Speechless, it was like the first time they collided in the Navy Commissary all over again. The group of his pilots and her SEALs flowed around and then pass them.

Epilogue

Stacy slid into bed aboard the super aircraft carrier and curled into Benny's warm embrace.

"Do you think getting them together face-to-face is going to work?" Benny asked.

"The only easy day was yesterday. I can only hope this meeting and the time they spend on the island will give them a chance. Their story so closely paralleled ours before we finally found each other."

He kissed her mouth, luxuriating in her taste. "Hey, babe, you must have a short-term, memory-loss problem. You had me at hello the night I met you in one of the Pentagon's cafeterias. You pressed all of the right buttons for me the first time I saw you, just as Helen has done for Shawn. After talking with you for an hour, I also knew no one has a greater dedication to duty than you do, no matter what the task or risk. You placed your commitment above all else, including us. Although I'm enormously proud of you and your accomplishments, you disappeared from my life for five, long, agonizing years before I found you again. After that, I had to work hard to prove to you we could have a life together and remain in military service. Shawn is going to have the same obstacle course to run with Helen."

Stacy looked up at him, her eyes shining with deep and abiding love. Palming his jaw and running her thumb over his mouth, she said, "I admit it was a hard sell until I understood what I was fighting so fiercely to protect included you, the rest of our family, and America. You're my hero, Benny. Helen has the same kind of dedication I have. She just has no frame of reference yet and hasn't learned family is important, too. That's exactly the way I was at the beginning of our relationship."

"I hope my pilot and your SEAL learn the same thing. Their daughter wants and needs both of them."

"We certainly bent the rules enough so Shawn and Helen have an opportunity to talk and perhaps give their daughter the two-parent home she asked me and you for in her letters to us."

"Since it was our eight-year-old sons who gave her the idea to write letters to us, I hope the next communique we receive from that little girl is a mission accomplished, thank-you note."

From the Author

Greetings all—

I trust you enjoyed both the novel *When You Know* and the novella, *Dedicated to Duty*. However, *Dedicated to Duty* is not only intended to entertain you, but also to highlight the extraordinary sacrifices and contributions women make (1) in the military, in all branches of the service and (2) to the safety of our lives 24/7 and 365. Today, there are approximately 214,100 women in active duty roles of military service, including 69 generals and admirals. That number comprises about 6,790 in the Coast Guard, 13,677 in the Marine Corps, 53,385 in the Navy, 63,552 in the Air Force, and 76,684 in the Army. Women in the reserves number approximately 118,781 and 470,851 in the National Guard.

At one point in US history, women were denied entry into certain segments of military careers. Those sections usually involved duties which included the expert use of weaponry. The fear was women needed to be protected because they were considered to be delicate, the weaker sex. Yet, women found themselves in non-traditional roles, caught in firefights through no choice of their own and served valiantly. Although approximately 300 women have been wounded in Afghanistan alone, more than 700 gave the ultimate sacrifice in both Iraq and Afghanistan. Still today, women serve in valuable segments of the services for the protection of their counterparts and combat partners.

In August 2015, President Barack Obama ordered the US Defense Department to open all uniformed service position to women. Though there remains opposition by a few to the Presidential Order, the same or similar arguments in opposition were raised as regards to the admission of people of color, certain religious affiliation, and with a same-sex orientation. However, women continue to argue that, if they can meet the physical and mental tests and are of "good moral character," no rank or position in the military should be denied them.

Only an enlightened citizenry will turn the tide on the naysayers and come to learn the color of ones' skin, religious beliefs, the orientation of ones' private, intimate life, and the gender of a person is no barrier to becoming a warrior in the fight to protect Americans from terrorists and insurgents, whether on domestic or foreign soil.

If you would like to read other novels in my Family Reunion—In the Wisdom of the Ancestors series, you are invited to visit my website at www.annjeffries.net.

Until the next time, I remain faithfully yours,

Ann Jeffries

About the author...

Ann Jeffries, the critically acclaimed author of the Family Reunion—Wisdom of the Ancestors Series, is a native of Washington, DC. As an only child, she enjoyed the benefits of a private school education at Allen in Asheville, North Carolina, and a public education at the University of Maryland. Ann began writing fiction for her own amusement.

Ms. Jeffries is the recipient of many awards for leadership and public service. A keynote speaker at colleges, universities, conferences, and conventions, she has extensively traveled the North American continent, Asia, and Europe. Among other endeavors, she is an entrepreneur, an avid supporter of public television, a genealogist, and a voracious reader.

Her pride and joy are her family, particularly her Fabulous Four grands. She lives in Maryland and South Carolina.

Follow Ann on her website: www.annjeffries.net, Facebook @ Ann Jeffries, on Twitter @Ann Jeffries and her publishing house site: www.newviewliterature.com. Her novels are available in both e-book and paperback. Her autographed copies can be found through annjeffries.net and also un-autographed on Amazon. com and barnesandnoble.com.